The

WEDDING THIEF

The
WEDDING
THIEF

A Novel

MARY SIMSES

BACK BAY BOOKS
Little, Brown and Company
New York   Boston   London

Copyright © 2020 by Mary Simses

Hachette Book Group supports the right to free expression and the value of copyright. The purpose of copyright is to encourage writers and artists to produce the creative works that enrich our culture.

Back Bay Books / Little, Brown and Company
Hachette Book Group
1290 Avenue of the Americas, New York, NY 10104
littlebrown.com

First Back Bay paperback edition, July 2020

Back Bay Books is an imprint of Little, Brown and Company, a division of Hachette Book Group, Inc. The Back Bay Books name and logo are trademarks of Hachette Book Group, Inc.

The publisher is not responsible for websites (or their content) that are not owned by the publisher.

The Hachette Speakers Bureau provides a wide range of authors for speaking events. To find out more, go to hachettespeakersbureau.com or call (866) 376-6591.

ISBN 978-0-316-42162-1 (paperback) / 978-0-316-42163-8 (hardcover, library edition)
LCCN 2019955206

10 9 8 7 6 5 4 3 2

LSC-C

Printed in the United States of America

In memory of Ann Depuy

The
WEDDING THIEF

CHAPTER 1

THE LIE

It was my mother's lie that brought me back home that July day. Not some inconsequential fib, the kind she occasionally told when my sister and I were young, like saying that Grover's was out of chocolate chocolate-chip ice cream when the truth was, she'd forgotten to put it on the shopping list. This was different. She said her health was failing fast and that she needed to be with her girls. It didn't matter that I was thirty-eight and Mariel thirty-five. We were still her *girls*.

Of course I believed her. Why wouldn't I?

It was a Monday morning and I was at my desk, working on the arrangements for the fall senior-management meeting. Two hundred fifteen people converging on Scottsdale, Arizona, to hear the company's plans for the coming year, get face time with one another, take jeep rides into the desert, have dinners around bonfires, eat too much, drink too much, and, if all went well, leave with a good feeling about Kelly Thompson Pierce Financial.

I'd just looked up from my computer and was gazing at the traffic on Lake Shore, wondering where all the sailboats in the harbor were off to, when my cell phone rang. It was Mom. Her voice sounded weak, shaky. And strangely distant, as though she were calling from someplace much farther away than Connecticut.

"You have to . . . come home . . . right now," she said, breathy spaces between the words. "Before it's too late."

"Before what's too late?"

"I'm ill, Sara. Very, very ill. I can't explain it . . . over the phone. I need to see you. Just come home."

Every nerve ending in my body stood at attention. "I'll get an afternoon flight from O'Hare." I was already searching the internet, my hands trembling, my fingers clumsy and numb when I needed them to be efficient.

"Your sister's coming" was the last thing she said, spoken as though it were a footnote.

It should have been the title.

I tried not to think about that as I booked the flight. Tried not to imagine Mariel packing. It wasn't even seven o'clock in Los Angeles, but I was sure Mom had called her first. She always sought her out first. After eighteen months of not speaking to my sister, I didn't want to think about the two of us being in the same place at the same time. Somehow, I'd survived last New Year's Eve, the first anniversary of the night I'd realized there was something going on between her and Carter. The night that ended my relationship with him. And with her. But I'd always thought I'd have a choice about whether to see her again and on what terms. I was wrong.

On the plane, I stared out the window at the clouds while my brain kept grinding away, wondering what was happening to Mom. I was prepared for the worst when I pulled into the driveway in my rented Jetta, a little after six that evening, Jubilee and Anthem hanging their heads out their stall windows, the late-day sun casting a faded glow on the white clapboard house.

In the mudroom, music drifted from the ceiling speakers, the last few bars of "What I Did for Love" from *A Chorus Line*. A stack of newspapers sat in the recycling bin, an edition of the *Hampstead Review* on top, and sun hats were piled on a shelf. Mom kept those sun hats there even through the winter, displayed as hopeful harbingers of spring. A black-and-white photo of my parents at the Broadway opening of *Right as Rein* stared down at me, the last play my father produced before his death from a cardiac arrest almost five years ago.

In the hallway, I charged past Martha, the housekeeper, who was carrying two boxes wrapped in silver-and-white paper. She looked surprised to see me.

"How is she?" I asked, but instead of waiting for an answer, I raced toward the stairs.

"Your mother?" Martha called out. "She's in the kitchen."

The kitchen? I thought she'd be in bed. But I was heartened that she was up. As I got closer, I could smell food. Something cooking. Tomatoes and onions, garlic, red wine. It smelled like spaghetti sauce, although I couldn't imagine Martha cooking spaghetti sauce for my mother—or cooking anything, for that matter. She broiled or boiled the taste out of any food, and Mom had stopped letting her near the stove.

Still, I expected to find Mom at the table, looking peaked and wilted, cloaked in a bathrobe, a little cup of tea in front of her. But she was standing at the Viking range, her back to me, seeming as fit as ever in a pair of pale gray pants and an ivory sweater, an apron around her waist. Her light brown hair shone as though she'd had it washed and blown out no more than a few hours before. And she was singing along with Frank Sinatra's "Fly Me to the Moon."

She held the lid of a large pot in one hand and a wooden spoon in the other. Empty cans of tomatoes and tomato paste were strewn across the counter. A chunk of onion and a clove of garlic rested on a chopping board. This was not a woman who was on her way out of the world.

"Mom?"

She spun around. "Oh, there you are!" She put down the lid and spoon and hugged me, squeezing me tight. She hadn't lost any strength, and her weight appeared unchanged from when I'd been there in March. "I'm so glad you made it." She studied me. "You look a little tired. Long flight?"

"Mom, I thought you'd be—"

"Well, you can catch up on your sleep here. And see? I'm making one of your favorite meals. I also picked up a peach pie from the Rolling Pin. I know how much you love their pies."

I felt as though I'd just walked into a *Twilight Zone* episode and Rod Serling was about to appear by the refrigerator: *You're looking at Sara Harrington, product of a dysfunctional family. Her sister has betrayed her; her mother has lost her mind. Sara thinks she's come home. But in fact, she's just entered* The Twilight Zone.

"Mom, what's going on? You call sounding horrible and tell me to come home because you're ill. 'Very, *very* ill' is what you said. So I tell my boss I'll have to be out for a week, maybe longer. I scramble for a flight. I pack. I get here as fast as I can, and you're cooking dinner? I thought you were at death's door." Maybe all actors were overly dramatic, especially the ones with a few Tony Awards under their belts. But this was going too far.

Mom dipped a spoon into the pot and tasted the sauce. "Needs a little salt."

"Mother!"

"I never said I was at death's door, sweetie."

There was a name for the crime of killing your mother...was it *matricide?* I wanted to have the correct term because I felt I was getting close to committing it. "Yes, you did. You said your health was *failing fast.* You implied you were terminally ill." My voice was ratcheting up a few decibels with every syllable. "You said you needed your girls here." I glared at her until I knew she felt the burn.

She dropped the spoon into the sink. "Well, my health *is* failing fast. My *mental* health. It's failing very fast, and that's because I worry all the time about you and Mariel and why you two can't make up."

I'd been frantic for an entire day, missed an important meeting, and spent my three-hour flight next to a guy who snored and drooled the whole way. For this. "You made me come back to reconcile with Mariel? I can't believe it."

She took a step closer, her hand outstretched.

I backed away. "No, you can't bring us together. And look at you, doing it under false pretenses. You made it sound like you were dying."

Mom put her hand on her chest. "Well, I *am* dying...of a broken heart. Two weeks, Sara. Your sister is getting married in two weeks, and you refuse to be a part of it."

Of course I refused to be a part of it. She was marrying my guy, for God's sake. The man who used to look at me as though I were the most fascinating and fabulous person in the world—the only person in the world. The guy who knew how to make me smile no matter how bad my day or his day had been. The one who understood what I needed and gave it to me—a sympathetic ear, a funny story, a bit of advice, some silence and a gentle touch. The man I could count on to calmly steer the way through any stormy crisis. My rock.

How could Mom forget the big deal she'd made about Carter being *my* boyfriend when she'd first met him? After I introduced her to him in LA, she'd said, *Oh, Sara, I adore him. He's so easy to talk to. I feel like I've known him for years. No wonder he's such a successful lawyer. And he's clearly smitten with you. I think he's going to be the one. You make the perfect couple.*

"Mom, stop the dramatics," I said. "You tricked me to get me home. I know very well when Mariel's getting married. And I'm not staying."

She grabbed my hand. "Oh, honey, come on. You girls have got to put this behind you. I've seen you inflict the silent treatment on each other plenty of times, but this situation's gone on way too long. You two haven't talked in forever."

"Forever wouldn't be long enough."

"You don't understand what it's like to be a mother and be in the middle of your two daughters not speaking with a wedding coming up." She pulled a box of penne pasta from the cabinet. "I love you both. I just want you to act like sisters again. Why can't you put the past aside and get back to the way you used to be?"

Mom continued to labor under the delusion that Mariel and I had once been close. I wondered if all parents had blind spots when it came to their children. True, this was the longest we'd ever gone without speaking, but there were always old wounds just beneath the surface that never seemed to heal.

And had she seriously asked why I couldn't put the past aside? She made it sound as if it were the kind of tiff Mariel and I had gotten into as kids, like arguing about who would sit in the front seat of the car or which restaurant Mom and Dad should take us to for dinner. My sister had stolen Carter Pryce, the only man I'd ever really loved, and in two weeks she was going to marry him. I felt as though my heart was about to shatter all over again.

I wanted to rewind the clock and do everything differently so they would never meet. Rewind it back to the day I'd met Carter, when I was still living in LA, working for Spectacular Events. I'd gone to Santa Monica to see a bank CEO who had hired us to plan a birthday party for her husband. I left her twelfth-floor office and stepped into the empty elevator, stuffing notes in my briefcase as the car descended and stopped on the seventh floor.

A man got in. Tall, tan, with a full head of blond waves, he looked as though he should have been out racing a sailboat. Except he was wearing a bespoke charcoal-gray suit and carrying a red stapler. The door closed; the elevator descended again. Then the car stopped with a loud *clunk*. I waited for the door to open, but nothing happened. I pushed the button for the lobby, but the button didn't light up. Several more pushes produced no result except my heartbeat gathering speed.

"Not working?" the sailboat racer asked, pushing the button on his side.

I began to sweat. "I think we're stuck." I could hear the tremble in my voice.

The sailboat racer seemed to hear it too. "Don't worry," he said, laying a hand on my arm. "We'll get out of here soon. It's no big deal."

He pressed the red emergency button on the elevator panel, and a few seconds later a woman's voice came floating down from a speaker somewhere above us. "Can I help you?"

"Yes, I'm trapped in an elevator," Sailor said. "It's not moving, and the doors won't open." He glanced at me. "And I'm with a lovely lady who looks like she wouldn't mind getting out of here as soon as possible."

Oh God, I hoped I didn't have sweat stains under my arms.

The woman told us she'd contact the fire department, but she couldn't say how long it would take for them to come.

"It's okay," Sailor told me. "We'll be out before you know it." He lowered his voice to a whisper and said, "Actually, I didn't even need to make that call. I have special skills learned from watching years of *MacGyver* reruns. And I can get us out of here with just the objects I have on hand."

It took me a moment to realize he was kidding, and I laughed in spite of my damp armpits and shaky knees.

"Let's see what I've got." He held up the stapler. "One Swingline. Red." He handed it to me and then emptied his pockets, reciting the contents as he displayed them: "One pack of Doublemint gum, one set of keys on a key ring."

"What's that other thing on the key ring?" I asked. He told me it was a flashlight. That *was* very MacGyver-like. Maybe he wasn't kidding.

"One black leather wallet stuffed with credit cards," he went on. "One brown lacquer and gold Dupont fountain pen. One cell phone. And one book of matches. With these, I can create an explosive device that'll blow the door right off this thing."

I laughed again. He had beautiful eyes, deep blue, and I sensed there were some well-toned muscles under his suit. "I'm so relieved. How do we start?"

"You don't think I can do it. I find that a bit insulting, Miss—uh, are you a miss?"

"Yes, I am. Harrington. Sara Harrington."

"Carter Pryce," he said. "I'd shake your hand, but I'm holding the key components to an explosive device. I don't want to trigger it accidentally."

I liked his sense of humor. "I understand."

He wadded up a couple of pieces of gum and stuck them between the elevator doors and the jamb. "That's the first step. We need a good seal."

"Right. And you're telling me you learned these skills from watching *MacGyver*?"

"I did."

I didn't want to tell him I wasn't really a *MacGyver* fan. I listened to him recount the plot of an old episode, something about a Bigfoot-type creature, and I stopped thinking about the elevator walls closing in on us. All the while he added things to the wad of gum—credit cards, the ink barrel from his Dupont pen, the battery from the miniature flashlight. "Now all I have to do is set it off with this." He held up the book of matches. "Are you ready?"

Fortunately, he didn't have to do it, as firefighters from the Santa Monica Fire Department began calling to us from the other side of the doors. Within twenty minutes, we were out.

I remember the feeling of relief when the doors opened and I saw the foyer stretching in front of us with its creamy interior and silvery recessed lights, the receptionist busy behind her desk as if nothing were amiss. But I felt something else as well: the sense that I might have been able to stand being trapped in that elevator a little longer just to be with Carter Pryce.

Two days later he called and asked me out. We went to Balboa Island and walked around eating frozen bananas like tourists. We talked about the elevator rescue and I told him I'd been a lot more afraid than I'd let on.

"You're a pretty good actor, then," he said.

I thought that was funny, because of the four people in my family, I had the least amount of dramatic talent.

"I knew when I woke up that morning something good was going to happen," he told me. "I don't know how I knew, but I did. And then we met."

I remember being surprised, not knowing how to respond. Here was a guy who spoke his mind, wasn't afraid to say what he felt, wasn't playing games. How refreshing. I was the luckiest girl in the world. Or so I'd thought at the time.

Mom dumped the box of penne into a pot of boiling water. "Can't you, Sara?" she asked.

"Can't I what?" I watched the steam rise.

"Put the past aside."

She made it sound as though Mariel stealing Carter was ancient history, but it had been only a year and a half ago. I'd given a New Year's Eve party at my place in LA, the bungalow with the blue door I rented in Venice. I'd hired a caterer and a bartender, gone all out. My Christmas tree was still up in the living room, the scent of evergreen hung in the air, and a piece of mistletoe decorated the kitchen doorway. I'd dimmed the lights; candles flickered everywhere. The place was packed with guests, and Carter was there, of course. We'd been dating for almost two years by then.

I was mingling, going from the living room to the den, making sure everyone was having a good time, occasionally dashing into the kitchen to confirm that things there were under control. Once an event planner, always an event planner. Carter and I were pulled in different directions, but every now and then we'd make eye contact. At eleven forty, I went into the kitchen to check on the caterers and get ready for the champagne toast and the cake. The bottles of Veuve Clicquot were on ice, and my old stainless-steel Waring blender was whirring, mixing up a fresh batch of margaritas. Then, suddenly, it was almost midnight.

The guests began screaming, "Two minutes to go!" At eleven fifty-nine, they started counting down the seconds. I looked for Carter, and I couldn't find him. I almost went outside, but it was a cold night, and I knew he wouldn't have wandered out there. Finally, I saw him standing in a darkened corner of the den with Mariel. They were talking, but I could see, even in that crowded room, that something more intimate was going on. They stood too close, smiled too much. Their gestures seemed too familiar; their eyes never strayed from each other. Something had happened between them. Or was about to.

I walked out of the room, trying to steady myself. Carter. My Carter. With Mariel. My sister. I'd thought they barely liked each other. God, how wrong I'd been. I felt dizzy as I left the house. Outside it was fifty-five degrees, and I shivered in my sleeveless dress. In a daze I headed down the street, a video running in my head: Carter and Mariel, Mariel and Carter.

When I got to Abbot Kinney Boulevard, it was more hectic than ever, people driving by, honking horns, tooting party blowers, leaning from car windows to yell "Happy New Year," all a blur of sound. I walked on through the noisy, drunken crowds, passing places I'd seen a million times. Now they looked foreign to me. Finally, I stopped and leaned against the wall of a café, hugging myself in the cold, wondering how all these people could go about their night as if nothing had happened.

Eventually I went home. After the guests were gone and the caterers had cleaned up and I was left with a pile of tattered party hats and blowers, I confronted Carter. Part of me wanted him to deny it, to convince me I was way off base. But he didn't. He told me they hadn't planned it, never wanted to hurt me, that it had been going on for only a couple of weeks, that they were waiting for the right time to tell me.

When would the right time have been? That's all I said before I told him to leave.

I saw them together once, a couple of months later, in Beverly Hills. I was in my car at an intersection, and they crossed the street in front of me. He held her hand, laughed at something she said, gave her a little tug as if she were a child. Four months after that, Mom told me they'd gotten engaged.

"You want to know why I can't put the past aside?" I asked my mother now as she gave the pasta a stir. "I can't put it aside because it's not the past. They're together. It's the present and the future."

"That's why you have to move on. Or you're going to stay stuck right where you are. I'm sure Mariel would be willing to put it aside."

Of course Mariel would be willing. She wasn't the one who'd been betrayed. "She's got nothing to lose. She's got Carter. She's not the victim here."

Mom turned down the burner under the sauce. "Sweetie, do you know where the word *compromise* comes from?"

Oh no. I'd just landed in the world of etymology again. Mom never let me forget she had a degree in English from Yale. *Language is everything,* she liked to say. Theater, which she'd minored in, was the area she ended up pursuing as a career, but she'd never lost her obsession with words.

"Well, it includes the word *promise,*" I said, "so it's probably something about making promises."

"It comes from the Latin *compromissus.*" She took a colander from a drawer and put it in the sink. "Past participle of *compromittere.* 'To make a mutual promise.'"

"Yes, okay, fine."

"Pity you never learned Latin."

"I've survived so far," I said. "And I'm not compromising with Mariel in *any* language." Didn't she see how awful this was for me?

I'd thought I was going to have love, a wedding, and children with Carter and now here I was, almost forty, without any of it.

Mom let out a breath like a deflating balloon. "But I know she would forgive you."

"Forgive me for what? I didn't do anything."

"For not speaking to her in such a long time."

"I haven't spoken to her because of what *she* did to *me*," I said. "I feel like we're having two different conversations here. Did I ever tell you you're like a walking non sequitur?"

She placed a bowl of salad on the table. "Now, there's a great Latin phrase! *Non sequitur.* 'It does not follow.'"

"That describes you perfectly," I said. "Nothing follows with you. You refuse to hear what I'm saying. You always side with her."

"Oh, Sara, there must be a way to make this better. It wasn't really your sister's fault."

That was it. "I can't talk about this anymore." I held up my rental-car key. "I'm leaving. You lied to me. There's not a thing wrong with you."

Mom followed me out of the kitchen, her kitten heels clicking on the hardwood floor. "Sweetheart, come on. I'm sorry I brought you here under false pretenses, but this really does break my heart. I wish you'd stay. And not just for Mariel. For me. I want to catch up a little, do some mother-daughter things."

"Some other time," I said. "When she's not going to be around."

I walked down the hall, my mother's voice trailing behind me as I passed the photos on the wall. Mom in a summer-stock production of *A Little Night Music* in upstate New York. Mom in *The Importance of Being Earnest* at a regional theater in Connecticut. Mom in

Dragonfly Nights on Broadway. There were dozens of photos. Her wall of fame.

I stepped into the mudroom, relieved to be getting out of there. I wondered if the Duncan Arms, which was right here in town, had any rooms available. And then the door opened and in walked Mariel. For a second, I didn't recognize her. Gone was the bohemian look of beaded tunic tops and woven handbags; she'd swapped those for a pair of skinny white jeans and a coral-colored top that looked stunning against her tan skin. Four-inch heels had replaced her flat leather sandals.

She'd also cut her hair, which for years she'd worn in one length, down past her shoulders. Now it was up to her chin, in layers, and blonder than it had ever been—platinum. But she could get away with it. She could get away with anything. She'd inherited the beauty gene. When she walked into a room, everyone—men and women—noticed her. And now there was one more thing to notice: that rock she was wearing. Even the plastic stones on the rings I'd worn as a kid during my princess stage weren't as big as the diamond she was sporting.

I stood there feeling like a wilted flower in my wrinkled clothes, my hair frizzy from the July humidity, wondering how she could look fresh after traveling all day from the West Coast. For a second, we just eyed each other like a couple of feral dogs.

"So you're here," she said, a little scowl on her face as she pushed a Louis Vuitton suitcase into the room.

No more nylon zipper bag for her. She'd moved up in the world with Carter. I wondered who'd designed the clothes she was wearing. And the shoes. Jimmy Choo? Prada? I was sure Carter had paid for all of it. At thirty-five, Mariel had never supported herself. And now she'd moved her dependency from the Bank of Mom to the Bank of Carter. She'd never have to stand on her own two feet. "Actually, I'm leaving."

She planted her hands on her hips. "What? You're running out on Mom?"

I stepped toward the door. "She's not dying. Not even close."

"What are you talking about? She called me and said—"

"It was a lie. Go ask her. She's in there making dinner." I nodded in the direction of the kitchen.

"Why would she lie?"

"Why do you think? You're getting married in two weeks to the guy you stole from me, remember? Mom wants us to reconcile so I'll go to the wedding. Which I refuse to do."

"I didn't steal him," Mariel said. "Carter wasn't in love with you anymore. Why can't you believe that?"

"He was in love with me until you stuck your big nose in the picture."

She flinched, then touched the side of her nose. "It's not big. And he started it."

"See, this is why I can't even talk to you. I told Mom she was wasting her time."

"I tried to apologize. I called you, I texted you. I wrote you a letter. You sent it back to me with spelling corrections."

"You never could spell."

"That wasn't the point."

"It was *my* point. He's way too smart for you and someday he'll figure it out. He'll realize he's bored, that he needs more than arm candy, and he'll go on to someone else. Then the shoe will be on the other foot." I glanced at her four-inch heels. "And don't try to tell me you didn't steal him. You've been stealing guys from me since you were in middle school."

"What? That's so not true."

"Robbie Petler? Does that name sound familiar? He lived on Apple Ridge?"

"*That* kid? He just helped me with my homework."

"As soon as he thought you were interested in him, he didn't want to have anything more to do with me. He said you looked like a movie star. How could I compete with that?"

"Oh, get over it, Sara. If it did happen, it was ages ago."

That didn't matter. It was still relevant. "It proves your history of stealing boys from me."

She cocked her hip. "Like you were so perfect. Throwing my Barbie into the pond? Cutting up my favorite jeans?"

I didn't remember the jeans, although I had a vague recollection of the Barbie incident. "You could have gotten her out."

"She landed next to a snapping turtle, Sara."

"Well, you shoved my sneakers down the storm drain. And they were brand-new."

"You stuck that rubber snake in my backpack. Scared the hell out of me."

"Right," I said. "But you got Carter."

If she had a response to that, I didn't wait around to hear it. I sidestepped her Louis Vuitton suitcase, opened the door, and walked out.

CHAPTER 2

COLLISION COURSE

I woke up the next morning in a four-poster bed on the second floor of the Duncan Arms, a fireplace and love seat across the room, vintage paper of pink cabbage roses on the walls. At the window, I pushed aside the drapes and raised the sash. The sweet scent of fresh-cut grass drifted through the screen, along with a chorus of birdsong. On the lawn, a man and a little girl were throwing a softball. It might have been a scene from thirty years ago; the man could have been my father, the girl me, and the field the one behind our house.

In the bathroom I washed my face, brushed my teeth, popped in my contacts, and dragged a hairbrush through my hair. Yikes. There were new grays sticking out on either side of my part. I tried moving the part, then tousled my hair with my fingers to hide it altogether. That looked a little better. Highlights and a cut would be in order when I got back to Chicago. How had my hair gotten down to my shoulders? And where had all those new grays come from?

I packed my suitcase and got ready to leave. I'd booked a flight back to Chicago at seven in the evening so I could drive upstate and look at a new resort. It might be a good option if I needed to plan an off-site meeting at a quiet place in New England. I rolled my suitcase out the door, the wheels screeching. Not all of us could afford a Louis Vuitton travel bag like Mariel's. Some of us supported ourselves.

Why couldn't I stop comparing my life to hers? I liked being self-sufficient. I was proud of it. Proud of the fact that I didn't take advantage of Mom's generosity. Besides, there was nothing wrong with my suitcase. So what if the color had been out of style for a decade? Asparagus green wasn't all that bad.

A sign in the lobby said breakfast was being served in the Pub Room. A cup of coffee to go was all I needed, so I headed there. Inside, the tables were covered with red-and-white-checkered cloths. I walked past mahogany bead-board walls displaying paintings of foxhunting scenes and a pen-and-ink portrait of George Washington (had he slept here?). At the buffet, I grabbed a piece of orange-cranberry bread and a cup of coffee.

Five minutes later I'd checked out and was in the Jetta in the parking lot, sipping the coffee and devouring the bread, wishing I'd taken an extra piece. I was a sucker for pecans. My phone rang; Mom flashed across the screen. The image of my supposedly dying mother looking healthy as she cooked pasta whirled through my head, along with a picture of my soon-to-be-married sister, looking better than ever with her new hair and clothes. And that rock. I let my mother's call go to voice mail.

What was up with that rock anyway? I glanced in the rearview mirror and put the car in reverse. That diamond was obscene. Too big to be nice, when you really thought about it. Had Carter picked out that engagement ring himself? Or had Mariel seen a ring like that on the hand of one of his celebrity clients and given him instructions to duplicate it? That would be just like her. I pressed my foot on the gas. Had he gotten down on his knee to propose? The image made my stomach twist. And what had he said? What were his exact words? More twisting, but I couldn't stop myself now. Did he say—

Crunch!

There was a loud cracking sound behind me, like splintering wood. Or was it a splintering car? I gasped. I pulled forward. In the rearview mirror I could see it. I'd hit a picket fence? Where had that come from? And there was a man standing behind my car. Had I hit him too? Oh God, I hoped not. I jumped out. The man, who looked around forty, was dressed in khakis and a dark blue polo shirt. He was standing to the side of the car, tearing bubble wrap off something huge—six feet high, almost as wide, and a few feet thick. I could see green through the plastic.

"Don't you look where you're going?" His brown eyes bored into me. He had the kind of week-old beard I'd never liked. It always made me suspect the guy couldn't decide whether to really grow one or not.

"Did I hit *you?*" I said, my heart speeding up.

"No, you didn't hit *me*. You hit *this*." He turned away, continuing to unwrap whatever it was.

I didn't appreciate his tone. I knew it was my fault. "I'm sorry I hit your...your thing there." I pointed. "I didn't mean to."

He had the bubble wrap off now and I could see it was a giant hand, painted in shades of green and made from something that looked a lot like papier-mâché. The thumb, index, ring, and pinkie fingers were crushed and bent at ninety degrees, while the middle finger pointed straight to the sky.

"What is that?" I asked. "Some kind of a costume?"

He shifted the hand toward a white van nearby. "A *costume*? No. This is a sculpture. An Alex Lingon." He sounded almost insulted that I hadn't known that.

"Alex who?"

He wheeled around, glaring at me. "Alex *Lingon*. You haven't heard of him?"

"I don't think so."

"There was a big article about him in the *New York Times* just a couple of weeks ago. Sunday's Arts and Leisure section."

"I live in Chicago."

"They don't sell the *Times* there?" That tone of voice again. I could have done without it.

"I don't usually read the *Times*."

"Maybe you should, then. He's been called a national treasure. You ought to look him up." He stepped closer to the hand, slowly shook his head, and blew out a loud puff of air. "Well, this is ruined. Four fingers bent, smashed."

"Look, I'm really sorry. But maybe you should have packed it a little better. I mean, since you're an art handler—"

"I'm not an art handler. I'm in real estate development."

Well, no wonder. That was a different story. I thought about someone I'd once dated who'd worked for a company that built

23

houses. I wondered if this guy did that. "What kind of real estate development do you do?"

"What kind?" He took a step away from the hand and considered the question. When he spoke again, he seemed a little calmer. "We buy and sell buildings. Apartment buildings, retail buildings, mixed-use." He wasn't talking houses. "Sometimes we build or renovate. It depends on the situation."

I guessed that made us about even as far as art expertise went.

He looked back at the hand, touched the bent section of the pinkie, and grimaced as though it were his own finger that had been damaged. "I only did this as a favor for Anastasia. And now she'll probably lose her job."

"Anastasia?"

"My girlfriend. She's Alex's assistant."

"Oh." The pieces of the puzzle were starting to fit together. "So, you drove this from..."

"Brooklyn."

"As a favor for your girlfriend."

"Yes. There was a mix-up with the art-transport company. And now I've got this crisis to deal with."

"There has to be some way to resolve it," I said. I knew from years of planning events that there was always a way to fix a problem. "I assume it's insured?"

He looked at me as though I'd lost my mind. "Of course it's insured. But that's not the point. It's supposed to be in a show of Alex's work at the Brookside Gallery. It opens a week from Friday."

I'd been to the Brookside Gallery. It was right in town. They exhibited a lot of contemporary art and had a large following. I was about to tell him I thought it would be best to let the artist know and then help him make an insurance claim, but then I had another idea. "Let me ask you something. What's this made of?" I reached out.

"Don't touch it!"

I drew back my hand. "Okay, okay."

"It's papier-mâché. Alex does a lot of work with paper." He stepped closer to the hand, staring at the thumb, as if by some magic trick or mind game he could get it to straighten itself.

"And when did you say the show opens?"

"A week from Friday."

The day before Mariel's wedding. Today was Tuesday. That was ten days away. Ten days was an eternity in my line of work. In my fifteen years as an event planner, I'd solved all kinds of crises. Usually in a couple of hours, and sometimes much faster than that. I'd tracked down a best man who'd gone missing, found him drunk by the hotel pool, sobered him up, and written his speech just minutes before he had to give it. When a guest knocked over a dessert table, sending a wedding cake to the floor, I'd substituted two sheet cakes from Costco and had them sliced and plated. And all that was just one wedding…

"Ten days is plenty of time," I said. "What about repairing the fingers with more papier-mâché? You know, fill them in or whatever so they'll stand up straight, fix the parts that are crushed and bent."

The man squinted at me as though he were trying to figure out if I was real or not. "Are you kidding? I can't do that. It's a piece of art. I'm not in the art world, but I've learned enough about it from Ana. Even if I could straighten the fingers, the paint is another thing altogether. Alex mixes his own colors and he uses lots of different shades and pigments to get the effects he wants. It's complicated."

I stepped closer to the hand and took a long look. Sure enough, there were all sorts of green shades in there—fern green, olive green, kelly green, hunter green, and dozens of others blended together. Still, as he began to rewrap the hand, I continued to think the problem had to be fixable. After all, I'd had ring bearers lose the wedding rings or swallow them. I'd cleaned up red wine spilled on brides' dresses, stopped fistfights at bachelor parties, and halted at-the-altar confessions by brides and grooms who'd had sex with each other's college roommates. I was a fixer. It was in my nature.

"I have an idea," I said. "Why not take the hand to Carl's?"

"Carl? Who's that?"

"Carl's Arts and Crafts. It's a store here in town. See what they say about fixing it. Get a professional opinion. You know, I've done a little work with papier-mâché in the past, and I doubt repairing this will be as hard as you think." Sure, they were Christmas ornaments and I'd been five, but it was still papier-mâché.

He opened the van's back doors, lifted the hand, and slid it inside. "Oh, right," he said. "I walk into the local crafts shop and ask for their opinion on repairing a hundred-thousand-dollar sculpture."

A hundred thousand dollars? I'd had no idea it was that valuable. I swallowed hard, hoping we could pull this off.

"Why take that kind of risk when we might end up making it worse?" he said.

"Because we might end up making it better. I'm sure it can be fixed. Everything can. Well, most things. If there's a problem, there's a solution. That's what my father always said."

The man looked at me for a moment as though he could see inside me, and his face softened. "You honestly believe everything can be fixed, don't you?"

I smiled bravely. "Yes, I do. Maybe not matters of the heart..." I wasn't going to get into that. "But most things. Look, I'll go to Carl's with you. It's my fault, and, well, I'm actually very handy to have around when it comes to disasters."

He broke into a smile. "You mean you can do something besides *cause* them?"

I couldn't help but laugh. "Yes, I mean I can fix them. I'm an event planner. I handle disasters all the time."

He shut the van's back doors. Then he looked skyward as if he couldn't believe what he was about to say. "All right, Miss Fix-It. I'll go along with your suggestion. Let's see what they have to say at Carl's."

I offered my hand. "The name's Sara Harrington."

He shook it. "David Cole."

What a morning. And the day had barely begun.

CHAPTER 3

CARL'S

We got in the van, David at the wheel, and headed down the long driveway of the Duncan Arms, passing a cluster of Adirondack chairs on the lawn. The van rattled and shook as we flew over a speed bump.

"Sorry." He tapped the brake. "I don't usually drive this thing. It's a rental and the suspension's awful."

I asked him what he normally drove, and he told me a Range Rover. That was definitely a cut above what we were in.

"Take a left at the bottom there." I pointed. "Carl's is just a few miles from here, a little after the downtown area."

We pulled onto the main road, passing a field that stretched lush and green for twenty acres, the property bounded by a post-and-rail fence, horses grazing at one end.

"I take it you've been here before," David said.

I grabbed my sunglasses from my handbag. "I grew up here. My mother still lives in town."

"But you were staying at the Duncan Arms."

I understood the confusion. Why would someone come back to a place where she had a family home and go to an inn? "I didn't want to stay at the house. My sister's there right now and...well, we're not exactly speaking."

"Families can be complicated," he said.

I turned away and looked out the window as we passed an antiques shop. What could I say? How could I explain the way things were with Mariel? Sometimes the ice on our chilly relationship would thaw, and we'd become friendly again. Then we'd argue—usually over a topic we'd quarreled about too many times before. I'd tell her she should stop asking Mom for money. She'd say I should stop telling her what to do.

What I really wanted was for her and Mom not to exclude me from their conversations. It hadn't bothered me as much when Dad was alive, because he and I were close. But in the years since his death, I'd felt like Mom and Mariel were living together in one bubble and I was off in another one.

"I hadn't talked to Mariel in a year and a half," I said. "Until last night. And I'm not sure I'd really count that as talking. We just happened to be in the same room for a couple of minutes." We stopped at a traffic light; the engine idled. "Do you have siblings?"

"I don't," David said. "Not anymore." Two girls walked their bikes across the road. "I did have an older brother. Beau. But he died when I was twelve." His comment would have seemed matter-of-fact if I hadn't caught the sadness in his eyes.

"I'm sorry. Was he...was he ill?" Too late, I realized I shouldn't have asked, shouldn't have pried.

"Nope. Not ill." David stared through the windshield. "He dove off a cliff into a lake. He didn't know the water was shallow. 'Cervical spine injury secondary to blunt trauma.' That was the official cause of death."

"How awful. I'm so sorry." I couldn't begin to imagine the effect that must have had on David and his parents.

"It was a stupid, stupid thing to do." His voice was tinged with anger, almost as though he were speaking to his brother instead of me. "We were really close. He was two years older, but we did a lot together. Played Nintendo, fished, skateboarded, watched movies from the video store. But he had this wild—no, careless—he had this careless streak. I wish I'd been with him that day, but I wasn't."

I could hear the regret in his voice, and as the light turned green and we drove on I wondered what it would be like to be that close to a brother or sister and then lose them. Especially that way. *Devastating* was the only word I could come up with.

I studied the dials on the dashboard, the bottle of water in the cup holder. "My sister and I were never very close," I said. "It was better when we were young, but even then, she was always trying to compete with me. I took violin lessons; she took violin lessons. I learned to ride a pony, so she had to ride. When I was a senior in high school, I quit the school paper because she'd joined as a freshman. I had nothing of my own; she was always chasing me. The worst thing, though, was when she stole the guy I was in love with. Still am in love with. She's marrying him in two weeks. Right here in town."

David turned to look at me. "Your sister is marrying your ex-boyfriend?"

30

"Yes."

He let out a low whistle. "Oh, boy."

"Obviously, I'm not going to the wedding. I'm leaving town tonight."

"Did she *think* you were going?"

"I don't know. And I don't care. I just want to get back to Chicago."

We passed a grassy hill, the site of an old Indian burial ground. "So home is the Windy City?" he asked.

Was it? "I guess so, although it doesn't feel like home. Not yet, anyway. I've been there only a year, so maybe that's not surprising."

"Where did you live before Chicago? Were you here on the East Coast?"

"No. I lived in Los Angeles. I went to UCLA and never left after that. I loved it there. Even after Mariel followed me to LA to go to Cal State, I stayed. And we got along for a while. But now she's wrecked California for me. There isn't enough room there for the three of us."

"The three of you?"

"She and Carter and me."

"Oh, yeah. Carter."

"I got lucky and found a job in Chicago. Moving seemed like a good solution. I would have taken almost any job to get out of LA. So home is definitely not Chicago, but where it is, I don't know." We drove alongside the stone wall that bounded Four Winds, a boarding school. "What about you? Do you live in Brooklyn?"

"Brooklyn? No, that's where Alex's studio is. I live in Manhattan. Upper East Side."

Upper East Side. He looked like an Upper East Side kind of guy. Nice clothes. That almost-beard thing. A Range Rover. I could imagine his apartment: on a high floor, all windows, modern furniture, no food in the fridge because he ate out every night, like Carter.

"Where are you from?" I asked. "I mean, originally."

"I'm from here," he said.

"Connecticut?"

"No, the East Coast. I grew up in New York. Pound Ridge."

"I've been to Pound Ridge," I said. "It's pretty." It wasn't that far from Hampstead, about fifty miles, but far enough for our paths never to have crossed.

"My parents are still there. They have a business in the area. They're accountants. Semiretired, though. Funny, I'm the son of two accountants and I'm terrible at math. Go figure."

"I'm terrible at math as well." I heard the hand rattle in the back as we went over a bump. "So why did you have to drive that sculpture here?" I asked. "Doesn't Ana do that kind of stuff?"

"She had to catch a plane to Aspen to meet with Alex and a couple of his clients. To help her out, I stayed at his studio to make sure the art-transport company got everything off all right. But the hand was in another room, and I didn't realize until it was too late."

I didn't know anything about art or art-transport companies. I'd never thought about how things ended up at art shows or museums, but I was sure there had to be an inventory.

"And there was some confusion with the inventory," he added, as if reading my mind. "Anyway, I felt like an idiot. And I don't want this to be Ana's problem. She's got a tough enough job as it is. Alex can be a real pain in the ass."

I tapped Alex Lingon into my phone's browser. Up popped dozens of pictures of a man with . . . what *was* he with? "I'm looking at pictures of him. What are these things? They look like giant fish heads."

"They are giant fish heads. That's what he used to do. It's how he got started, back in the eighties."

"Are they papier-mâché as well?"

"They're made from some other kind of paper substance."

I scrolled on, through oversize body parts, arteries, a kidney— his more recent work. I'd seen enough. I put away the phone and rolled down the window. The breeze smelled like summer, trees, and sunlight, and you could almost touch the sky.

We arrived in Hampstead's downtown, with its clapboard colonial buildings, mullioned windows, wraparound porches, and window boxes of purple dahlias and pink hydrangeas. There was a sign in front of the Book Nook, probably advertising an author event. People were going into the Rolling Pin bakery and the cheese shop. A banner at the park by the town hall advertised the annual Sunflower Festival at Grant's Farm, the big antiques weekend, and the upcoming outdoor movie night where *North by Northwest* was going to be shown.

"How are the restaurants around here?" David asked, glancing at the people eating breakfast on the porch of Abigail's.

"They're very good."

"I would think they would be, with so many people coming out here from the city."

"New Yorkers like you," I said in a teasing tone.

"Ha. Except I'm not like most New Yorkers that way. I'd rather cook than eat out."

That was a surprise. I had friends in Manhattan and they always ate out. "You must be a good cook, then."

He grinned. "I'm an excellent cook. I'd never want to do it professionally. Too crazy a business. And horrible hours. But I like cooking for myself and Ana, and for friends. It's relaxing."

Relaxing? "That's the last thing I'd ever do to relax. I hate to cook. Except the occasional dessert. I have a sweet tooth." Cooking took too much time, my kitchen was small, and it got really hot in there. But good for him that he found it relaxing. "What do you like to cook?"

"Pretty much anything. I can make chicken in about thirty different ways. I do some nice meals with swordfish and salmon and tuna. And I can't resist a good steak every now and then. But I'm happy cooking just about anything, as long as people enjoy it. I always try things out on Ana first, though. Then I tinker until I get it the way I like it."

I hoped Ana appreciated having a man who cooked for her.

"What do you do to relax?" he asked.

Lately I wasn't doing much at all, letting my job fill a lot of my time. "I don't know. Read books, watch movies. I used to ride. Not too much anymore, though. That was when I lived here."

"You mean ride horses?"

I nodded. "Yes. My mother still has two of them. They're semiretired, but I hop on every now and then."

"I'd never do *that* in a million years."

"Why not?"

"To start with, you could fall off, get thrown, break a leg. It's not safe."

"Everything has some risk," I said.

He was silent for a moment. "Yeah, it does. Not everyone considers that as much as they should, but I do." I wondered if he was thinking about his brother.

The business district was behind us and the road quiet again. We drove by the turnoff that went to the river and the covered bridge, the place I'd once hoped would be the location of my first kiss. Instead, it happened behind the school gym, Tom Parker having suffered from a distinct lack of imagination.

Carl's was up ahead, a converted wooden barn surrounded by a field. David pulled in, parked, and opened the van's back doors. We slid out the hand and carried it into the store, where Carl stood behind the counter, talking on his cell phone. His slight frame seemed overwhelmed by his full head of curly salt-and-pepper hair. "That's him," I said. "He'll know what to do." At least I hoped he would.

I started to walk toward the counter, but David grabbed my arm. "Hold on a minute. I was just thinking—what if he recognizes Alex's work?"

He had a point. Alex had just been in the *New York Times* and he had a show coming up here in town. I didn't see any way around it, though. "I think we have to take that chance. Besides, the hand looks a little different from his previous work. And if you don't want Ana to lose her job..."

"Just let me do the talking."

"Of course. I'm only trying to help."

"That's what I'm afraid of," he said, but I could see he was struggling not to smile.

"What's this?" Carl asked as we approached the counter. "A giant hand giving people the finger?"

"It's not supposed to be giving people the finger," David said. "It's supposed to be a regular hand." He placed the sculpture on the floor and turned it to display the palm and the four crushed and bent fingers. "It's been in an accident."

Carl rubbed his chin. "I'll say."

"I was hoping you could tell me the best way to repair it. You sell materials to make papier-mâché, right?"

"Papier-mâché? Yeah, sure. Plain newsprint, liquid starch—I think that works better than white glue and water." He examined the hand closely, the palm, the wrist, the bent fingers, all the while muttering to himself. "You're going to need some wire mesh, wire cutters, masking tape..."

We followed him down several aisles, Carl pulling things off shelves and tossing them into a shopping cart. When we were finished, he placed everything on the checkout counter. "I've also got a book on papier-mâché you might want to buy. Has detailed pictures and all."

"We'd better take that," David said.

"And then for the paint..." Carl ran his hand along the surface of the pinkie. "Looks like acrylic."

He led us to the paint aisle, stopped at the acrylic section, examined the colors, then began pulling down tubes—Prussian blue, ultramarine blue, yellow ocher, cadmium yellow light. "You'll need to mix the blues and the yellows to make the greens."

I moved a couple of steps down to the green tubes. Chromium oxide green, emerald green, permanent green light, phthalocyanine green. I couldn't even pronounce that last one. "Couldn't we just use these? I mean, they're already mixed."

"Not for this," Carl said. "That hand's been painted with a lot of different shades of green. They've all been carefully blended."

So I'd heard.

We went back to the counter, but just as Carl was about to ring everything up, David turned to me and said, "This is never going to work. It's way too complicated. The whole idea is crazy. I can't go messing around with this."

As much as I hated to agree, I was beginning to think he was right. Repairing the damage did seem complicated for two people who weren't artists. If I was being honest, I'd have to admit that even my Christmas ornaments hadn't been that great. Although I'd always loved art classes in school, loving something and being good at it didn't necessarily go hand in hand. My art teachers were nice to me, but I'm sure it was because of my enthusiasm, not because I had any real talent. And now my enthusiasm had taken me down the wrong path.

"Oh God, David. I'm sorry. I was just trying to help. I thought this would be easier than it is." He didn't say a word as we went through the aisles and put everything back on the shelves. I felt like I was at a funeral.

We loaded up the hand and got back in the van. "Look, there has to be another way out of this," I said. I wasn't ready to give up.

"There isn't any other way out of it. I'm going to call Ana and tell her what happened. And then I'll call Alex and tell him so Ana won't have to. He can't fire her for this. It wasn't her fault. It was mine."

Except it wasn't his fault either.

37

Back in the lobby of the Duncan Arms, I grabbed a business card from my wallet. "At least let me know what happens. Please?" I handed him the card. "Text me or call me or send me an e-mail. Something. And if there's anything else I can—" I stopped myself before uttering the last word, realizing too late it was the wrong thing to say.

"I think you've done enough," he said.

I could tell he didn't mean it in a good way.

CHAPTER 4

MOM IN HER ELEMENT

I opened the door and entered the darkened auditorium of the Hampstead Country Playhouse. It was a little after four. I'd long ago abandoned my plan to check out the resort upstate, and now I was meeting up with Mom. I hadn't completely forgiven her for luring me to Connecticut with her fabricated story, but the sideshow with Alex Lingon's hand had distracted me enough for my anger to lose most of its edge, and I didn't want to leave town without saying goodbye.

The acting class for adults Mom was teaching had ended, but the stage was still bathed in light. The auditorium reminded me of a little theater Carter had taken me to soon after we began dating. We'd gone to see the daughter of one of his clients perform in *Big River,* and I remembered thinking life couldn't get much better than the moment he put his arm around me, pulled me close, and told me how glad he was that I was there with him. He said it as though he couldn't possibly have gone with anyone else.

Mom was on the stage now with a few stragglers, students who were still hanging around, talking. I headed down one of the aisles, wondering how far into the ten-week session they were. She taught the class only every couple of years, but the structure was always the same, each session culminating in the performance of a one-act play. I'd seen several of them, and some hadn't been too bad. There were usually a couple of people who could act fairly well.

Mom never would have agreed to hold the workshops if Dad hadn't talked her into it. She didn't think she'd be a good teacher, but he had a knack for seeing beyond what people saw in themselves. By the time he got her to accept the suggestion, she was convinced it had been her idea all along, a strategy he often used in his work.

"Oh, I agree with you," Mom said as she smiled and tilted her head at a man in a chambray shirt. "He's a brilliant playwright. Just brilliant, although he's gotten very dark lately. He wasn't that way when I first knew him." She rested her hand lightly on the man's forearm. "I could tell you stories..."

"I'll bet," he said.

I stopped a few rows before the stage. "Hi, Mom."

She waved to me. "Hi, honey. We're just finishing up." She turned back to the students. "All right, great work, everyone. Same time next week."

The group disbanded, and Mom walked down the stairs and came over to me. "So glad you called." She gave me a hug. "I was afraid you'd already left."

"My flight's at seven."

"How about grabbing a cup of coffee? Or a snack?"

"I don't think I have enough time."

She glanced at her watch. "Oh, I guess you're right. Well, we can just sit here for a few minutes and chat if you want." She moved into one of the rows of red velvet chairs. "I'm always happy to be in a theater."

We sat down and I thought about how my father would have said the same thing. He loved the theater. Loved rolling up his sleeves and getting into the details. *Let's use candles here, but let's not have them all come up at once. It should be gradual, a progression.* Sometimes it drove the directors crazy, how much he got into the nitty-gritty, but he knew what he wanted—mood and tone, visual effects, sounds. And in the end, he was right every time. The awards in his office—five Tonys and four Drama Desks—proved it.

"How did your class go?" I asked, steering away from the elephant in the room, knowing if we talked about Mariel, we'd only lock horns again.

"The class? Oh, it's great. Nine people. An easy group. And a couple of them are quite good. One actually did some summer stock in college."

"And who was the guy?" I suspected Mom would feign ignorance.

"What guy?" she asked with perfect nonchalance.

"The one you were flirting with."

She smirked. "Owen? Oh, don't be silly, Sara. I wasn't flirting with him."

"He's got to be ten years younger than you."

There was a beat of silence. "Really?" She looked surprised. "That's all?" She looked relieved.

"Mom!"

She shook her head and sighed. "All right, maybe I was flirting a little. What harm does it do? Nothing will ever come of it. And besides, you know your father was my one and only love." She gazed across the rows of empty seats. "I sang that song to him, you know. At his thirtieth birthday party. Did I ever tell you about that?"

"I don't think so."

"It was at Twenty-One. In New York. You girls weren't around yet. We had a wonderful band playing, and some people started in on me to sing. Of course, I didn't want to."

"Ha," I said. Mom had never met a microphone she didn't like.

She gave a little shrug. "But they finally persuaded me. And I sang 'My One and Only Love.'" She looked down, fiddling with the strap on her handbag. "It was one of your dad's favorite songs. Of course, he loved Sinatra's version, but that night he told me my version was the best."

The story made me smile. I imagined my parents in their younger years, before my sister and I came along. "I'm sure it was beautiful."

"Well, my point is, I'll never find that again. And that's okay. *Je comprends*. One true love is more than many people ever get." She sounded wistful. "But having a nice-looking fellow on your arm when you go to a charity dinner isn't all bad," she added, glancing at me as though she thought she needed my permission.

"I never said it was." In fact, I'd told her plenty of times she should date if she met someone she liked. Mom was a pretty woman with a warm smile that made people gravitate to her. And she still had a nice figure. I'd seen men look at her. And I knew how hard it was to be alone. Not to share your life with someone you loved. The years since Dad's death had been difficult for her, as they would be for anyone whose spouse was also her best friend. She'd told me once she felt she had to get her bearings and, in a way, start her life all over again after he died. I wasn't sure she'd actually gotten her bearings yet.

"I haven't met anyone my own age," she said. "They're either twenty years my senior or ten years my junior. It gets harder and harder the older you are. The pickings are few and far between. What am I supposed to do at sixty-five? Start hanging around Teaborne's?"

Teaborne's was a bar a mile outside of town where the twenty-something crowd gathered. Famous for its pickup scene, it was full of bare-midriffed girls in micro-miniskirts, guys shooting pool, and people dancing on the bar after midnight.

"I just want some male companionship. I get lonely."

I almost said *Me too,* but I was afraid I'd go into a rant about Carter and Mariel, and I wanted to mend fences with Mom, not tear more holes in them.

She took a compact from her purse and reapplied her lipstick. Then she pulled out her phone. "Excuse me a second, honey. Siri, please remind me to call Barbara Knox at eight o'clock tonight."

Siri's voice came back: *Okay, I'll remind you.*

"Thank you, Siri." Mom turned to me. "I'm sponsoring Barbara's daughter and son-in-law at the club."

"Why do you always do that?"

"Do what? Sponsor people?"

"No, say *thank you* to Siri. And to that Google thing in the kitchen. They're computers."

Mom looked at me as though I'd asked her to go out in

public with no makeup. "Sara, we should *always* be polite." She lowered her voice. "And besides, someday it'll probably be them running the planet, not us. We might as well start building up goodwill now."

Who knew? Maybe she was right.

Mom's phone lit up, vibrating in her hand. She glanced at the screen. "Sorry, let me just take this. Hello?"

She listened, nodded, and said, "Sure, that's fine. I can do it then." She hung up and turned to me. "They want to do tomorrow's photo shoot at two o'clock instead of one now."

"What photo shoot?"

"The civic association is giving me an award for fund-raising, and *Connecticut* magazine wants to do a little article and photo."

"Oh, that's nice."

"Mariel's going with me in case my hair or makeup needs a touch-up. And she wants to watch them take the photos." Mom pushed a lock of hair behind her ear. Then she looked around the auditorium and sighed. "I wish you'd stayed at the house last night."

"I couldn't, Mom. Not with her there."

And I'd thought we'd be able to have just one conversation that didn't involve Mariel. The two of us sat there, not speaking, and I knew we were both thinking about her. "I'm sorry about yesterday," Mom said, finally breaking the silence. "I shouldn't have done that to you. Or to your sister."

I wished she hadn't added Mariel to the equation. She'd barely been inconvenienced. She would have been coming to Connecticut soon anyway to get ready for the wedding, while I hadn't been planning to come at all. I'd had to leave work; Mariel didn't have any work to leave. The last job she'd had was as a receptionist at a place where people took yoga classes while they charged their electric cars, but she'd quit when she got engaged to Carter. I could have pointed all that out to Mom, but I didn't.

"I accept your apology," I said. More fence-mending. "But please don't ever do that again. Don't tell me you're terminally ill. I mean, unless you are. You had me so worried."

"I won't," she said, giving me a two-finger salute. "Scout's honor. But I wish you'd change your mind and stay for the wedding. Your sister could really use your help. She's in way over her head. She planned it all herself. I helped a little, but she's done the lion's share. She didn't want to use a wedding planner."

Probably because that would be giving my profession too much credit.

"She didn't think she needed one," Mom went on. "And now things are going off the rails. Something about the flowers. And a problem with the transportation people. I can't handle it. I wish she'd stuck to picking out the dresses and the tuxes. She's got a good eye for that. But she didn't, and she's driving me crazy. Can't you do something, Sara? You're the one with the level head. You always know how to deal with things. And this is your area—you're the expert. Please stay and help us."

Us? Now it was *us?* Why did she have to make this a personal favor for her? "Mom, I'm not going to be her wedding planner and pick up the pieces at the last minute. She made her bed. Now she can lie in it."

"Just talk to her, then," Mom said. "Before you leave."

"And say what, exactly? I have nothing to say to her."

"Sara, with all the quarreling you and your sister have done over the years, you should know things are never one-sided."

"What's that supposed to mean?"

She gave me an exasperated look, as though she were dealing with a recalcitrant child. "It means I remember that it wasn't perfect between you and Carter, especially toward the end. Sometimes we want to imagine what happens to us is someone else's fault or responsibility when it's not."

Ah, there it was. She was sticking up for Mariel again, suggesting this wasn't her fault. I got up. "Why do you act this way? You tell me you're sorry and then you go right back to siding with her."

"I'm not siding with her." Mom stood up too. "I'm just asking you to be honest with yourself and think about the good and the...well, not so good."

"I have thought about it. I've thought about it for the past eighteen months. And I wish you could see it from my side for once. She should get the acting awards in the family. She plays the victim so well." I stepped into the aisle.

"Honey, wait." My mother grabbed my arm, but I wrenched it away and dashed toward the doors.

"I'm sorry," she called out. "I love you. And if it makes you feel any better, Mariel thinks I'm always sticking up for *you.*"

CHAPTER 5

JUST ONE

The text message came through the second I left the playhouse: Delta telling me my seven o'clock flight had been canceled and to contact them to rebook. But that flight was the airport's last departure to Chicago for the day. That meant one more night in Hampstead. One more night at the Duncan Arms.

The man at the reception counter booked me into another room on the second floor. This one didn't have a fireplace, but there was a tiger maple four-poster bed, cheery blue-and-white wallpaper, and a nook with two windows and an L-shaped banquette.

I freshened up, changed into a pair of jeans and another top, and took out my planners—the rose-colored one I kept my personal appointments in and the blue business planner—so I could do a little work, but the distant thrum of a headache told me I needed food. Five thirty was way too early for dinner on a normal day, but this day had been anything but normal and it felt like ages since I'd eaten that orange-cranberry bread.

The Tree House was the inn's more upscale restaurant, and although I thought about going there, I decided against it. For one thing, I was underdressed. For another, I wasn't in the mood to eat alone in a place with candlelight, flowers, white linens, and couples. The Pub Room, with its dark paneling and checkered tablecloths, seemed a better choice.

"I'd like to get some dinner, please," I told the girl at the hostess stand. There were about a dozen people in the restaurant.

"Just one?" she asked.

As if she needed to remind me. "Yes. Just one."

If Carter had been here, he would have committed the name on her tag—Onyx—to memory. Like my dad, he never forgot a name or a face. He'd meet people once and remember them the next time he saw them—guys who pumped his gas, receptionists at other law firms, his clients' assistants, and the *assistants'* assistants.

And he knew the owner and manager of every one of his favorite restaurants and even his not-so-favorite ones. He'd always reserve the best table for us, order something delicious ahead of time, and have a wonderful bottle of wine waiting. He knew how to take care of things.

Looking around at the couples, I felt more alone than ever. I didn't want to sit by myself at a table. A few women were having drinks at the bar. "I think I'll eat over there," I told the hostess. I took a seat at one end and set my planners on the mahogany surface.

"What can I get you?" a bartender asked.

The name tag on his fitted white shirt said JEROME. He had a little sparkling dot of an earring, like a diamond stud, in each ear. He might have been younger than me, but not by much. I told him

I wanted to order dinner and asked if he would bring the dessert menu as well. Nothing wrong with planning ahead.

"Something to drink?" he asked.

"Sure. A glass of wine." I glanced at the bottles behind the bar, amber light bouncing off their surfaces. "How about a glass of Riesling?"

"I have a Dr. Loosen Blue Slate that's very nice."

"Perfect. Thanks."

A moment later he placed my wine and a dinner menu on the bar. I put the glass to my lips and took a sip. The wine was crisp, cold, and slightly sweet, with the citrusy flavor I loved. I studied the dinner menu, starting with the appetizers, and quickly landed on a mixed baby greens salad with caramelized pears, aged goat cheese, candied pecans, and champagne vinaigrette. My mouth watered.

It was hard to select an entrée because there were so many good choices. The sesame-encrusted ahi tuna steak (seared rare, sliced, and served with stir-fried vegetables) looked amazing, but so did the prosciutto-wrapped breast of chicken (stuffed with ricotta and spinach, served with marsala sauce, red bliss mash, and asparagus).

I finally decided on the tuna, which left the dessert menu. The blueberry crumble seemed like the perfect choice. I was set. Jerome took my order, and I opened my business planner.

"What are you reading?" he asked as he set a place mat and flatware on the bar in front of me.

I looked up. "This? Oh, it's not a book. It's a planner. For work."

He tapped some keys on a computer, inputting my order. "I'm reading that book *Rx for Romance.*" He sighed. "It's sad romance is so confusing we have to read books to figure it out."

I was familiar with the book. It had been on every bestseller list for months. I'd purposely avoided it, hoping my love life would improve on its own. "Maybe I should read it. I haven't had the best luck with men."

Jerome leaned toward me and whispered, "Hon, that makes two of us."

True confessions, here we go. I laughed to myself, went back to the planner, and reviewed the list of things I had to do for the August board meeting, writing notes under some of the items. When Jerome placed my salad on the bar, I was happy to put the work away.

The caramelized pear was delicious, sweet and nutty. How did they make pears taste like that? I'd eaten here ages ago and vaguely remembered the old menu, which had been more of a meat-loaf-and-potatoes kind of thing. "I like the changes they've made to the menu," I said as Jerome walked by.

"When was the last time you were here?" he asked.

"Oh, it's been at least fifteen years. I think it was a Sunday brunch with the family."

"The menu's probably been changed a few times since then." He put a saltshaker and a pepper mill on the bar by me. "Do you live in town?"

"I used to." I slid another piece of pear onto my fork and popped it in my mouth.

"Still have family here?"

"My mother. I came to see her."

"Oh, nice." He poured a glass of water for me.

"Yeah, well...it's complicated."

"Mmm," he said, half under his breath, "isn't every family?"

Probably so, but I wondered if they were as complicated as mine. I tilted the glass of Riesling to my lips and took another long drink. The wine was having its effect, slowing me down, making me relax. I told him the story—about how I'd ended up back in town, about Carter and Mariel's upcoming wedding.

"So, back up," Jerome said. "What happened after the New Year's Eve party? Didn't your sister realize the terrible thing she'd done?"

"We didn't talk after that."

"You mean she never tried to get in touch with you to say she was sorry? Or anything?"

I stabbed a few pieces of lettuce with my fork. The dressing was beginning to taste a little bitter. "Oh, she called me, she texted me, she wrote me a letter. I basically ignored everything. I mean, there was nothing she could say. I met him first. We were in love. And then she, well..."

"But why would she do that to her own sister?"

Why did Mariel do anything she did? I'd been her sister for thirty-five years and I still didn't know. Why did she always copy me? Why did she take up everything I was interested in, try to impress my friends, go to college in LA, want my boyfriend? Because she felt she had to compete with me? Or was it just something in her DNA? I didn't know.

"We've never been that close. We've had our ups and downs. She was always jealous of my relationship with Dad. But she's the one who's close to Mom."

One of the servers asked Jerome for a dark and stormy and a jackrabbit. He mixed the drinks and set them at the end of the bar.

"My sister doesn't appreciate Carter," I said as I took the last pecan from my plate. "I mean, he's smart. He really cares about people. And he's a wonderful attorney. He's honest with his clients and he does what he says he'll do. He's also great at dealing with all kinds of personalities. You know, some of the folks in LA can be pretty crazy."

"Yeah, I've been there. I know," Jerome said.

I remembered Carter handling more than one actor who wouldn't be in a film with a rival star unless he had more lines, as well as several singers who didn't want their drivers to start a conversation with them or even *look* at them in the rearview mirror. Maybe Carter reminded me a little of my dad, who had worked with some challenging people but never got ruffled, always kept things under control.

Carter was good at managing difficult situations. He could solve almost any problem, legal or not. If you had a child who needed to attend a special kind of school, Carter would know the right place and the person who ran it. He'd make the introductory call. If you were looking for a contractor to renovate your home, he'd give you the names of two or three people whose work he'd stake his life on. If you were traveling to Rome for the first time, he'd connect you with a friend who lived there and could tell you everything you needed to know about the city.

I twirled the stem of my wineglass. "Like I said, she doesn't appreciate Carter. How kind he is and how willing he is to listen to people, to understand them. She's just interested in being around his celebrity clients." I could imagine her talking about them, making it sound as though Carter's clients were her personal friends. *Oh, yes,*

Katy's starting to work on a new album and Leo's going to London to shoot that movie.

Jerome wiped the bar in front of me with a towel. "Sounds like you're still in love with him."

I looked at my empty salad plate. Of course I was still in love with him. I wished he were sitting next to me at that moment. I could feel my eyes begin to burn. I was grateful when Jerome told me he was going to check on my entrée.

I sliced into my ahi tuna steak and took a bite. Crisp on the outside and rare on the inside, just the way I liked it. The sesame seeds were crunchy; the ginger and lime sauce was tangy.

"How is it?" Jerome asked as he walked by.

I told him it was perfect, and he gave me a thumbs-up and headed to the other end of the bar. When he came back, he asked if I wanted another Riesling. I said yes, and a minute later he brought me a new glass. "So what kind of work do you do that you have to take your notebooks to dinner?"

I laughed. "I don't have to take my notebooks to dinner. I just thought I'd catch up a little. I'm an event planner."

"Oh, you do weddings and parties and things?"

"I used to, but now I plan corporate events for a financial services company. Mostly meetings, client outings, company picnics, that kind of thing. But when I lived in LA, I was with a group that did weddings and parties."

"Weddings and parties in LA. Umm. Sounds like fun. Was it?"

People often assumed my job was fun, and I'd have to explain that, like most other jobs, it basically involved a lot of hard work.

Few people knew what went on behind the scenes at a big event. Clients and guests expected everything to go smoothly and according to plan, but it almost never did. "A lot of it was fun. But it's like any other job. It has its good and bad points. So many things can go wrong with an event, and you have to make it right."

"Yeah, I'll bet. Things people don't even know about. Not the guests, anyway. You've probably seen everything."

"Well, maybe not everything, but I have survived plenty of near disasters."

"Oh? Like what?"

Everybody wanted to hear the disaster stories. I rattled off a few, including one involving a sprinkler system and another involving a photobombing guest. "And once, when the bride made her own centerpieces, half the people at the wedding broke out in hives. We had to get bottles of Claritin and hand them out. We put pink ribbons around the bottles to make them look like party favors."

"Nice touch."

"I thought so."

"I was at a wedding once where the groom couldn't get the ring on the bride's finger," Jerome said. "They had a huge argument right there at the altar. She said he got the size wrong. He said she'd gained weight." He paused to refill my water glass. "You can imagine how the bride took that. I mean, what was the man thinking? She physically attacked the guy. The minister had to pull her off. I thought they were going to call off the wedding."

"You mean they still got married?" How could a marriage survive that kind of beginning?

He nodded. "Divorced a year later, though."

That didn't surprise me. People don't like to be told they've gained weight. "I had a bride who couldn't fit into her gown on the morning of the wedding. We were lucky because the whole thing was held at a hotel, and the hotel seamstress saved the day. She took some fabric from the train and stitched it into the gown. She literally sewed the bride into it."

"A good seamstress is worth a lot," Jerome said, then turned away to fill an order. I watched him pour champagne into a couple of flutes and bourbon into a glass.

"Weddings and parties," he said when he returned. "That's sort of a timely topic because I'm moving into that field myself."

"Oh, you mean as a bartender?" I was surprised he wasn't already doing some of that work on the side.

"No, as a photographer. I've had cameras ever since I was a kid, from little plastic things to Nikons. A couple of years ago I started looking for jobs I could do when I wasn't tending bar. A friend asked me to take some headshots for a book jacket, and he loved them. A couple of other friends asked me to take pictures for their Christmas cards. And word kind of spread. I've been buying more equipment, and I started doing weddings this summer. So far, it's going pretty well. I haven't had time to think about a website, but that's next on the list. Maybe in a few years I'll be able to stop bartending and become a full-time photographer."

"That would be nice. There's nothing like doing what you really love."

"Can I give you my card?"

"Uh, sure. But like I said, I've got a corporate job now. I don't do private events anymore except an occasional thing for a friend. Plus, I'm in Chicago. That might be a little far for you to travel."

"Oh, right. I forgot. Yeah, that would be a little far."

He removed some wineglasses from a dishwasher and put a cocktail shaker in the sink. "It's kind of funny—I mean funny-peculiar—that you're an event planner and your sister's getting married, but you're not planning her wedding. And you're not even going."

I finished my Riesling and set the glass on the bar. "It's just as well. If I were in charge of her wedding, I'd probably think of a million ways to ruin it."

"Sounds like a good title for a book—*A Million Ways to Ruin a Wedding.*"

"Yeah, well, I could definitely write that one."

A man at the end of the bar raised a hand, and Jerome went to take his order. I looked at my empty glass and began thinking about all the ways I could ruin a wedding if I really wanted to. Anybody's wedding. Even my sister's. If I really wanted to. But I wouldn't. That would be a little crazy. Besides, I didn't even know what she'd planned for the big day. Although whatever it was, I was sure I could unravel it. It wouldn't be hard. But I'd never do that. The whole idea was too far out there. Even for me. The one whose boyfriend Mariel had stolen. The one who couldn't go back to LA because she was there with Carter. The one whose life she'd ruined.

I ordered another glass of wine and looked around, studying the people in the restaurant as the place began to fill up. But I couldn't get the sabotage idea out of my mind. Maybe it was worth a little more consideration, just as a what-if. Just for the sake of argument.

Okay, then, if I was really going to unravel my sister's wedding plans, what would I do? Tinker with the music for the ceremony? Sure. Change the transportation plan so people would arrive late? Of course. Hide the wedding rings? Absolutely. Or substitute some costume jewelry. I could revise the playlist for the reception, revamp the seating arrangements, and hide the box after people put all the cards and checks in it. And that was just off the top of my head. I could even work on getting Carter back, so rather than wasting my energy feeling sorry for myself, I'd be proactive. I'd be doing something. The thought of it made me sit up a little straighter.

But hold on. This was crazy. Even if I wanted to ruin Mariel's wedding, how would I figure out who the vendors were, the contacts, what the timetable was, the details? I'd have to try to break into her computer. Or Mom's. Although Mom's was easy. She still used that same old password with our birthdays in it. I could go over to the house when they were out, get into her computer; maybe there was even a paper file around with copies of the contracts and...

"Here you go," Jerome said. He placed another glass of wine in front of me.

I took a long sip. "You know, that's not a bad idea."

"What's not a bad idea?"

I leaned in and lowered my voice. "A million ways to ruin a wedding. I could do it to my sister."

"Oh my God," he said, taking a step back. "You're serious."

CHAPTER 6

A GOOD FEELING
IS HARD TO IGNORE

The first thing I did the next morning was e-mail my boss to tell her I had to stay in Connecticut for a couple of weeks. I figured that wouldn't be a problem, because she'd been expecting me to be out for a while, and with my phone and laptop and planners I could work from almost anywhere. Sitting at the banquette in my room at the inn, I called the front desk and extended my stay. The sabotage plan was on. I just needed to figure out the details. And to do that, I had to have information.

The wedding ceremony was being held at St. John's Church in Hampstead at four o'clock a week from Saturday, with the reception taking place afterward at the Hampstead Country Club. I knew that because it was on the invitation and response card I'd thrown out the day they arrived. Beyond that, however, I didn't have a clue. I needed names and contact information for the vendors. I needed to know who was in the bridal party and what music was being played. I needed the guest list and the seating chart and the dinner menu.

I needed to know who, what, when, and where for every minute of that day in order to determine the best way to attack it.

And I needed some supplies, like a notebook for jotting everything down and a flash drive for copying anything wedding-related I might find when I broke into Mom's and Mariel's computers. I thought about the gift shop downstairs and decided to check it out.

The shop was called This and That and it consisted of one bright, cheery room with large windows, whitewashed floors, and walls covered in pale green ivy-patterned paper. The office supplies were limited, but they did have a few spiral notebooks, and I got the last flash drive on the shelf.

As I was heading to the checkout counter, an object on a table caught my eye—a snow globe with two horses and a red barn inside. The bay and buckskin looked just like Two's Company and Cracker-jack, the ponies Mariel and I had had as kids. Something about that scene tugged at my heart, and I found myself picking up the snow globe, shaking it, and watching the flakes fall. I'd just placed it on the checkout counter along with the notebook and flash drive when I heard a familiar voice.

"Okay, tell him to send it to me and I'll take a look. I think that could work."

David. I thought he'd gone back to New York City.

"Yeah, have him e-mail me the photos." His phone pressed to his ear, he made his way toward the table where I'd just been standing. "We could try to get a variance, but I think it's going to be an uphill battle."

Real estate talk. I wasn't interested in that. I wanted to know what was going on with the hand.

"No, I've gotten delayed," he said. "But I'll be back in the office in a day or two. In the meantime, maybe you could..."

He walked across the room, out of earshot. But I kept an eye on him and when I saw him put away his phone, I approached him. He seemed surprised to see me, but he didn't seem angry. That was good.

"You're still here, Miss Fix-It?" There was a glimmer in his eyes I liked, and I had to smile at the nickname.

"Yeah, looks like I'm sticking around for a little while after all."

"I guess that makes two of us," he said.

A playful mood struck me. "By the way, there are plenty of things I *can* fix, you know."

"Oh, I'm sure there are," he said, his tone matching mine. "Just not sculptures by famous artists." That twinkle again.

"True. But I have to draw the line somewhere. I mean, I can't be an expert at everything. I've already got a lot of areas covered, and there are only so many hours in the day."

"Hmm." He tilted his head back, assessing me. "But I was under the impression, given what you said yesterday about your experience with papier-mâché, that you were well schooled in art restoration."

Why did he have to remember that? "Ah. Well, sadly, I realized my skills in that particular area are more suited to pieces created on a kindergarten table during the month of December."

He peered at me in a suspicious way. "Are you saying your experience with papier-mâché was making Christmas ornaments as a five-year-old?"

He'd nailed it. I gave a sheepish nod. "Yep."

He smiled. "You should have seen my papier-mâché ornaments.

60

They were awful. I remember one year we were supposed to make a snowman and mine ended up looking like something out of a horror movie. It had this misshapen nose, and the eyes were dark and evil-looking. My mom was afraid of it. She wouldn't put it up."

I stifled a laugh.

"I bet yours were great compared to that."

"Oh, I don't know…"

He was being so nice. It was making me feel a little nervous, a little fidgety, like I might *jump off the cliff.* That was the term my father gave to my habit of rambling when I was anxious. It was as if the reasonable part of my brain shut down and let the other part go wild.

"So you didn't go back to Manhattan," I said.

"I was going to, but I got a lead on some properties out here and decided to stay and take a look at them."

Why did I feel a little surge of excitement when he said that? I picked up a box of note cards from one of the shelves and tried to shake off the feeling. "Do you think anyone still uses these?" I held up the box. "It seems like a lost art. Although I do. Use them, I mean. My mother taught us when we were little that we had to write thank-you cards. She was a real stickler about it. She said she'd give the gift back if we didn't send a card within a week. She was like a drill sergeant that way. I remember one time when…" I glanced at David. He was staring at me. I was doing it. "I'm sorry. I didn't mean to—"

"I use them sometimes," he said. "Note cards."

"You do?" I wondered if he really did or if he was just being nice. Either way, I felt better.

"Yeah. My mom was tough about that too."

I liked the idea that our mothers shared that trait. I put the box back. "What's going on with the hand? I've been wondering."

"Not much," he said, sounding a little frustrated. "Ana and I haven't been able to get a hold of each other. And I'm not taking it anywhere until I find out exactly what Alex wants to do."

Ana. So much was riding on her. It bothered me that she hadn't returned his call. "You mean you haven't spoken to her?"

"She called me back last night, but it was really late, and I was asleep. I tried her again this morning, but the call went right to her voice mail. I can't leave the story about what happened on her voice mail." His brows angled inward and a little ridge appeared between them. "I know she's been in meetings with Alex and his clients, and there's that time difference, but I really need to talk to her."

"Time difference?" I glanced at a woman trying on an ivory-colored shawl.

"She's in Aspen."

Oh, right. Aspen. I'd forgotten. "I was in Aspen once, when Mariel and I were young. Dad was meeting some people about a play. It was summer and we went on the gondola up Aspen Mountain. Eleven thousand feet. Wow, that thing is…" I began to feel dizzy just remembering it. "It goes up and up and up. And you keep thinking you're near the top, but you're not. I had kind of a problem with it, fainted about halfway up."

David winced. "You fainted?"

"Oh, I wasn't out for long. Mom had a spritzer of Poison in her handbag. Do you know it? The Dior perfume? I guess she thought it might work like smelling salts. She sprayed it all over the place. It did work. Brought me right around. I've carried my own little spritzer ever since. Have you been on the gondola?" God, I was rambling again. I had to stop.

"Yes, I have," David said. "I know what you mean. It's disorienting."

I wondered again if he was saying this sort of thing for my benefit. If he was, it was working. "What are you looking for?" I asked. "Anything in particular?"

He shrugged. "Something to bring back for Ana. She's hard to buy for, though."

Did that mean she was hard to please or that she already had everything she needed? "Is she picky?"

"Yeah, she is kind of picky."

Kind of picky. "Would she return a gift you gave her if she didn't like it?" I never returned a gift unless it was a piece of clothing and the size was wrong. I didn't want to hurt anyone's feelings.

"She's done it, yes. But that's fine. She's got very particular tastes."

She was a gift returner, then. "Well, I guess as long as it doesn't hurt your feelings..."

"I just want her to be happy."

How sweet he was. I hoped Ana appreciated it.

I looked at the woman trying on the shawl. She'd switched to one in lavender, and when she turned, I thought for a moment she was Christy Costigan from my class at Hampstead High. Christy had sat across from me in three-dimensional art. I could still see those long tables and the cabinets filled with sculpting tools and paints and brushes. I could smell the paper and glue, the clay, the paint thinner. And I could see the teacher—petite, blond, pretty. She was a little bit of a free spirit. What was her name? Miss Bain, Miss Blair, something like that. No, wait a minute. It was Miss Baird. Jeanette Baird.

She taught sculpture. She *was* a sculptor. She showed us pictures of her work. Some of it was in galleries. An effervescent feeling enveloped me. Miss Baird could fix the hand. If she was still in the area, I'd find her and get her to do it. It was a brilliant idea. So brilliant I could have danced around the room. I'd figured out a way to resolve the hand dilemma. I turned to David, who was leafing through a coffee-table book. "I've got an idea about the hand. We can ask someone to help us."

He closed the book and put it back on the shelf. "What? No. Definitely not. We tried that at the art store, remember? It turned out to be way too complicated."

"I mean we could ask an artist. A real artist. I was thinking of Miss Baird, one of my high-school teachers. She was a wonderful sculptor. She could fix that thing in her sleep."

"Your high-school art teacher?" One eyebrow went up so high, it looked as if it were about to take off. I could hear the skepticism in his voice. "Sara, thank you, but I can deal with this. When Ana calls me back, I'll let her know what happened and take it from there."

He was probably right. I needed to stay out of it, let him handle it. But it seemed crazy to give up now when there might be someone who could really help. I had a good feeling about this plan. And a good feeling is hard to ignore.

"I'll be right back," I said. I walked into the hall, took out my phone, and put Jeanette's name into a couple of people-search web-sites. No luck. Maybe I could find her through Hampstead High. Except it was July. Would anyone be there to answer the phone? Then I remembered summer school would be going on. I looked up the phone number and tapped it into my phone; the girl who answered sounded like a student herself. When I explained that I was trying to track down my art teacher from twenty years ago, she told me there were no art teachers at the school who had been around that long. I asked if they had records for past teachers, and she assured me they did but that those *really old* records, the ones *on paper,* were stored off-site.

Really old. Paper. I felt like a dinosaur.

"And we can't give out teachers' personal information without their permission," she said. I thanked her, hung up, and went back into the gift shop, where David was still browsing. "Well, so much for that idea."

"What idea?" he asked. Then he realized, shook his head, and stared at the ceiling. "Oh no. Not the art teacher."

"Well..." I grimaced.

"God, you're stubborn."

"People have told me that."

"I can see why."

"I just thought I'd give it a try, but I couldn't find her."

"Welcome to the real world, Sara. Things aren't always as easy as you think."

"I don't always think things are easy. I just hate to give up."

He picked up a handblown wineglass from a set on a shelf. "I understand that, but you have to admit, some of your ideas are a little *out there.* I'm going to talk to Ana and see what she and Alex want me to do. I just need some instructions so I can get back to Manhattan. I have a lot to take care of in the next couple of weeks before Ana and I fly to Paris."

Paris. I'd been to Paris twice, both times for weddings I'd planned.

I'd never been there on a personal trip, although Carter and I had talked about going. Carter. I used to think about us strolling across the Pont Neuf under a sunny sky or gliding down the Seine on a boat, Notre-Dame winking in the night as we passed. How romantic. The City of Light. The City of Love.

"Paris is such a romantic place," I said. "Are you going on vacation or for business?"

"Definitely not business."

Something in David's demeanor had changed, and I got a strange feeling I knew what this trip was for. "Are you proposing?" The words leaped out before I could stop them.

"How did you know?" His cheeks turned pink as he put the glass on the shelf.

"Then this is a really special trip. Where are you staying?" I grabbed his arm, startling him. I was in full planning mode. "You have to stay at the Meurice or the George Cinq. That's all there is to it." I didn't mention those were the only hotels where I'd ever stayed in Paris. "I personally prefer the George Cinq, but the Meurice is wonderful as well. I'd recommend either."

"Uh, thanks for the tip. But I've booked a suite at the Plaza Athénée. I've stayed there before."

Of course. He actually *knew* Paris. What a jerk I was. My face tingled with heat. "That's a great choice too. Lovely rooms, wonderful service." I'd only passed the place in taxis and seen photos on the internet, but it did look great and I was sure the service was wonderful. "She'll love it."

David took out his phone. "I hope so." He began scrolling, then passed the phone to me. "Here's a photo of Ana."

She was beautiful—high cheekbones, short, blunt haircut, long neck. She looked graceful, like a ballet dancer. "She's very pretty." I tried to picture them together, but my mind went a little cloudy.

"Yeah, she is." He put the phone away.

I picked up a sachet bag from the table and held it to my face, inhaling the scent of rose petals. "Have you figured out how you're going to propose?" I wondered if he'd planned something unusual or if he was going to stick with a more traditional approach. I also wondered if I should offer my help with their wedding plans, but I really didn't want to help Ana. She sounded too picky.

"I made a reservation for dinner at Le Jules Verne in the Eiffel Tower. I've already spoken to the manager and they're going to decorate a dessert plate with the words *Will You Marry Me, Ana?* The ring will be in a box in the center, and I'm putting a photo of the two of us in the box. They'll have a bottle of Krug Clos du Mesnil ready."

"That's lovely, David." And it was. Just the right touch. I felt a little pang of jealousy. Ana was a lucky woman.

"She's kind of traditional. I thought that would be a good approach."

"I agree. I see so many outrageous, showy proposals, all for the sake of social media, I'm sure. That's not what I'd want."

"I know what you mean," he said. "It's as though there's no limit to what people do these days."

I told him about all the will-you-marry-me fireworks displays I'd set up—enough to make the idea trite. And about the man who'd had me commission a private air show that ended with his proposal written in the sky. "Oh, and speaking of Paris, I had a client who asked me to arrange a boat ride on the Seine, and at a prearranged place, two scuba divers popped up with a little treasure chest. The ring was inside."

"Way over the top," David said as he picked up a pale blue throw blanket and felt the fabric. It looked handwoven and very soft. He glanced at me. "So what would you want? For yourself, I mean."

"For myself?" I'd never really thought about what I'd want. I'd never gotten that close to being engaged. "Well, not skywriters or scuba divers, that's for sure. Definitely something more low-key. I guess I'd just want it to be romantic. Kind of like what you're doing."

David nodded. Then he put the throw blanket under his arm, and I knew he'd found his gift. We paid for our purchases and I followed him as he went outside to put the box in the van. Sunlight poured onto the lawn as we walked down the front steps, and puffy pink clouds drifted across the sky as though pulled by strings. I kept thinking about David and Ana's wedding, wondering what it would be like, where they would get married, how many people they would invite. What would her dress look like? (And how many dresses would she try on before she found the right one?) Would she take his last name or keep hers? Or want a hyphenated version of the two?

At the foot of the steps I stopped. "I just thought of something. Maybe she's using her *married* name."

"Who's using her married name? What are you talking about?"

"Miss Baird. My art teacher."

"We're back to her? Sara, listen to me—"

"No, wait. Hear me out. Please. She got married the year I was in her class—my senior year. But she never used her married name.

Not at school, anyway. Maybe she's using it now." We crossed the grass toward the parking lot.

"But websites that give out people's addresses have all that information," David said. "They have maiden names. You would have found her if she was in Connecticut."

He was probably right. Still, if I could remember her married name, it would be worth a try. I had a vague recollection of it being complicated. And I thought I'd seen it printed somewhere—her maiden name and married name together. But the memory was like a slippery fish I couldn't grasp. *Jeanette Baird, Jeanette Baird.* I said it to myself as we headed toward the van. And then I recalled a photo with her name under it.

"I've got it. I know where I can find her name. My high-school yearbook. It's in my room at the house. At least, I think it's still there."

"Sara, this is too far-fetched. Even if you could find her, how do you know she's capable of fixing that sculpture? It's a valuable piece of art. And even if she is capable, how do you know she'll do it? I'm going to wait until I hear from Ana."

"All I'm saying is it's worth checking out. I told you she's really talented. And I know we could get her to do it. Look, I understand what you're saying. But until you do hear from Ana, why not explore this idea? Let me at least find the yearbook and get her name. See if I can track her down. There's no harm in that, is there?"

"I guess trying to talk you out of this would be a waste of time."

"I'll stop at the house this afternoon. My sister will be out, so I won't have to run into her. She's going with Mom to some photo-shoot thing." I could do my sleuthing at the same time. See if I could get into Mariel's laptop or Mom's. Look for papers. Find some information on the wedding.

"Photo-shoot thing?"

"My mother's getting an award. Something to do with fund-raising for the Hampstead Country Playhouse. She does a lot of stuff with them. She has an acting class there."

"Your mom takes an acting class?" David said. He unlocked the van and put the box inside.

I laughed. "No, she teaches one. Every couple of years. She's an actor."

"Really?" He closed the door.

"Yeah, plays, musicals, that kind of thing."

"Where? Regional theater?"

"Regional, Broadway. She's done it all."

He gave a quick shake of his head, like he hadn't heard right. "Broadway. What's your mom's name?"

"Camille. Camille Harrington."

He mumbled the name as we started walking back toward the inn. "What plays was she in?"

I used to think it would be a good idea to carry a copy of Mom's bio with me for situations like this. I could just hand it over. "Well, on Broadway she was in *Dragonfly Nights, A Quiet Evening at Home, Who's Pulling the Rickshaw?* The original, back in the late nineties, not the revival that was on Broadway a few years ago."

"I saw the revival of *Rickshaw*. It was great."

"Mom had the part of Cora."

"The lead. Wow," David said as we passed a family emerging from an SUV.

"Let me think, what else…oh, *Eggs and Bacon, Hold the Toast.*"

"The play about the diner? I never got to see it, but I heard it was great."

"Again, she was in the original, not the revival."

"I'm impressed. What about your dad? Is he an actor too?"

I kicked away a little branch that had fallen onto the pavement. "My dad died several years ago."

"I'm sorry," he said, his voice quiet.

"Thanks. He was a great guy. Creative, too, but in a different way from Mom. He produced plays."

"So they were both in the business."

"Yeah. Except he always used to say he was the one with more experience, because he'd produced his first play when he was twelve. He did a streamlined version of *Hair* with a bunch of neighborhood kids. It lasted half an hour and ran for two nights in his family's garage."

We were at the edge of the parking lot where a shuttle bus was filling up with hotel guests. "That's a great story. I guess you never got the bug, though? Never wanted to be onstage?"

"Me? An actor?" I giggled.

"What's funny about that? You'd probably be good at it. You've proven you can talk people into things. I would think you could talk them into believing you're someone else. And you're charming and pretty. Why couldn't you do it?"

I had no interest in being onstage in any capacity, but I liked what he'd said about me being charming and pretty. "Thanks, but it's not my thing."

"Did your parents meet through the theater?"

"Yes, when Dad was doing *Dragonfly Nights.* He always said it was his favorite show because that's how he met my mother. My parents were kind of an odd couple because Mom is—well, she can be a little dramatic, and my father was more down-to-earth. Very creative, but he could figure things out and make decisions one, two, three. A great businessman.

"Some people even called him a genius, but he always scoffed at that. I think he just had a talent for picking interesting stories and adapting them for the theater. He called it *rounding them out.* I remember right after *Miss Keaton Returns* won a bunch of Tonys, a reporter for the *Boston Globe* interviewed him and asked why so many of his shows had been so successful. You know what he said?"

David shook his head.

"*Sheer luck.* It wasn't true, though. He was brilliant. But like I said, he was different from Mom. He loved that whole dramatic side of hers, but he was also good at reining her in when she needed it. He helped keep her grounded."

A large group of hotel guests were walking toward us, probably heading to the shuttle bus. "Why did she need reining in?"

"She just gets crazy ideas sometimes. The reason why I'm in town is that she told my sister and me she was terminally ill. She hoped that would get us both here and we'd reconcile."

"It's too bad you and your sister don't get along," David said. "My brother and I were such good friends. I'd give anything to have him back." He looked away, and I could tell he was reliving some memory of their time together, some skateboarding adventure or the construction of a Lego neighborhood. "People are always shocked when I tell them I was only twelve when Beau died. They say, *How young you were, that's terrible*. But I didn't think about it that way back then—that I was young or that he was young. All I knew was that was my life. My brother was dead, and I had to go on without him. As I get older, though, I understand what they were really saying. That I got cheated losing him so early. I have friends with brothers, and I think how lucky they are to still have them around."

"I know what you mean, at least a little bit. Most of my friends still have both their parents, but I don't have my dad anymore."

We were back at the steps of the inn. On the wraparound porch, an elderly man and woman sat in wicker chairs, sipping what looked like lemonade. David glanced at them. "Do you think people make better couples when they're more alike or when they're different?"

I didn't know the answer to that. "I'm not sure. I guess I've seen it work both ways." I wondered why he was asking. I wondered which of those scenarios fit his relationship with Ana.

We walked up the steps and into the lobby. "I'll run by the house this afternoon and grab that yearbook. And if you've already spoken to Ana, then we'll drop it. I'll call you and let you know what I find." I handed him my cell phone. "Put your number in there, okay?"

He took the phone, tapped in David Cole, and added his number. "All right, Sara."

"I have a good feeling about this."

He winced, but at the same time he was sort of smiling. "You say that about a lot of things."

CHAPTER 7

A PROPOSAL

The house looked quiet when I pulled into the driveway. Jubilee and Anthem were in their paddocks, grazing, their tails swishing at flies. I looked in the garage window and saw both bays empty. Mom's Mercedes was gone, as I'd expected, but so was the Austin-Healey, a 1965 3000 Mark III convertible in British racing green Dad had paid a fortune to restore. It was just like Mariel to help herself to that car. I shuddered thinking how awful it would be if she scratched or dented it.

I unlocked the mudroom door, stepped inside, and walked down the hall. The only sounds were my footsteps on the wooden floor and the heavy clunk of the pendulum in the grandfather clock. In the kitchen I helped myself to some strawberries and ate them at the counter as I stared at an old photo in a silver frame. Me in my cap and gown at my high-school graduation with Mom and Dad and Mariel. A moment after that picture was taken, a little group had gathered around Mom, asking for her autograph. Out-of-towners who just couldn't resist, who didn't know you were supposed to leave people alone. But she loved it.

Next to the frame was a coffee mug, *The Best Mommy in the World* on it in curlicue letters, fancy writing for my then seven-year-old hand. Underneath, Mariel had drawn a stick figure of Mom. I recalled our collaboration on that mug at a pottery-painting studio. How had the two of us arrived at this place where we wanted nothing but to avoid each other?

I saw a stack of unopened mail on the table. Maybe there was something wedding-related in there. I thumbed through the envelopes. Water bill, electric bill, invoice from the feed store. Nothing helpful. On the other side of the table was a leather three-ring binder, PHOTOS embossed on the cover. We had several albums in the house like it. Mom must have been taking a trip down memory lane.

I flipped through the pages. Mariel and me at Disney World, waiting in line at the Barnstormer, the mini–roller coaster in the Magic Kingdom. The two of us in front of Minnie Mouse's country home, all that lavender and pink. Pages later I was graduating from preschool, holding a rolled-up "diploma." Further along were Halloween parties and Christmases and birthday parties and school events.

I paused at a photo of Mariel with her hair covered in spaghetti and tomato sauce. She was six at the time, and I'd gotten so angry about something she'd done that I'd dumped the bowl of pasta on her head. For years she'd complained about that photo being in the album. I was surprised it was still in there.

There were other pictures she'd complained about as well, like the one from her middle-school years where she was imitating Britney

Spears in her famous "... Baby One More Time" video. Mariel's hair was in braids like the singer's and she was in an outfit like the schoolgirl uniform Britney had worn, with the miniskirt and knee socks. I remembered how she danced around the house, singing that song. You couldn't even mention Britney Spears's name to Mariel now without her having a fit, she was so embarrassed about that period of her life.

As I flipped to the next page, something fell out and floated to the floor. A newspaper clipping from the *Hampstead Review*, August of last year.

Mariel Harrington to Wed Carter Pryce

Camille Harrington of Hampstead announces the engagement of her daughter Mariel Harrington to Carter Pryce, son of James and Sandra Pryce of Rye, New York. The bride is the daughter of the late John Harrington. She is a graduate of California State University and was most recently a receptionist with YogaBuzz in Los Angeles. The future bridegroom graduated from Cornell University and Georgetown Law and is a partner with Bingham Keith Rodrick, LLC, a Los Angeles law firm.

The couple is planning to wed next summer.

And there they were in a photo, the two of them smiling, Carter with his arm around Mariel, her head resting against his shoulder. They stood on a terrace, the blue California ocean in the background. I recognized the terrace. I knew the restaurant in Malibu.

Carter and I used to go there, and after dinner we'd walk on the beach as the sun set, heading toward a tiny strip of land far down the sand that was immersed in that golden sunlight that comes at the end of the day. I could almost smell the salt air and the woody-scented aftershave Carter wore, could almost feel his hand in mine the way I did then as we strolled toward that light.

I took a picture of the photo with my phone. I'd edit Mariel out and keep Carter. He looked so handsome.

I needed to get into Mom's computer, but I also wanted to find that yearbook. Upstairs in my room I scanned my bookcase, the shelves of which were full of horse-show trophies, novels, and trinkets from my childhood. I pulled my senior-class Hampstead High yearbook from the bottom shelf and paged through to the teachers' section. Miss Baird was there, wearing a white gauzy top and a beaded necklace. Her hair, the color of corn, was styled in a braid. Her large green eyes made her look perennially curious. I tried to guess how old she'd been then. Early thirties, maybe. The name under the photo was *Jeanette Baird Gwythyr*. Gwythyr? What kind of a name was that? No wonder I couldn't remember it. I wasn't even sure how to pronounce it, all those consonants.

My phone seemed to digest the information when I put the name into the people-search website; a blue bar proceeded across the top of my screen. A moment later she popped up: Jeanette Gwythyr, 516 Upland Road, Eastville, Connecticut. The words danced in front of me. She was still around here; Eastville wasn't more than a forty-five-minute drive. This was going to work.

I tapped her number into my phone and took a deep breath. *Pick up, pick up.* I heard a click and then a woman's voice. *Hi there. You've reached the home of Cadwy and Jeanette Gwythyr.* She pronounced it "Gwith-er," like *zither.*

Leave us a message, she said. *Share your story.*

A message. My story. How could I explain it in a message?

"Hi, Mrs....uh, Miss Baird. This is Sara Harrington. I don't know if you remember me, but I graduated from Hampstead High twenty years ago. I know it's been a while, but you were my three-D-design teacher in twelfth grade. And I still recall what a great artist you were. *Are.*" A little flattery couldn't hurt.

"If you don't remember me, you might remember Christy Costigan. She made a huge cat out of clay. Claws and whiskers and everything. I sat next to her." Maybe she wouldn't even remember Christy. "Or Julia Feretti? She re-created sections of Michelangelo's *Last Judgment* in miniature on a set of rubber spatulas." They were beautiful, although I heard her mom had used them by mistake and the paint came off in the dishwasher. "Oh, wait, that was painting class. You might not have taught Julia.

"Anyway, I'm in Hampstead for a few days and I could really use your help with something—a piece of art, a sculpture. I'd love to talk to you about it. It's kind of important. Would you please call me as soon as you can?" I left my number.

It was probably a long shot. Still, I had a good feeling as I texted David and gave him the update. He replied, telling me to let him know what I heard back. Maybe he was actually going to go along with this. Amazing.

I was about to take a quick look at Christy Costigan's picture when I heard footsteps in the hall. I figured Mom had come back early. But then I heard Mariel's voice. She was coming up the stairs, talking on her phone. A moment later she stood in my doorway.

"I have to call you back." She clicked off the phone, slipped it into her handbag. Her nails, the color of pink grapefruit, looked as though they'd just been done. "I'm glad you're here," she said.

I closed the yearbook and put it on the bed as she strolled to my bureau and began to look at the things on top—a jar of loose change I'd collected from foreign countries, an old photo of our parents, a silver baby cup, a bottle of perfume. She picked up the baby cup, turned it around, and looked at my initials engraved on the front. "Can we, uh, chitchat for a minute?" She flashed me a little smile.

Chitchat? "It depends on what you want to chitchat about." I wasn't going to talk about the wedding. Or Carter. Or any of that. I stood by the bookcase, waiting for her to say whatever she was going to say.

She took a large coin from the jar on the bureau. "I think we need to move forward. Get beyond this." She turned the coin over and then dropped it back into the jar; it landed with a clank. "I feel like we're in a war. Like we're in *The White Queen*."

"White Queen?"

"The TV series. Haven't you seen it? It's *sooo* good. One side of this family is fighting with the other side because they both want to rule England."

"I haven't seen it."

"Oh, you should. It was made...I don't know, years ago, but it's good."

"I already know the story. I studied it in history."

She started. "You mean it's *true?*"

I thought she was joking, but she didn't laugh. "Yes, of course it's true." How could she not know that? Oh, I forgot. She spent her four years of college taking History of Lipstick or something instead of real history. "It was referred to as the War of the Roses. You might look it up sometime."

She picked up the perfume, sprayed it into the air, sniffed, and put the bottle back. "Look, that's not what I wanted to talk about. I wanted to tell you I'm sorry about what happened. So is Carter. I mean, we're not sorry we're together..." She twirled her engagement ring around her finger. "But we're sorry about how you found out. You know, New Year's Eve and everything. And that we never told you things were...happening the way they were."

Well, that was at least something. Her phone messages and texts and e-mails had never included such a straightforward apology.

"So, like I said, I thought we should try to put it behind us."

She was sounding more and more like Mom. *You girls have got to put this behind you.* Could I put it behind me? Oh God, a part of me wanted to, I had to admit. Deep down inside I knew the anger was eating me alive. But I didn't know how to put it behind me. Too many things had changed forever because of what she'd done.

"I don't know what to tell you," I said. "I need to think about it. I need some time to process what you're saying. To figure out if...and how..." You couldn't just snap your fingers and expect the past to glide away, could you?

Mariel walked to the closet door and glanced at herself in the mirror. "Well, okay, that's fine. Think about it. For sure. Because I'm dealing with a lot of things right now, and I'm getting stressed out."

She straightened one of the straps of her dress. "So I just think we should, you know, move forward."

Move forward? Was that like putting your foot on the gas pedal and driving to another town? I wished it were that easy. Maybe it was for her. I knew it wasn't for me. And yet, I was tempted to say that, yes, we should see what we could do to start putting things back together, or as back together as they could be.

"But don't think about it for too long," she said, "because I'd like you to be in the wedding. Be a bridesmaid. The way we always planned."

I flinched, my elbow bumping a photo on the bookcase—me at seven, riding Crackerjack. The frame fell to the wood floor with a smack; the horse-show ribbon clipped to it went flying. I picked up the frame and put it back on the shelf. A little piece of glass had been chipped off. This was all happening way too fast. I hadn't even said I could move forward, let alone go to the wedding, let alone be *in* the wedding. How could I be a bridesmaid at the wedding of the man I was in love with?

And why did she say, *The way we always planned*? That was teenager talk, years ago. We hadn't spoken of it in ages.

Mariel must have mistaken my shock for delight. A smile bloomed on her face. "You're surprised," she said, sitting on the bed. "I know." She picked up the yearbook and began leafing through it. "Here's the thing. It's kind of weird the way it worked out, but I think it's all good. See, my friend Baily...you remember her? From Newport Beach? Tall, blond, cute?" That could have described half the women in California. "She can't come because she broke her leg in two places. Skiing in Argentina." Mariel turned a couple of pages.

"We're supposed to have a maid of honor, a best man, three brides-maids, and three groomsmen. And now we're short a bridesmaid. So I thought you might want to take Baily's place."

She couldn't be serious. She wanted me to sub for another bridesmaid? The one she picked first? "You've got to be kidding. You're asking me to be a second-stringer?" I could barely get out the words.

"You can use her dress," she went on. "The bridesmaid dresses are gorgeous. In this mauve color. They call it rose quartz. With a little ruching here." She ran her hands across her bust. "And a cinched waist." She grasped her sides. "I had Baily send it to me. She's taller than you, but we could get it altered." She closed the yearbook. "I need to get my gown altered too. The waist needs to be taken in a little. We could go together."

A stand-in bridesmaid with a stand-in dress. She wanted me to be in *her* wedding to *my* former boyfriend as a stand-in for *her* girl-friend to even out the bridesmaids-groomsmen count. And with a mauve dress. I couldn't wear mauve. It made me look completely washed out. She must have known from my expression that I wanted no part of it.

"This is my wedding," she said. "And you're my sister. You're supposed to help me out here. It's my big day. You have no idea what it's like being the bride. I know you've planned a lot of wed-dings, but you've never been on the other side of one. I've got a lot of anxiety about this, Sara. Carter's invited some of his partners and clients. Everything has to be perfect. It has to be right. I really need your help."

I was about to refuse when I realized she'd presented me with a fantastic opportunity. Being in the wedding party would give me the chance to gather all the details I needed about the event. It would also give me the perfect excuse for staying in town. I'd leave the Duncan Arms and move right here, into my old room, where I could be in the middle of everything.

I waited for a minute, pretending to give a lot of thought to what she'd asked. "You're right," I finally said. "We should put our differences aside. What happened in the past needs to stay in the past. Let's look to the future."

Mariel's eyes brightened. "You think?"

"Yes, I do. I'll be your bridesmaid. And I'll do more than that. I'll even be your wedding planner for these last couple of weeks so you don't have to deal with any more stress."

Mariel flopped down in the middle of my bed as though she were exhausted. "Oh, that's great."

I smiled. "Leave it all to me."

CHAPTER 8

ALTERATIONS

I checked out of the Duncan Arms and brought my suitcase to the house. I'd barely finished unpacking when Mariel appeared in the doorway of my room and insisted we bring our gowns into town to get them altered.

Twenty minutes later, we walked into Marcello's Tailoring with our garment bags. A black-and-white cat curled up in a chair near the door opened his eyes, raised his head, squinted at me, and collapsed back to sleep. Halfway across the room, Bella, mid-fifties, olive complexion, thin frame, knelt in front of a small platform with a mirror around it and directed a customer to turn as she pinned the hem of her dress. Bella had been running the business since her father, Marcello, retired a few years back.

"I'll be right with you, ladies." She glanced at us and pushed a couple of dark curls behind her ears, revealing silver hoop earrings.

We took seats near a wall of wooden shelves filled with bolts of cloth. I remembered going there as a child with my father and being mesmerized by all that fabric, organized by color, from pale yellows to peachy pinks and teal blues to the darkest, inkiest blacks. There was another room in the back where the work was done, a room Dad and I got to glimpse once when we were there. How surprised I was to see two women working away on old sewing machines. I'd always imagined Marcello did everything himself, like a singular Santa's elf.

"It's the Harrington girls," Bella said, greeting us after her other customer left. "Nice to see you. It's been a while." She eyed the garment bags, a pincushion in her hand. "What can I help you with?"

"Well," Mariel said, hanging her garment bag on a rod by the counter, "I'm getting married, and I have a very special wedding gown that needs some final alterations."

Bella's eyes danced. "Ooh! You're getting married. Congratulations. When's the big day?"

"A week from Saturday," Mariel said.

"And I have a bridesmaid gown that needs to be altered," I added as I hung my gown on the rod next to Mariel's.

"You've worked on wedding gowns before," Mariel said in a tone that was half question, half statement.

"Of course," Bella said, turning to glance at a calendar on the wall. "A week from Saturday. That's coming right up. Go try them on so I can see what I'll need to do."

Mariel and I took our gowns to the dressing room in the back. She unzipped her garment bag, and my first glimpse of her gown took my breath away. It was exquisite. Sheath silhouette, a scoop neckline, fitted waist, and a simple but elegant train. There had to be five layers of fabric in that dress, the one on top being the most gorgeous floral-patterned lace I'd ever seen. It looked like the kind of lace someone's great-grandmother had made by hand a hundred years ago in a tiny little town in Italy. I looked at the label: Valentino. No wonder.

"That's quite a dress," I said, running my hand over the fabric. It was thick, luxurious. I'd never felt anything like it. Or seen anything like it. I stared at the minute patterns in the lace. Every square inch was a work of art.

It must have cost a fortune. I knew Carter had paid for it because Mom told me he'd insisted on buying the gown. I couldn't believe Mariel had asked him to buy such an expensive one, though. I would never have done that. But then, I understood the value of a dollar. Mariel, who had always depended on others for her financial well-being, did not.

She stepped into the dress and I zipped up the back. She turned, studying her reflection in the mirror. The gown looked spectacular—the cut, the fabric, the lace. If only I were the one wearing it. If only I were the one marrying Carter. I pictured us at the altar, Carter saying his vows to me. *To love and to cherish . . .*

"Hello," Mariel said, waving a hand in my face. "You need to try on your dress."

"Right," I said, unzipping the other garment bag. The bridesmaid's gown was tulle over silk with a ruched, crisscrossed top and flowing skirt. I put it on. It was at least four inches too long. Baily Richardson was one tall girl.

"Hmm." Mariel stood back and studied me. "Not sure that's the best color on you."

No kidding it wasn't the best color on me. "Couldn't you have gotten it in a different color? You know I don't look good in mauve."

"Hey, you weren't even coming to the wedding when I picked out that dress."

"Well, I'm here now."

"And you have to wear it."

There was a knock on the door. "Excuse me. Do you need some help with zippers or buttons or... anything?"

Bella. She'd probably heard us. "We're okay," I said.

When we emerged from the dressing room, Bella clasped her hands and I could see her eyes were misty. "Look at you! What a beautiful bride you're going to be." She circled Mariel, studying the gown, touching the fabric, nodding. Then she turned to me as if she'd suddenly remembered her manners. "Oh, and you too. You look very nice."

I forced a smile.

She directed Mariel to the platform. "I can see it's a little big for you—"

"It's way too big," Mariel said. "I can't believe the bridal shop didn't get this right. I have a tiny waist. I'm swimming in this."

Bella gathered some fabric on either side of Mariel's waist. "If we take it in a bit here and here... I think... yes, that should do it."

"Don't you see?" Mariel said, looking in the mirror, angry little lines crossing her face. "Don't you see how tiny my waist is? How could they have thought this would fit me?"

If she said *tiny waist* one more time, I was going to choke her.

Bella picked up a pincushion and began pinning the dress. "Who's the lucky man?"

Mariel's face relaxed. "His name is Carter Pryce. He's a lawyer in Los Angeles. An *entertainment* lawyer. He works with movie stars."

"Movie stars." Bella sounded impressed.

"Yes, movie stars, singers, writers. Producers too. He has all kinds of celebrity clients. He's very successful."

Oh, please. Did we really have to hear this?

"We're going to the Telluride Film Festival next month. Or maybe it's the month after. I don't remember." She smoothed the bodice of her gown like a preening bird.

In the beginning, I'd been excited about those things too. The parties, the benefits, the industry events. Black-tie this, black-tie that. I remembered how impressed I'd been by a Thanksgiving dinner at Carter's, early in our relationship, with a lot of Hollywood A-listers and food catered by some trendy new restaurant. A little part of me had longed for a simple family meal, but I'd tried to think of it as a once-in-a-lifetime experience.

"You'll probably like the film festival," I said. "Personally, I'm glad I don't have to do that kind of thing anymore. All those crowds and starstruck fans."

"I'm looking forward to it."

"Not to mention the altitude. It's hard to breathe."

"Then it's good you won't be there," Mariel said, sounding cheerful, as Bella gestured for her to turn. "I'm sure you'll be happier in Chicago. With those cold winters. And the crime. And the pollution."

I wanted to remind her she was the reason I'd had to escape LA and go to Chicago, but I bit my tongue. I had to keep my eyes on the prize.

Bella finished pinning the right side of the dress and was about to start on the left when the door to the back room opened and in walked a small man, slightly hunched over, bald, with bushy eyebrows. Marcello. He stared at us for a few seconds and then burst into a grin.

"The Harringtons. My, my. How long has it been? Three, four years?"

"At least," I said.

He looked at Mariel. "And what's this? You're getting married?"

She smiled. "I sure am."

"Congratulations! Such a surprise." He glanced at Bella. "Nobody tells me anything."

Bella shook her head, her brows raised. "I didn't know, Pop."

"Who's the lucky man?"

Did we really have to go through this again? "She's marrying an entertainment attorney," I said. "In Los Angeles. Carter Pryce." I needed to speed things up here.

"And you're a bridesmaid."

"Yes, I'm a bridesmaid." I was clenching my teeth.

He turned to Mariel again. "Are you going to live in Los Angeles?"

"Yes, we already live there. But we're looking for a new house."

They were? Carter had a gorgeous home on a hill overlooking Santa Monica. Who wouldn't want to live there? I remembered those lazy Sunday mornings, the two of us sitting on his terrace, reading, drinking coffee, the city skyline visible through a clearing in the trees, the ocean wild and blue beyond it.

"My fiancé has a house," Mariel said. "But I think we should start with something new. A place we can make our own, not a house he already has. My designer has a lot of ideas and I'm sure when we find the right place, it will turn out to be perfect."

Her designer? She was talking about Carter's designer. I was ready to explode.

"I thought you retired," I said to Marcello, hoping to change the subject.

He smiled a patient smile. "Sure. I did. I'm almost eighty. But, you know, retirement isn't something you do all at once. I get bored. So I come in sometimes and help my Bella." He gave her a gentle clap on the shoulder.

"Don't believe it," she muttered, putting a final pin in the dress. "He'll always be the boss." She stepped back. "There. What do you think?"

Mariel looked in the mirror, turning in one direction and then the other. "I think this will work."

"Okay, next," Bella said, nodding to me.

I stepped onto the platform as Mariel walked back to the dressing room. Bella pinned the hem and made a couple of adjustments in the shoulders as I stood there fuming. Couldn't Carter see Mariel was manipulating him into buying a new house when he didn't need one?

"There," Bella said when she was done. "How does that look?"

It looked better, but it was still mauve.

"All right," she said as Mariel came out of the dressing room. "Let me get your information down. Phone numbers and all."

Mariel followed her to the counter, and I went to change. When I opened the dressing-room door, I saw her gown hanging there, pinned by Bella to ensure the perfect fit. I stared at the graceful neckline, the lace, the fitted silhouette, the layers of fabric, the train that would swirl gracefully around Mariel's feet. I imagined her floating down the aisle in the gown, a spray of orchids at the end of each pew, candles flickering, all eyes on her.

Then I remembered my client, the girl the seamstress had had to sew into her gown, and the image of my sister changed. She was still walking down the aisle, but suddenly there was a loud *rrrrip* and her dress split open, exposing a three-inch-wide strip of skin all the way down her back.

The bridesmaids shrieked and huddled around her, trying to block everyone's view. The guests gasped, and the priest looked as if he would rather be selling fire extinguishers door to door than be there. Carter was pale, clearly in shock. Then he saw me, sitting off to the side. Our eyes locked and I knew he was smitten. Again. It was as if no time had passed, as if nothing had happened.

I never stopped loving you, Sara, he said, loud enough for everyone in the church to hear. He grabbed the wedding rings from the ring bearer—who was only five but knew this wasn't how it had gone at the rehearsal—walked over to me, and said, *Sara Harrington, will you marry me?*

My sister fainted dead away. Even my spritzer of Poison didn't bring her around. They had to carry her off somewhere to revive her. Texas, maybe. But meanwhile, the wedding went on, except now *I* was the bride. I modified the ceremony a little and switched out a couple of the music selections. At the reception, I put all my favorite tunes on the band's playlist, changed Mariel's name to mine on the wedding cake, and...

"I don't know how they could have done that," Mariel was saying to Bella. "You do see how tiny my waist is, don't you?"

She thought she had a tiny waist? I'd show her a tiny waist. I took Bella's pins out one by one and moved them to make the dress an inch narrower on each side. Now, *that* was a tiny waist.

The sabotage had begun.

CHAPTER 9

GOING LAME

I heard someone call my name as Mariel and I left Marcello's. Tate Lambert was walking toward us, waving. I hadn't seen him since his wedding six years ago, although we'd exchanged the occasional e-mail, the last one coming about a year back, an announcement that he'd added a second vet to his formerly solo equine practice.

"Hey, Sara!" he said, his smile revealing the dimples I remembered so well.

"Tate" was all I could get out before he threw his arms around me and rocked me back and forth.

We'd been friends since first grade, and in high school we came close to a romance before one of us chickened out. I think I was the one. I was afraid to risk our friendship. And I was kind of in love with Scott Wilders at the time, although Scott wasn't in love with me. I heard years later that he'd moved to Alaska, which was way too cold anyway.

Tate looked a little different from the way he did in the photo

I remembered in the e-mail announcement. He still had that same hairstyle, if you could call it that—kind of tousled, like he'd just woken up. But now I saw gray flecks in his hair. And he looked leaner. Not that he'd ever carried much extra weight, but there was a stripped-down look about him that was new. He still had that impish smile, though, and the slightly crooked nose, the result of a run-in with a plate-glass door when he was fifteen.

"And Mariel," he said, giving her a hug as well, although it was slightly more subdued. "The bride-to-be." He studied her for a moment that ticked on a little too long. "Wow, you look great. Did you change your hair or something?"

Hair? He honestly thought that's all it was? Of course she'd changed her hair. She had that short platinum thing going on now, with the layers. But didn't he realize she'd changed her entire look, with the Escada bag and the Louboutins and everything else she had on?

"Yeah, I changed…something," she said, with a coquettish tilt of her head. Then she looked at me. "Tate's coming to the wedding."

"Oh. That's great." I guess I was a little surprised, although maybe I shouldn't have been. He was an old family friend, not to mention Anthem and Jubilee's vet.

"It's so good to see you," I said, giving his arm a little squeeze. He'd always been a sweet guy. And there was nothing like seeing an old friend who knew you from way back, who knew your history. Someone you could talk to like you'd never been apart even if you hadn't seen each other in years.

Sometimes I wondered if I should have acted on that romantic undercurrent I'd felt during those teenage years, but then we probably wouldn't be standing here talking now. I wished I could say he'd ended up marrying someone I liked, but that wasn't the case. I never really thought of Darcy as his type, although maybe I was too quick to judge. I'd met her only a few times, but she'd always seemed a little cold and self-absorbed to me.

"How's your business going?" Mariel asked.

"You mean his *practice?*" I said as two women jogged past us.

Tate smiled. "*Business, practice,* call it whatever you want. It's going well."

"That was a nice photo of you and your new vet in the e-mail you sent," Mariel said.

"It was," I added.

"Oh, thanks. Yeah, things have been a lot better since I brought Amy into the practice. For one thing, I don't have to be on call every night. She's young, but she's smart and she's a hard worker." He nudged me with his elbow. "Speaking of work, how's your new job and how do you like Chicago?"

I could feel Mariel's eyes on me. "Love the job, love Chicago," I said, hoping I sounded convincing. "It's a nice change, working in-house, planning corporate events."

"I'm sure you're good at it. You're so organized. You're a lot like your father that way. Now, there was a guy who could put things together."

The mention of my father's name in connection with mine made me smile. "Yeah, he was special, all right."

"So, are you ready for the big day?" he asked Mariel.

"I'm completely ready." She glanced at me. "Sara's helping me with some of the final details, but I did everything else myself. I thought, *If Sara can plan a wedding, why can't I?*"

Tate laughed. "You were always following in your sister's footsteps."

Following in my footsteps? She was stealing my life. Didn't he remember how she used to do that? And now she'd finally pulled off the ultimate heist—my boyfriend. Clearly Mom hadn't filled Tate in on the situation with me and Mariel and Carter during any of his visits to our barn, probably because she'd convinced herself my sister and I would reconcile before the wedding.

"I have a feeling it's going to be a really fun wedding," Tate said. "And you'll make a beautiful bride."

Why was he gushing like this? He couldn't take his eyes off Mariel.

"You're so nice." Mariel gave him a little kiss on the cheek. "Gee, if you'd talked to me this way in high school, you might have ended up being my boyfriend."

Oh my God, she was pulling out all the stops, just like we *were* in high school. She hadn't been interested in Tate back then. And she wasn't now, but she was going to compete for his attention anyway.

"Yeah, I'll bet you say that to all the guys." Tate made a dismissive brush with his hand, but I noticed the rosy sheen on his face.

We stood there for a moment. The door of the Rolling Pin bakery opened, and a boy with a skateboard under his arm walked out. I caught a whiff of cinnamon in the air.

Tate glanced at his watch. "Hey, what are you guys up to?"

"You mean *now?*" I asked.

"Yeah. Now."

"I'm not doing anything right this second. Why?"

"I was wondering if you two wanted to ride with me out to the Darrells' on Indian Spring. They have a mare that's gone lame. We could catch up and I could drop you here after. I'll be coming back through town."

"Sure, I'll go," I said, happy to have more time to talk to him.

Mariel pulled out a pair of sunglasses and put them on. "I wish I could, but I've got a few things I need to do in town."

"So you're helping Mariel with the wedding?" Tate asked as Mariel headed in one direction and we went off in another.

"You seemed very attentive to her," I said.

"I haven't seen her in a long time."

"You haven't seen me in a long time either."

"Oh, come on, Sara, I was just being nice. What's wrong?"

I shook my head. I didn't want to talk about it. We walked on, and I spotted his white LAMBERT VETERINARY SERVICES pickup truck parked in front of Juniper Apothecary, a store where I'd worked one summer.

"You know," he said after we got into the truck and closed the doors, "I always felt a little sorry for your sister."

"You felt *sorry* for her?" Had he lost his mind?

"I never told you because you would have gotten mad at me, but it always seemed like she was unsure of herself, like she couldn't really find her stride."

"Don't tell me you really believe she's insecure."

"In a way I do, yeah."

"Looks like she's hypnotized you too."

"She hasn't hypnotized me. You're just too close to the action. You don't see it."

I thought my vision was pretty clear. "What's my mom been saying about me?" Maybe she'd put some of these thoughts in his head.

"Let me think. Last time I was out there...let's see, that was a few months ago...she said you were getting ready to start your own business."

I put the window down and rested my elbow on the open frame. The flag in front of the post office rippled in a soft breeze. "That's what drives me crazy. I mentioned to her one time, back in the winter, that I *might* want to go out on my own someday. And she tells you I'm about to start a business." It was like that game of telephone, where you had a group of people and a message that got repeated from one person to the next, and by the time you got to the last person, the message had been garbled beyond recognition. Except that you didn't need the group of people. My mother did all the garbling herself.

Tate gave me a sympathetic smile. "Well, she's always been a little prone to exaggeration."

"It's worse since my dad died."

"Yeah, that's true." He slowed the truck as a black SUV pulled in front of us. "She's never boring, though. You've got to give her that."

As we headed away from downtown, Tate glanced at me, a playful smile on his face. "Remember in high school how we used to forge our moms' signatures so we could get out early?"

I cringed and laughed at the same time. "I still can't believe we got away with it for as long as we did. And then to get caught on the first warm day of spring." There was nothing like the start of spring weather in Connecticut after a gritty, gray winter, that morning in April when crocuses pushed their way up from the hard ground, petals stretching for the sky, and the air felt alive again. Who wanted to sit inside a classroom on a day like that?

After a couple of miles, we turned into a driveway that sloped upward, bisecting a large field. A white, late-1800s farmhouse stood at the hilltop, and behind it was a large red barn with a gray gambrel roof that sported two cupolas. In a paddock to the side, a bay gelding watched the truck approach, his ears erect.

"That's Shadow," Tate said. "The mare's inside."

He parked and we walked around to the cargo area in the back of the truck, which was filled with bandages and syringes, medicines, salves, dressings, and equipment for ultrasounds and X-rays. He took out a hoof tester. "Do you ever get to ride?"

"Not really. Once in a while I hop on Anthem when I'm home. But that's about it."

"Too bad. You're a great rider."

He was nice to say that. "Oh, I don't know. A long time ago, maybe. What about you? Do you still have horses?"

"No. I ride other people's horses when I ride at all. I do have a pony, though. A Welsh gelding. For Emily and Claire."

"They're riding? How old are they now?" I vaguely remembered the baby pictures Tate had e-mailed me.

"Four and five."

"How did they get to be four and five already? Has Emily started kindergarten?"

"She will in the fall."

Tate with a daughter in kindergarten. That didn't seem possible, especially when I realized that he and I hadn't been much older than that when we'd met. How could all that time have come and gone? I felt as though my life hadn't moved in the right direction at all. The only thing I had to show for it was a job. I wanted love. I wanted to be married. I wanted to have children.

"People warn you they'll grow up fast, but you don't believe it." Tate leaned against the back of the truck, crossed his arms, and looked toward the field and the hills, where dozens of green hues collided. The corners of his mouth sagged. "Did your mother tell you the news?" he said in a low voice.

I didn't like the sound of that. "We've only talked a little bit since I've been here. What's going on?" A bee hovered over a nearby thatch of goldenrod, its gentle buzz reaching my ears.

"Darcy and I are getting a divorce."

I must have stood there with my mouth open, that's how surprised I felt. I'd had my misgivings about Darcy, but I hadn't expected to hear that. Or maybe I just felt bad that my hunch about them had been right. "Oh, Tate." I put my hand on his arm. "I'm sorry."

"Yeah," he said. "Me too."

"I feel so bad for you."

He looked over at the bay gelding, who was nuzzling the neck of a buckskin in the adjoining paddock. A hawk soared overhead. "I think it was inevitable. We almost split up a year ago." This was news to me. I should have been better about keeping in touch. I'd have to do that in the future. "But we decided to give it another try." He kicked a stone, sending it skidding down the driveway. "We couldn't make it work. So I moved out and we've started the whole divorce thing."

"That's...I'm..." I didn't know what to say. All I could think of were old clichéd lines. Here was a friend in a moment of need and I was coming up empty. "How are the girls taking it?" I finally asked.

"It's kind of a mixed bag. We're only telling them little bits, things they can digest and understand. At least, we hope they can understand."

"I'm sorry," I said again, wishing I had some magic words to offer him.

"Thanks, Sara. We're very different people, Darcy and me. I just didn't see that going into it. She's not happy being a vet's wife. It's better now—with Amy in the practice, I mean. It does take some of the burden off me, but that's not really the answer to our problems. Darcy doesn't even like horses that much. I think she just pretended to in the beginning. But you know what? I've got two incredible kids, and for that I wouldn't trade a thing. I just have to figure out how to go on from here."

Sometimes life seemed like one big how-to-go-on-from-here. "You will," I said. And I knew he would. He'd do a lot better than I was doing.

We walked into the barn, where the air smelled of sweat and manure, hay and leather. Three stalls were empty; in the fourth, a chestnut mare turned to scrutinize us, poking her head over the door and nickering as we approached.

"That's Brontë," Tate said, picking up a halter and a lead line hanging by the stall.

"How did she go lame?"

"I don't know. Jodie, the owner, said she got on her this morning and could tell something was up. But she wasn't sure where it was coming from." That wasn't unusual. It was often hard to determine the origin of a horse's lameness, to pinpoint the exact source.

"Hey, pretty girl." He opened the stall door, slipped the halter over the mare's head, and led her into the aisle.

"Aw, she is pretty." I ran my hand down her neck, admiring her copper coat, feeling her warmth, inhaling the earthy scent of animal and grain, an aroma I'd always loved. When we were kids, Mariel and I used to talk about creating a perfume called Eau de Horse. It wouldn't have had wide appeal, but we were sure every girl who rode would buy it.

I followed Tate as he led Brontë through the barn, her shoes clip-clopping on the floor, and into a ring outside. "Do you want me to walk her?"

Tate handed me the lead line. "Sure, if you don't mind. You can be my assistant."

"You can't afford me." I led the mare about thirty feet away and brought her back as Tate studied her gait.

"Would you mind trotting her?"

I gave the lead line a little tug and jogged out and back again, Brontë trotting beside me.

"Looks like the right foreleg," Tate said as I brought the mare to a stop. He ran his hands over her neck, back, and rump, then examined her legs, flexing the joints and looking for a reaction. There wasn't one. I stroked her cheek and she snorted a puff of warm air at me.

Tate picked up the hoof tester, which I'd always thought looked like a giant pair of pliers, and examined her hoof. "It might just be a stone bruise," he said after discovering a sensitive area. "She could have stepped on something or landed too hard going over a jump. Can you take her inside while I grab some things from the truck?"

I walked Brontë into the barn and clipped her halter to the crossties. Tate came back in with an armload of supplies, including a cloth diaper and a roll of elastic tape. He mixed some Epsom salts and warm water in a bucket and eased the mare's leg into it.

"You know, we should go riding sometime," he said, "since you're going to be here for a little while."

"I'm pretty rusty, Tate."

"That's okay. We could take a couple of quiet horses. Go on the trails like we used to."

I thought about the woods, the oak and hickory trees, the red and white pines, the lichen-covered boulders that had been strewn around thousands of years ago by glaciers, how the sun flickered through the trees, creating a million shades of light. "I don't know. Maybe."

Brontë put her head down and exhaled, making a deep, fluttery sigh. "So tell me," Tate said, "what's going on with you? Is there a man in your life these days?" His impish smile reappeared. "Give me the lowdown."

I rubbed the mare's neck. "Oh God. It's a long story, Tate." I gave him the short version.

"I had no idea all that was going on," he said when I finished. "And you're helping her with the wedding anyway. That's pretty big of you." He took the mare's hoof from the bucket, packed it with Epsom salts, and wrapped her leg in the diaper.

"Yeah, well, it's more of a favor to my mother," I said, leaving it at that.

He called the horse's owner and gave her an update while I put the mare back in her stall. After we gathered up the supplies, I gave her a final scratch on her head. It was almost four o'clock, and outside the air had cooled a little, the afternoon sun losing its strength. Tate took me home, and as we came up the driveway, he eyed Anthem and Jubilee in their paddocks.

"There are a couple of quiet horses we could ride," he said.

"Yeah, we could take them out sometime."

"How about now? I'm done with work for the day. It'll be fun. Like when we were kids. I have such good memories of us as kids. Maybe I'm just getting nostalgic in my old age."

"Hey, I'm the same age as you, and I don't consider thirty-eight old."

"You know what I mean." He nudged me. "Come on, it's a beautiful afternoon. Not so hot out anymore…"

"I don't think I have clothes. Boots. Stuff." I looked at his jeans and work boots. "And neither do you."

"I have some things in the back." He shot me a look that told me he wasn't going to give up.

"Okay, all right." It would be pretty on the trails in the late afternoon. I wasn't going to protest anymore.

I went into the house, rummaged through my closet, and found a pair of riding breeches. My old field boots were in there as well, covered in a haze of dust. I cleaned them off and pulled them on. As I was closing the closet door, I caught a glimpse of myself in the mirror. It didn't seem like that long ago when I'd stood in that same spot as a teenager, dressed in my show clothes—white shirt, navy jacket, black boots.

I remembered that feeling of butterflies in my stomach as I waited to enter the ring on Mayfair, the Dutch warmblood I rode then, reviewing the course in my head one last time while the rider before me finished up. Oxers, gates, verticals, walls, and water jumps with the correct number of strides between each one in order to take off and land in the right spots.

A part of me really missed that phase of my life and wished I'd stuck with it longer than I had. Wished I hadn't let Mariel's interest in riding make me feel claustrophobic, make me feel as though I had to find something else to do, something I loved as much, because I never did.

Tate and I walked to the paddocks, and I gazed at the green lawn that stretched for twenty acres around the barn and house, lines visible where the wheels of the riding mowers had driven. Where the cut grass ended, a meadow began, and where the meadow ended, the woods took over, its trails passing by a string of neighbors' houses and barns. I knew every inch of that land, from the place deep in the trees where the stone wall marked our property's boundary to the pond and the weeping willows and the paddocks bounded by the split-rail fence.

We brought the horses into the barn, brushed them, and tacked them up. As I slipped the reins over Anthem's neck and slid the bit into his mouth, I remembered how complicated bridles had seemed when I first learned to ride—all the straps and buckles—but after a short time, I could have taken one apart and put it back together blindfolded.

"How long has it been since we've ridden together?" Tate asked as we brought the horses outside. "Ten years?"

"I think so." Again I felt that stab of regret that I'd let our friendship wane.

We mounted, retightened our girths, and got settled. It was odd how quickly I felt at home in the saddle. Gazing at the paddocks and fields and the hills in the distance, I thought about how lovely and different the world looked from up there.

We warmed up in the ring for a little while, Anthem slipping easily into his gaits and responding well to my touch.

"How do you feel?" Tate asked as we slowed from a canter to a walk.

"He's in good shape, but I'm not."

Tate eyed me up and down. "You don't look out of shape."

"Ha. I meant riding shape."

We left the ring and he asked which trail I wanted to take.

"How about the one that goes by the Tillys' barn?" The Tillys moved when we were in college, but for Tate and me, the barn would forever be known as the Tillys'. "I haven't been down there in ages."

"Neither have I," he said. "Let's do it."

We crossed the grass toward the pond, where weeping willows hung over the water on one side, looking like maidens letting down their hair. "Remember how we used to grab the willow branches and swing over the water and try to knock each other off?" Tate asked.

"You always won. I always got wet first."

"I think you won a couple of times."

I think he might have let me win.

We walked around the pond; blue flag irises and purple pickerelweeds bloomed around the edges, nestled among the rushes.

We trotted across the field and entered the meadow, where the tall grasses swished against the horses' legs, and wildflowers sprang from the soil in riots of color—black-eyed Susans, golden sunflowers, yellow coreopsis, purple lupine, and blue bachelor's buttons.

We entered the woods, walking the horses two abreast where the trail was wide. The waning sunlight fell through the trees in patches as birds chattered in the canopies. The air held a faint scent of pine. Somewhere in the distance, a woodpecker tapped out a staccato rhythm.

We picked up the pace, trotting past stone walls that started and stopped at random, marking the boundaries of farms that had once existed there. Wild turkeys with bright red necks and striped plumage stared at us; gray squirrels darted across our path. I signaled to Anthem with my legs and he cantered up a hill, his hooves pounding out a comfortable three-part rhythm. We were flying. I felt as if I'd been set free.

At the top of the hill, the trail ended, and we walked into a swath of cleared land, then stopped to take in the view of the valley below and another hilltop in the distance. To the left, farther along the ridge, stood a large, white clapboard farmhouse.

"Is that the Tillys' house?" I asked. It looked familiar, but there was a glassed-in walkway between the house and garage that hadn't been there before, and the woods seemed much closer to the house than I remembered.

"Yeah, that's their house, but I don't see the barn."

I'd once carved my initials and Gary Decker's inside a heart on a post in that barn. How old was I then? Thirteen, maybe?

"They must have torn it down," Tate said.

A feeling of wistfulness stirred inside me. We walked the horses past the house and down the hill to the woods, where the trail picked up again. We hadn't gone far when I spotted the barn. "Look, Tate." The red paint had faded to pink; there was a gaping hole where the double wooden doors had been, and a sapling had grown through one of the window openings.

"They've let the woods go wild and they've let the barn go to ruin," he said.

We stared in silence as if paying our respects, then rode on through the woods, letting the horses drink at a stream before we crossed it. Fifteen minutes later, at the top of a hill, we stopped on another ridge. The fields below were full of oxeye daisies and coppery goldenrod and dotted with a few houses. I was taking pictures with my phone when Tate pulled Jubilee up next to me.

"Hey, take a look behind us."

I turned and saw that the sky had gone from blue to gray-silver, the color of an old metal saucepan. In the distance it was smoky gray.

"I don't like the looks of that," Tate said.

I didn't like the looks of it either. A shower wouldn't be a problem, but a bad storm could make the trail slick and dangerous. "Let's head back."

We turned and cantered back along the ridge, the clouds chasing us, a breeze picking up and blowing the grass. Anthem pricked his ears forward and snorted. The air was filled with the sharp, metallic scent of ozone.

We were back in the woods when I felt the tap of raindrops on my arm. Suddenly they were hitting the leaves, pinging my arms and face, landing on Anthem's coat. Thunder rumbled and the rain picked up and began to pelt us; wind gusted down the trail, shaking the trees. Anthem let out a squeal and lowered his head as we cantered on.

We'd just reached the Tillys' barn when the clouds tore open and water fell in sheets, thick and gray, pounding the horses, our helmets, our clothes. I could barely see.

"Let's get them inside," Tate shouted as the rain lashed us.

We slid out of the saddles and led the horses into the barn. A dull gray light came through the window openings and the holes in the roof, illuminating the empty stalls, the cracked water buckets, an old lawn mower in the aisle.

The horses settled down, sniffing the new environment, pricking up their ears occasionally at the sound of rain pinging against a metal gutter. Jubilee pawed the concrete floor, and in the dim light we watched the rain cascade in waterfalls over the doorway and windows. I shivered in my wet clothes as I looked for the heart I'd carved on one of the posts so many years before. I told Tate I couldn't find it.

"That's probably good," he said. "I remember when you had that crush on Gary Decker. I always thought he was a jerk."

I laughed. "I never knew that. I was convinced Gary and I would get married someday. The naïveté of a thirteen-year-old." Anthem chomped on his bit. I stared at the rain.

"You know," Tate said, "my mother always told me I should have married you."

I stood still and drew in a breath. "What?"

"Yeah. She thought you and I would have made a good couple."

He paused. "That was a long time ago, before I met Darcy. But she used to say it."

I wasn't sure how to respond. Why was he telling me this? Did *he* think he should have married me? Did he wish we'd gotten together years ago? Seeing him again made me wonder what that would have been like. Or could be like now. But my thoughts rushed back to Carter. Maybe Carter had taken up all the room I had in my heart.

I was about to come right out and ask Tate why he'd told me that when sunlight spilled through the window openings, brightening the inside of the barn.

"Well, look at that," Tate said. "Storm's over. Guess we can go back."

We rode the horses up Mom's driveway, walking them over the wet gravel. They tossed their heads, eager to get to the barn. I was still thinking about what Tate had said, but I couldn't work up the nerve to ask him about it now that the moment had passed.

I pulled off my riding helmet and tried to shake my hair loose, but it was stuck to my neck in sweaty clumps. My clothes were soaked, my breeches and boots speckled with mud, and I could feel a layer of grit on my face. I couldn't wait to get the horses untacked, toweled off and groomed, and put in their stalls so I could take a long, hot shower.

We were almost to the house when I heard tires on the gravel behind us. I glanced over my shoulder and saw a black SUV moving slowly up the drive. We stopped and watched as the vehicle passed us and pulled up at the front door.

A driver emerged; he went around and opened the rear passenger door, and a man got out, a little ray of light bouncing off his sunglasses. His gray suit fit so well, it could only have been custom-made. By his favorite tailor in Beverly Hills. He turned and stared at me. Then he took off his sunglasses. "Sara? Is that *you?*"

Eighteen months. Eighteen whole months away from him. And now here he was, standing in the driveway, looking at me. My breath caught in my throat and everything around me—the house, the trees, the sky—fell away. Only Carter was there. I wanted to throw my arms around him, press my face to his chest, inhale his scent.

"Carter." I said his name. Felt those two syllables leave my mouth. Heard them in the air.

"Did you get caught in the rain?" he asked, smiling that smile I'd missed for so long.

The rain. Oh God. I looked down at my mud-spattered clothes, my sweat-soaked shirt, felt my hair hanging around my head like Spanish moss. I wished Anthem would bolt, take off into the field, into the woods, anywhere Carter couldn't see me looking like this.

"Yeah, we got a little wet." I could hear the nervous tremble in my voice. What was he doing here this early? Why hadn't I known he was coming today?

He ran a hand through his hair. I ran a hand through my own. I put my helmet back on. Then I took it off again. Then I put it back on. Then I gave up, because there was no way to tame my hair. No improving this picture.

Anthem tugged on his reins, telling me he'd had enough standing around, that he wanted to go to the barn. Tate was looking at me and I realized I'd ignored him. Just as I was about to introduce him to Carter, the front door swung open and out stepped Mariel, moving like a swan with a breeze at her back, graceful in her dark, stretchy jeans and wedge sandals. Ferragamo? Prada? Fendi? Her top, cornflower blue, made the blue of her eyes pop, and every layer and strand of her hair looked as though it were held in place by magic.

"Moo-Moo," she shouted, a big smile on her face.

Moo-Moo?

I watched her skip off the porch, her arms reaching for him. I could smell jasmine and rose in her perfume. I could smell the sweat under my arms. I wanted to die.

CHAPTER 10

A MILLION WAYS TO RUIN A WEDDING

I didn't see Carter for the rest of the day. By the time Tate and I finished with the horses and I'd showered and changed and gotten myself looking human again, he and Mariel had gone out to dinner with some of her friends, and I fell asleep before they came back.

But the next morning I was wide awake at seven, my heart drumming in my chest because I knew Carter was in the house. I opened my bedroom door and peeked into the hall. The doors were closed, everything quiet. I was the first one awake.

I took out my spiral notebook, got back in bed, organized my thoughts, and listed my sabotage ideas:

Alter the wedding gown

I put a checkmark next to that.

Change the transportation plan for the church—get people there late, send some to the wrong church

Change the flowers for the church
Change the photo on the wedding program
Change the music for the ceremony
Hide or switch the wedding rings
Change the menu for the reception
Hide the box with the cards and checks in it
Change the seating chart for the reception
Change the music for the reception

That sounded pretty good.

A door closed in the hall. Someone was up. I jumped out of bed and opened my door a crack, just in time to see the back of Carter as he headed toward the stairs. I stuffed the notebook under some clothes in a drawer and got dressed. White jeans, a blue linen shirt, some earrings, some makeup, and a little dab of Antonia's Flowers, my favorite perfume, the one I knew he would remember.

By the time I got downstairs, I could smell coffee. Carter was sitting at the kitchen table. Dressed in an oxford shirt and khakis, he had a mug in front of him, and he was leafing through the *Hampstead Review.*

"Hey, good morning," he said when I walked in.

"You're up early." I poured myself a cup of coffee and added a shot of milk. "And you made coffee."

He stifled a yawn. "I guess I'm still on LA time."

I took a sip. "Well, this should fix you right up." I held up the mug.

He pretended to look surprised. "Too strong?"

"No, it's perfect." I smiled. He smiled. It was an old joke. His coffee had always been too strong for me.

He put down the paper. "It's good to see you, Sara."

It was? Did he really mean that or was he just being polite? "It's good to see you too. Are you catching up on the local news?" I sat down across from him.

"I was reading an article about tomatoes."

"That doesn't sound like news."

He closed the paper and looked at the front page. "Well, the top stories today are '*Farmers' Almanac:* Connecticut Winter to Be Colder Than Usual' and 'Scavenger Hunt Draws Record Crowd.'"

"I see your point. Well, it's a small town."

I'd always assumed I'd be the one to bring Carter here on his first visit to Connecticut, that I'd be the one to show him the covered bridges, the hiking paths, the old movie house, the conservation center, the wine trail. I never imagined it would be Mariel.

"It seems like a nice town," he said, but I knew from the hitch in his voice that he could never live here.

"It's not LA, I know."

He shrugged. "Every town or city has its pros and cons."

"I miss it there," I said.

"What do you miss? Can't be the traffic."

"There's traffic in Chicago too. But you're right, it's not as bad. No, I miss the people, my friends out there. And I miss the place." I missed *him* most of all, but I couldn't say that. "I miss the neat towns California has. Something for everyone. Remember that time we went to Ojai? How much fun that was?" I'd lived in LA for years and had never been there before I met Carter.

"I remember carrying a case of olive oil to the car for you."

"Yeah, I did buy a case of olive oil. And you bought a pen at one of the antiques shops."

"An old Dupont," he said, staring across the room as though envisioning it. "I still use that pen."

My stomach filled with butterflies. He still used it. That had to mean something. "Was that the place where you told the owner you were an attorney and he started asking you about his lease?"

Carter chuckled. "Yeah. He was in a dispute with his landlord. I think I wrote a letter or made a couple of phone calls for him. Got it straightened out. He was a nice guy. I was glad to do him a favor." He sipped his coffee.

"We always said we'd go back there, but we never did."

"Things got busy."

Things always got busy with Carter.

I put some more milk in my coffee and took another sip. "I bet you haven't been back to the ostrich farm in Solvang."

"No, I haven't."

"That's too bad. See how I broadened your horizons?" I wanted him to think about that, about what he was missing.

"You did, Sara. I would never have gone to an ostrich farm and fed them if it wasn't for you. I guess I'm just a boring guy now."

I smiled. "You could never be boring." I could feel my heart skittering. But I couldn't help it. He was right there, and we were talking about things we'd done together, and it was all I could do not to reach across the table and touch him. And then I heard footsteps and Mariel appeared in a pink robe.

She stretched; she yawned. "Oh, there's coffee." She grabbed a mug and filled it. "Mmm, that's good, Moo," she said as she sat down next to Carter and gave him a kiss on the cheek.

I got up and put my mug in the sink. They were huddled over the newspaper and didn't even look up when I walked out.

Upstairs in my room, I grabbed the spiral notebook from my drawer. Where did that name Moo come from anyway? What a stupid nickname. Carter hated nicknames. I couldn't believe he was putting up with that.

I added some ideas to the sabotage list:

Rewrite the wedding vows
Cancel the photographer and instruct guests to take cell phone
photos and upload to a website
Change the flowers for the reception
Misspell names on place cards
Have baker print embarrassing photos of Mariel on the wedding
cake frosting

There. That was better.

Mariel had given me a manila folder containing all the wedding information and had downloaded some other documents onto my flash drive. I opened the folder and saw that she'd thrown everything in there with no order or organization. There were bills and vendor contracts, a list of songs she wanted played, another list of songs she didn't want played, screenshots of the wedding website Mom had hired someone to create, wedding vows and readings Mariel and Carter had chosen, notes about the cake and the dessert bar, and e-mails with the florist about the flower arrangements.

There was a seating chart clipped to a printout of a spreadsheet Mariel or Mom must have hired someone to make. The guests were listed, sorted by bride's and groom's sides and again by bridal-party members, friends, relatives, and "Hollywood," as Mom referred to the entertainment-industry contingent from California. There was even a column for the handful of children coming and a note about their ages. The seating chart seemed like a good place to begin, even though I knew there would be last-minute changes.

I entered all the guests' names into a seating-chart software program I used and then arranged and rearranged everyone until I'd created a plan I liked. I split up couples, putting them at different tables, and placed single people with guests who weren't single. The children were supposed to be seated together at one table, prob-ably an attempt to contain the chaos, but I scattered them among the adults, putting four-year-old Cal, whose nickname was Cal the Kicker, next to the actor Chris Grisham, who had a reputation for disliking children.

The misfits table included Mom's housekeeper, Martha, Mom's gar-dener, Joey, and my eighty-eight-year-old aunt Bootsie, whose run-on mouth and refusal to wear a hearing aid were legendary. I moved Boot-sie next to Matt Weston Woods, the hot young country singer who'd won all the awards at the last Grammys, figuring she'd have plenty to say to him, and I put Joey next to the model Eloise Cameron. He'd think he'd died and gone to heaven. I wondered what she'd think.

I reseated every guest, ending with my cousin Gavin. I placed him next to Rick, one of my other cousins. The last time the two of them were together at a family event, eight years ago, they'd gotten into a brawl—something about Rick's wife, Honey—and they hadn't spoken since.

After that, I turned to the music. The Orion String Quartet was coming in from Manhattan to play at the ceremony, and there'd also be a soloist, an opera singer named Cecelia Russo who lived here in town. Orion's selections included works by Handel and Brahms, Beethoven's "Für Elise," and Debussy's "Clair de Lune." Nothing unusual there. I pulled out my phone and called Joel Shibley, the first violinist and contact for the group. When he didn't answer, I left a message saying that I was Mariel Harrington's sister and wedding planner and asking him to call me about a couple of changes.

According to her bio on the internet, Cecelia Russo had sung with the Metropolitan Opera, had a PhD from Juilliard, had taught at Juilliard, was an opera stage director, and had won several awards. A note in the folder said she would be singing Puccini's "O mio babbino caro" and Dvořák's "Song to the Moon." I dialed her number and reached her assistant.

"I'm calling about a wedding Ms. Russo will be singing at," I told her. "I need to speak to her about making a change to the program." A minute later Cecelia was on the phone.

"I'm on my way out the door," she said after I explained that we had a change to make. "But if you come by this afternoon, we'll talk."

She wanted me to come by? I guessed that was okay. I'd never met an opera star. We agreed on one o'clock.

The band playing at the reception was called Eleventh Hour; they were from the New Haven area. I found several e-mails in the folder between Mariel and Brian Moran, the keyboardist. I called Brian and left him a message asking him to call me. I also left a message for Wade Wallace, the photographer. I was able to get in touch with George Boyd, the manager of the Hampstead Country Club, and we made an appointment to meet at the club the next day.

On to the bakery and the florist, both of which were in town. I stuffed the wedding folder in my briefcase, grabbed the keys to the car, and left the house.

Cakewalk was known for creating over-the-top cakes and desserts for special occasions. The bakery had been in business only a year but it had quickly become the go-to place for spectacular confections, so it was no surprise Mariel had chosen it for the wedding. Lory Judd, the owner, a large, soft-spoken woman, came out of the back to meet me at the counter.

"I'm Sara Harrington," I said, "Mariel Harrington's sister. You're making the cake and doing the dessert bar for her wedding."

Lory retied her apron strings. "You're her sister?" She studied me for a moment. "Yes, I can see the resemblance."

I gave her one of my business cards. "I'm also an event planner, and I'm handling all the final preparations for the big day."

She looked at the card. "Oh. Well, I'm sure she's glad to have the help."

"Mariel's got so much on her plate right now. You know how it is. Anyway, I wanted to talk to you about a little change she wants to make to the cake."

Lory brushed some flour off her sleeve. "She's changed her mind a couple of times already, but that's okay. It's her wedding. So, let's see…" She tapped the screen of an iPad on the counter. "Here we are. Her last selection was the Grand Marnier cake. And for the dessert bar—"

"Oh, she still wants the Grand Marnier cake. And the dessert bar can stay the way it is. But she wants to decorate the cake with photos. You know, on the sides of the tiers."

"You mean print the photos on the icing?"

"Exactly."

"I can do that."

"Perfect. I'll get the images to you in the next couple of days. And if you've got any questions, please call me. Mariel's under a lot of stress at the moment. That's why I'm trying to run interference."

Lory told me she'd be in touch once I'd sent her the photos.

Ginny Hall, the owner of Hall's Florist, had pictures of her kids and dog tacked up on the wall behind the counter along with dozens of photos of flower arrangements. I told her what I'd told Lory, that I was Mariel's sister and I was trying to help out.

"Mariel seemed kind of stressed," Ginny said as she unpacked a carton of ceramic pots. "Sometimes people don't realize how much work an event like a wedding really is."

"That's true. I see it all the time."

"What kind of changes does she want to make? I thought she was happy with the orchids and the calla lilies and—"

"She was, but now she wants to tone things down a little, do something simpler, more low-key."

"Simpler. That *was* the simpler option. I couldn't get her the orchids she originally wanted. They come from Ecuador, and my supplier is having problems right now. Some issue with customs. What she chose was the compromise."

Orchids from Ecuador. Trust Mariel to want those.

Ginny picked up a pad and pen. "Does she have anything particular in mind?"

"Oh, yes. She specifically said daisies and sunflowers. And maybe you could mix a few mums in there as well." Mariel was allergic to all of them.

There was a beat or two of silence. "Oh. That *is* a change. She seemed adamant about having orchids in the mix. Are you sure she doesn't want to use *any?*"

"I'm positive. As I said, she wants it low-key. Oh, and I'll be bringing over the containers in the next few days."

"Containers?"

"For the table centerpieces. Mariel picked them out herself. These really cute glass beer mugs. The flowers will look great in them."

On the way to Cecelia Russo's house I called David and told him I hadn't heard back from Miss Baird. "It's been more than twenty-four hours," I said. Which wasn't that long, but we didn't have any time to spare. "I think we need to escalate things."

"What are you suggesting?" David asked. "That we hunt her down?" He laughed.

Maybe he thought I was kidding, but that's exactly what was going through my mind. "Actually, yeah. I think we should drive up to her house. Today. Maybe she'll be home. And we'll have a better chance of getting her to help us if we talk to her in person."

I waited through several seconds of silence. Then: "All right. Let's drive up there. I guess it can't hurt."

I knew that meant he hadn't been able to talk to Ana. I told him

I'd call him when I got back to the inn and I drove the last mile to Cecelia Russo's home.

Cecelia lived in a stone mansion tucked behind a hedge of trees on Woodbine Grove. At one o'clock I rang the bell. Cecelia answered the door in a full-length orange silk shift, her black hair pulled back in a bun. At five foot ten, she towered over me.

"Miss Harrington, I presume."

"Yes, it's Sara. Thanks for seeing me, Mrs.—"

"Miss."

"*Miss* Russo." I followed her into a living room full of uncomfortable-looking antique French furniture. Three Grammy awards stood on the fireplace mantel. Photos of Cecelia with Zubin Mehta and Luciano Pavarotti, among other notables, dotted the top of a baby grand piano. I took a seat on a brocade-covered settee.

"I thought your sister and I had agreed on what I was going to sing," she said. "The Puccini and the Dvořák. What is it that she wants to change? And why?" She sat back in her chair, crossed her long legs, rested her hand on the arm, and began to drum her fingers.

"Well, there's a song she really loves. It's meant a lot to her ever since she was young. And she told me she wanted you to sing it, but I guess she was a little shy about asking."

Cecelia's head went back slightly, as if she couldn't imagine anyone being shy about asking her anything. "What is the song?"

She probably thought I was going to name something from an opera, *The Marriage of Figaro,* maybe, or *Madama Butterfly.* Or possibly a popular song, an old standard like "The Very Thought of You" or "All the Things You Are."

"It's called '…Baby One More Time.' It was Britney Spears's first hit. Quite a few years ago."

"Britney Spears? She's not an opera singer."

"No. She's a pop singer. I guess that's what you'd call her."

"I've heard of her. I don't know her music, though. And I'm not familiar with the song. What did you say it's called? 'Baby' *what?*"

"'…Baby One More Time.' As I said, it was a big hit quite a while back. And it's one of my sister's favorite songs. Maybe even her favorite. It got her through some tough times. If you could please sing it…" I took out my phone. "I can show you on YouTube." I brought up the music video and handed the phone to Cecelia. She took a deep breath as she watched the singer and her backup dancers cavorting around a school in their skimpy school uniforms, Britney mouthing the words and pouting at the camera.

"And she wants this instead of the Dvořák?" Cecelia said, her upper lip curling.

"Yes, she does. It would mean the world to her to hear this at her wedding."

It seemed like Cecelia Russo, with all of her awards and accolades, her PhD from Juilliard, and the thousands of hours she'd probably spent singing Mozart and Beethoven and Verdi and Wagner, wasn't about to stoop low enough to sing "…Baby One More Time." I wouldn't have if I were her.

I was about to tell her to forget it, that the Dvořák would be fine, when she thrust her shoulders back, raised her chin, and said, "I'll do it. But don't expect me to dance."

CHAPTER 11

¡VIVA LA REVOLUCIÓN!

I returned to the inn, and not long after, David and I carried the sculpture to the van and headed toward Eastville to find Miss Baird. As the road meandered past a hillside of grazing cattle, David turned on the radio and a song began, something I recognized. A couple of bars with a few quick piano notes, then the metallic clank of an accompanying cowbell. The piece would build to more percussion and eventually a saxophone and vocals.

"'Compared to What,'" I said as David muttered the same thing. We looked at each other and smiled.

"Swiss Movement." I named the album.

"Montreux Jazz Festival," he added.

"From the sixties."

"That's right," he said. "So you're a jazz fan too?"

"Ever since I was a kid."

He turned up the volume. "Eddie Harris and Les McCann."

"With Benny Bailey, Leroy Vinnegar, and Donald Dean," I said. He looked at me, his mouth open. "Wow. You win this week's music quiz, Miss Harrington. You get a set of steak knives and an electric can opener."

I laughed. "Great. I can use them."

"How did you get interested in this old stuff?" he asked.

"Mostly through my dad." I thought about his music collection, boxes and boxes stored in the back of the guest-room closet. The CDs had been digitized long ago, but the albums and cassette tapes just sat there.

"He was the Broadway guy, the producer, right?"

"Yeah, the producer. He had all these old albums and CDs. Miles Davis, John Coltrane, Dave Brubeck, Duke Ellington. And tons of Great American Songbook stuff. That's my favorite kind of music. The Gershwins, Irving Berlin, Jerome Kern. That whole era. He had it covered. I felt like I grew up with those guys. I used to go around the house singing their songs when I was a kid. I even sang 'You're the Top' in the fifth-grade talent show."

"You didn't." He grinned.

"Oh, I did. Other kids were doing the B-52s or Wilson Phillips. And I was doing Cole Porter." I cringed, picturing myself as I pantomimed the lines. Wavy hand motions for the phrase about the Nile; listing to the side for the Tower of Pisa reference.

"I bet it was cute. Any videos around?" His eyes had a mischievous glint.

"Not that anyone will ever see. Thank God there was no social media back then." I glanced out the window as we passed a lake where two boaters skimmed their kayaks over the water. "What about you? How did you get interested in jazz?"

"Me? I used to play the saxophone. A long time ago."

"You're kidding."

"Why do you look so surprised?"

"I don't know. I guess you just don't seem like a sax guy."

He recoiled, pretending to be insulted. "What do you mean? What's a sax guy supposed to seem like?" He glanced around the van as though one might be in the back seat.

"I don't know. You just seem like a real estate guy."

"That's because you know I am one. But that doesn't mean I can't also be a sax guy." He put on his hurt expression again.

He was right. I shouldn't have prejudged him. "Okay, all right. You're a sax guy. Tell me about it. Did you play for a long time?"

"Long enough to have a jazz band in high school. We were called...you ready for this?" He paused. "Jazzmatazz."

"Jazzmatazz?"

"I know. Pretty lame, right?"

"Actually, I kind of like it," I said. "What happened? You didn't stick with it?"

"Oh, I stuck with it for a while. All through college and a few years after I got out."

I tried to imagine David as a musician. Late nights in a basement club in a college town, brick walls, the floor sticky from spilled drinks, the air heavy with the odor of beer, David blowing the lid off his sax. I kind of liked the image.

"But I wasn't really going anywhere," he said. "I don't think I wanted it enough. And then a friend of mine's father who had a commercial real estate business told me if I got my license, he'd hire me. Seemed like a better way to make money at the time. Although I sometimes wish I'd never given up music."

I wondered what he missed about it. Playing before an audience or jamming with other band members? Or maybe just sitting alone in a quiet room, filling the space with notes? What magic that had to be. Perhaps he missed all those things.

"I think it's wonderful that you have a talent for music," I said. "I always wished I could sing. I mean really sing. But I don't have a good voice. You have the talent. You shouldn't waste it. You should keep playing. I love the sax. I bet you're great on it."

"Not anymore. You wouldn't want to hear me play these days."

A Dexter Gordon tune came on. I couldn't remember the name, but David identified it as "Cheese Cake" and told me he was taking back the electric can opener and the steak knives.

"I think we're here," David said, and I looked up to see a sign that said ENTERING EASTVILLE.

I felt a sudden stab of doubt. "Maybe Miss Baird won't remember me." I hoped I hadn't dragged him all this way for nothing.

We turned onto a narrow, heavily wooded road and after we'd traveled almost a mile with no houses or driveways in sight, the GPS announced we had arrived at our destination. David stopped the van and we looked around.

"Where are we?" I said. There was nothing but trees.

"No idea." He glanced at the GPS again. It showed the car as a dot and our destination as another dot, but the background was solid white and there was nothing connecting the dots. It was as if we were floating in space.

"Wait, what's that?" On the right a dirt road, barely more than a path, sloped upward at a sharp angle; there were tufts of wild grass growing between tire tracks and ruts carved like hieroglyphics into the ground. "Could that be the driveway?"

"You think we're supposed to go up *there?* In *this?*"

"I don't see anything else."

He looked around again and took a deep breath. "I guess I'll have to pretend I'm in my Range Rover."

He turned the van onto the path and we began to climb the hill, the van scrambling over rocks and ruts, stones and boulders grinding under the wheels, tree branches snapping against the windows. We bounced and jostled our way to the top.

The woods opened into a clearing and in the middle stood a two-story cottage, yellow with turquoise trim. Roofing and gables and dormers jutted out randomly, and little windows appeared in unexpected places. It looked as though the house had been an experiment by someone who hadn't made it through architecture school. A giant rainbow in pastel shades and a huge golden sunflower were painted on the front. The shrubs and ferns that grew tall and wild around the perimeter of the house had clearly never heard the whine of a weed whacker or seen the glinting edge of a scythe. Crows danced across the scruffy lawn.

"I guess we're here," David said, sounding hesitant. He turned off the engine. "Maybe we should keep the hand in the van for now. If we don't like the looks of things, we can leave."

I agreed. It seemed like a good plan.

We tramped across the grass to a small porch on the right side of the house. There was a stone bust of a young man in the corner. Broad nose, thick neck, long hair. Not an attractive face, but an interesting one. And the piece was beautiful in its execution, detailed and lifelike.

"I wonder if Miss Baird made that," I said, moving closer to get a better look.

"If she did, she's good," David said. "Really good."

A lantern hung over the door. Several wind chimes nearby attempted to respond to a slight breeze. A large bell with a rope attached was mounted on the wall, the kind of bell you'd see in an old Western movie. Someone would ring it at mealtime, and the ranch hands would come running.

"I guess that's the doorbell?" I looked at David.

He grabbed the rope and gave it a pull, which sent the bell into a clanging frenzy that made us jump. David reached out and grasped the clapper to silence it.

A moment later we heard a woman's voice. "Coming, coming." And then the door opened, and Miss Baird appeared.

Her hair, styled in a long braid, had turned silver-gray and was streaked with white. Her loose-fitting T-shirt covered a sizable paunch, and her flowy cotton skirt fell to midcalf, revealing a crescent-moon tattoo on her right ankle. She wore beaded leather sandals and held a small paper bag.

"You're the Howleys?" Miss Baird looked us up and down as though we weren't the type of people she'd been expecting.

"Excuse me?" David said.

She stepped onto the porch. "You're here to pick up the psyllium?" She held up the bag. "Psyllium husks? Constipation? You said you needed something for constipation."

David and I exchanged a glance. "No, we're not constipated," I said. At least I wasn't. "You're Jeanette Baird, right? I mean Jeanette Gwythyr."

Her forehead wrinkled. "You're sure you're not the Howleys?"

I almost laughed. "I don't think so." I turned to David. "Are we?"

"I wasn't a Howley when I woke up this morning."

I did laugh then, but Jeanette didn't seem to think it was funny. Or didn't understand we were joking. "You're not from the government, are you? You're not tax people?" She took a step back, her eyes darting from me to David.

This wasn't going the way I'd planned.

"No, we're not from the government," David said. "We're here because—"

"I know all about how they *spy* on people. They do it through their computers. I always unplug mine when I'm not using it." She stared across the yard at the woods, as though there might be IRS agents hiding there. "We pay our taxes!" she shouted at the trees.

"Please let me explain," I said. "I'm Sara Harrington. And this is David Cole. I grew up in Hampstead and I was in your three-D art class at Hampstead High. Back in 2000."

She pulled in her head like a turtle and squinted at me. "In 2000? That's the year Cadwy and I got married."

"Yes, I know. I remember. I was a senior. We all knew you as Miss Baird, though."

"You were in one of my three-D classes?"

I nodded.

She studied my face, scrutinizing me. Then she said, "No. I don't remember you."

"Maybe you'd remember Christy Costigan. Tall, long red hair. Always spent her free time in the art rooms. She made a huge cat out of clay. Siamese. It was fantastic."

"A Siamese cat?" Jeanette shook her head. "I don't recall that." But a moment later she held up her hand. "Wait, the redhead. I know who you're talking about. She had a funny voice. Kind of like gravel."

"Exactly. I sat right next to Christy."

"That was a long time ago. I really don't remember you." She nodded toward the door. "But come on in anyway. I can't stand out here all day. I've got a bad knee. Ever since that march to save the teak trees last fall."

"We'd love to come in, but we need to get something from the car," I said.

Jeanette peered at the van. "That gas guzzler over there's yours?"

"It's not mine," David said, sounding a little defensive. "I had to rent it to bring the—"

"He usually drives a Range Rover," I added, realizing too late that that wasn't going to help things.

"Actually, my Range Rover is fairly fuel-efficient," David said. "It's a diesel."

Jeanette gazed skyward. "Tell that to the ozone layer."

David and I walked to the van, debating whether we should ask her to fix the hand. "She seems a little odd," he said. "I don't think we should do it."

I glanced back to see Jeanette throwing birdseed on the lawn. "That sculpture's fantastic, though. And we're already here. Let's see what she has to say."

He shot me a look like he couldn't believe he was going along with the idea, and then he opened the back doors of the van and we pulled out the bubble-wrapped hand with its four crushed and bent fingers.

"What in the world...," Jeanette muttered as David and I carried the hand across the yard and onto the porch.

"We need your help," I said. "David has this sculpture, and it got a little damaged, and we were hoping we could hire you as a kind of consultant to fix it."

"You want to hire me to fix a sculpture?"

I nodded.

Jeanette gestured for us to follow her and we walked into a small kitchen. "Who made the sculpture?" Jeanette asked.

"Um, his daughter," I said, uttering the first thing that came to mind. "A school project."

She led us into the next room, where tapestries decorated the walls and shiny diamond-shaped pendants hung from the windows, sending rainbow patterns bouncing everywhere. Two sofas sat on opposite sides of a brightly painted coffee table, and behind each sofa, a row of what looked like giant seedpods hung from the ceiling.

"I see you're admiring my pods," Jeanette said, and I realized I must have been staring.

"Yes, they're very, uh, interesting," I said.

"They're made from all-natural materials."

"I can tell." They looked a little scary.

David peeled the bubble wrap off the hand, revealing the single pointed finger, a finger that seemed to fill the entire room with its presence.

Jeanette stepped back, crossing her arms. "Mmm. Yes," she said after a long moment of silence. "I see. I like this. I like it a lot." She nodded. "A statement against bureaucracy. Against the groupthink of society. Against materialism. Against tyranny of every kind. It's stunning."

"Um, well, it's not supposed to be giving people the finger." David turned the hand around to display the bent digits. "It's just supposed to be a hand. The fingers got damaged. That's why I need to get it repaired."

Jeanette's shoulders slumped, and her eyes lost their glitter. "Oh. Well, it's not going to make the same statement, then, is it?" She sat down on one of the sofas, and David and I took seats opposite her. "So what happened to it?"

"It was in a car accident," David said. "A little fender bender."

"Why isn't your daughter fixing it? She's the artist. She'd be the best person to do it."

"Uh, well, yes, I realize that, but I don't want her to know this happened."

"And it's supposed to be in an art show," I added. "Next week."

"Hmm." Jeanette got up, studied the hand, and ran her fingers over the bent thumb. "It needs a lot of work. Layers and layers of papier-mâché, coats of paint. This isn't something that can be done in a day, you know. I really don't have the time. I'm busy with my own work." She glanced at a couple of the hanging pods. "And then we've got our healing businesses. Our natural remedies, oils and herbs. Cadwy and I do that together." She sat down on the sofa again.

"You're healers?" David said.

"We sure are." It was another voice that answered.

I turned and saw a man in faded jeans, a tie-dyed T-shirt, and pink rubber flip-flops. He was short, built like a fireplug. His hair fell to his chin, and his crinkly eyes were half-hidden behind wire-rimmed glasses. I realized why he looked familiar. The stone bust on the porch was him, although a much younger version.

"Here's Cadwy now," Jeanette said, her face lighting up.

"Didn't know we had company." He raised a hand in greeting and then walked over and plopped himself on the sofa next to Jeanette.

"Sara says she was a high-school student of mine, but I don't remember her. And this is David, her boyfriend."

My boyfriend? I'd never said he was my boyfriend.

"Cadwy has wonderful skills," she said. "He's the one who insisted we get into healing. After my cancer scare. It was the herbs that made it go away."

"That's wonderful," I said.

Cadwy nodded. "Changed our lives."

"We're certified, you know," Jeanette said, a note of pride in her voice.

Cadwy let out a contented sigh. "It's probably hard to believe, but I used to sell insurance."

That was hard to believe.

"And Jeanette and I—we lived in an ugly little place with a garbage disposal, three TVs, and two cars that guzzled gas. Now we have this wonderful house and a car that runs on cow dung. We're so much happier."

"I can imagine," David said.

Cow dung?

Jeanette clasped Cadwy's hand. "And so much healthier. Right, honey? Thank God I've gotten him on a nutritious diet. For a while we ate only green, you know."

"Vegan?" I asked.

"No, I mean the *color* green. Broccoli, string beans, avocado, kale. But that was too hard on him. Cadwy loves his food. Took me forever to get him to give up sugar. I kept telling him, *Sugar's not your friend*. It was tough at first, but he's used to it now."

Cadwy stretched his brawny arms over his head. I heard something crack. "Let me tell you, there's nothing like having your own business. Jeanette handles the orders and I go out and do the local deliveries. Get to meet with our customers, do consultations. We have a lot of customers right here in Connecticut."

"We love helping people," Jeanette said. "In fact, I've been noticing, Sara, you look a little tired. Are you having trouble sleeping?"

"No, I'm sleeping fine, thanks." At least she wasn't still asking if I was constipated.

Her smile wilted as she fixed her gaze on me. "Umm. You don't look like you are. I'm only mentioning it because we're having a special right now on valerian-root tea. Good for problem sleepers. Brew a cup at night and you'll sleep like a baby."

"That's right," Cadwy said. "Buy one, get one free."

"Let me think about that," I said, wanting to stay on her good side. "Maybe I'll take some."

Jeanette continued to stare, and I wondered what was going through her mind. That I needed more herbal remedies? Or was she back to the IRS bit? Did she think I was there to arrest her? She leaned across the table, narrowing her eyes. "Were you by any chance in my class the year we had the fire?"

The fire. I couldn't believe she was bringing up the fire. I hadn't thought about that in ages. Connor Parish and his lighter. We were fooling around with it, flicking it and...but I'd always thought that was in Mr. Thurm's painting class. Wasn't I working on a painting when that happened? Wait a minute. Maybe not. I had a sudden vision of dozens of tiny plastic jars I'd coated with Mod Podge and food coloring. I was making my own interpretation of a Dale Chihuly blown-glass seaform installation. Minus the glass. And the talent. And Connor was there. He'd made a three-foot-tall wooden sculpture that looked like a stick figure.

"I think I might have been there," I said, now certain it had happened in her class, hearing my voice climb at the end, the way it did when I was nervous. Did she know? Was this a test to see what I'd say? I felt heat rise in my face.

"A fire," Cadwy said. "What fire was this?"

"There was a boy with a lighter," Jeanette said, staring across the room as though she could conjure his image. "And a girl sitting next to him…"

Connor's lighter. And the paint solvents. We hadn't meant it to happen. We were just fooling around.

Jeanette's mouth was open; she looked like a shark about to chomp down. "You did it. You sat next to him. You were the one!" She pointed at me.

She knew. She knew the whole story. She was never going to help us now. "Connor Parish," I said. "That was his name." There was no point denying it.

"Connor Parish. Connor Parish," Jeanette said. "That's right. How could I have forgotten him? Or you? We'd never had a fire in the art room. Until then. And we never had one after that. I remember the whole school evacuating. The fire engines, the police. The two tables charred."

David recoiled. "You caused a fire?"

"It was *very* small," I said.

"The bomb-sniffing dog," Jeanette added.

"And an *explosion?*" David stiffened.

"There was never an explosion. The dog was only there as—I don't know, as a precaution, I guess." I wished we could talk about something else.

"I remember that dog," Jeanette said. "German shepherd. He had a beautiful coat."

"Maybe they gave him safflower oil," Cadwy added. "Does wonders for dogs' coats. Do you have a dog? Need any safflower oil? Buy one, get one free."

"Please, that was a long time ago. I mean, we're talking high school. And it was an accident." David was staring at me as if he'd never heard of anyone causing a fire in an art room.

Jeanette looked a little shell-shocked, and I was sure this was it—she was going to order us to leave. I was about to stand up and head for the door when she said, "That was no accident, Sara. You can tell the truth. You're among friends here." And then she smiled. A warm smile. A conspiratorial smile.

What was she talking about, telling the truth among friends?

She turned to David. "That was the year the students were protesting everything. The food in the cafeteria, the color of the gym uniforms, the location of the parking spaces. They put up posters, got out and marched around, walked out on classes. But the fire... now, that was something else again. The biggest protest in all the years I taught there. Of course, I wasn't a protester back then. I was a little naive, but now I can see it for what it was."

Hold on. She thought I'd done it on purpose? To protest gym uniforms? "That's not what…I mean, I didn't plan for…it was the cleaning solvents. We weren't really thinking about—"

Jeanette held up a hand. "Don't apologize for being a radical, Sara. The world needs more of us."

"That's right," Cadwy said. "We're all here to do our part."

"I wish I'd done something meaningful back then like you, Sara." She slid to the edge of the sofa and raised a fist. "Take on the institutions. Lead the charge. Stick it to the man!"

I was about to repeat that the fire was an accident, then I thought, *What the hell.* I stood up, raised my fist in the air, and shouted, *"¡Viva la revolución!"*

David stared at me, his eyes wide, and I knew he wanted me to stop, to sit down. But then Jeanette stood up as well: *"¡Viva la revolución!"* And Cadwy did the same. Which left David the only one sitting. And then even he stood up and said it. I had to bite my lip not to laugh. I wanted to hug him.

"I'll tell you what." Jeanette's eyes met mine. "I'll work on your boyfriend's daughter's project."

"He's not—oh, never mind." She was going to do it. I was so elated I was ready to fly.

"Next week is going to be busy, busy, busy, though. I'll have to squeeze in your sculpture and get it done over the next few days." Jeanette closed her eyes. "What's today? Thursday?" Her finger moved through the air as though she was counting. "Uh, Sunday," she said, opening her eyes. "I'll have it done Sunday. Got it on my mental calendar right here." She tapped her head. "Come back at night, though. Eight o'clock. I'll need the whole day."

"That's great," David said. "I can't thank you enough. That means I can even go home for a few days, get some work done there." He turned to me. "What about you, Sara? When do you leave town?"

"Oh, I'll be around until the end of next week. I'm staying for the wedding."

He looked pleased. "Really? You've made up with your sister?"

"Um, well, kind of."

"Good for you." He gave me an affectionate thump on the arm. "And what do you charge for doing this?" he asked Jeanette, handing her his business card.

"Oh, I don't know. How about seventy-five dollars an hour plus materials? I'll have it figured out when you get here. You can pay me then."

"Sounds good," David said.

"I'm doing it in honor of dissidence," Jeanette said. "Here's to the radicals." She flung her fist in the air again. "Here's to solidarity."

Cadwy raised his fist. "Solidarity!"

David and I looked at each other. And then we raised our fists as well.

CHAPTER 12

UNDER PRESSURE

I spent the next morning sitting at one of the umbrella tables outside the Full Pot, drinking coffee and working on plans for the annual company picnic. A little before one, I closed my laptop and left to go to my meeting with George Boyd at the Hampstead Country Club. I was on my way there when Mariel called. There was a beat of silence after I said hello. Then:

"Mom's in the hospital."

Her voice had a shakiness to it that made my stomach do flip-flops, like I'd swallowed a live fish. How could Mom be in the hospital? I'd seen her early that morning and she'd been fine. "What do you mean? Are you there?"

"Yes, I'm at Ashton Memorial. She's in the emergency room. I came out because I didn't want her to hear me talking to you."

"Where's Carter? Is he there?"

"No, he's at a meeting in New York."

Damn. I wished he were there. He was the best person to have with you in an emergency. "What's going on?" I pulled into a driveway, turned around, and headed toward the hospital. In my whole life, my mother had been in the hospital only once, when she'd had Mariel, and I didn't remember that. She was rarely even sick.

"We were at the farmers' market. You know, at the park? And Mom was acting a little weird."

"What do you mean, *weird?*"

"We were walking around, and she had a hot dog and some French fries. And then she said she wanted to buy some corn from one of the vendors. She started to give him change, you know, along with the bills, but she couldn't figure out what coins to use. Then she said she felt dizzy. I took her to a bench and brought her some water."

"Did that help?"

"No, she was still dizzy. And she wasn't sure where she was, so I took her home. I thought she would feel better if she lay down, but she didn't. I called Dr. Griffin and he said to call 911 and get her to the hospital."

I pictured paramedics putting Mom on a stretcher, putting the stretcher in an ambulance. "Is she conscious? Is she talking?" Maybe she'd had a stroke. Oh God, I hoped not. And why couldn't the car ahead of me go any faster?

"She's talking. But she's still acting kind of weird. She thought one of the doctors was the guy who comes to fix the air-conditioning system at the house."

"You mean Ralph?"

"Is that his name? She kept asking him to check the vents in the kitchen."

"I'm on my way."

*   *   *

It's going to be all right.

Perspiration trickled down my back as I pressed the pedal and accelerated to fifty on a thirty-mile-an-hour stretch of road. This would turn out to be nothing or, at worst, something minor. Maybe Mom was just exhausted. She'd been helping Mariel a lot with the wedding, and she'd been teaching her class and doing who knew what else. That had to be it. But what if it wasn't? What if something bad *was* happening? I waited at a red light, my foot tapping the gas pedal like I was sending an SOS in Morse code.

At least I was in town. I was grateful for that. When Dad died, I was living in LA, and I still hadn't forgiven myself for not being here. Mom always told me there was nothing I could have done, that he'd died without warning. As if there were ever really a warning about death. It's not as though you woke up one day and got a text message that your time was up.

Four thirty in the morning, West Coast time. That's when my phone rang. I remembered hearing that ring, thinking I was dreaming. Then I woke up and saw the numbers glowing on the clock on my bedside table. I knew it was going to be something bad. People don't call at that hour with good news.

Your dad is gone, honey. He died in his sleep. His heart went. They couldn't revive him. Then came those raw, painful sounds. The kind of sounds I imagined a dying animal might make. I'd never heard those sounds coming from my mother. I sat there in the dark, trying to picture him, trying to put the pieces of his face together, wishing I could have said goodbye.

She'll be all right.

I made the turn onto Route 395. It had to be exhaustion. And maybe Mom was adding a little dramatic touch. Honestly, when did she *not* do that? In the grocery store, if one of the employees helped her find the coffee crunch ice cream or the little bottle of lemon extract she couldn't spot, she'd act like he'd thrown his coat over a broken jar of pickles for her. *Oh, you're too kind. What's your name again? Scotty? I've always loved that name. And you've got the most beautiful smile.* Mom would give him a hug and then glide on by, the other shoppers watching, poor Scotty not knowing what to say. Yes, she could be dramatic. I was betting that by the time I arrived, she'd be drinking a glass of ginger ale with lots of ice, smiling, ready to go home.

But what if I was wrong?

I pulled into the parking lot at the hospital and ran into the emergency room, past an old woman, a couple with a crying baby, and a dour-faced teenage girl and her parents. The receptionist told me Mom was in bed 8, and after getting a visitor's badge, I rushed into a large room with a nurses' station in the middle and curtained rooms around the perimeter.

I found Mom's cubicle, pulled back the curtain, and stepped inside. She was lying on a bed, an IV in her wrist with a line connected to a bag on a pole. A blood pressure cuff was around her other arm. Wires protruded from the sleeves of her hospital gown and terminated at a monitor on the wall; a small oxygen monitor was clipped to one of her fingertips, and everything around her was emitting beeps and bleeps. She looked pale and tired, but somehow her hair was still coiffed and her makeup mostly intact.

I took that as a good sign. Mariel sat in a chair on the other side of the bed.

"Mom," I said, relieved to be there. I kissed her, noticing a trace of freesia perfume, a welcome antidote to the smells of bleach and recirculated air. "How are you feeling?"

She looked surprised to see me. Almost shocked. "Sara? How did you get here so fast?"

"Fast?" It had seemed like a long ride to me, but maybe that was because I was in such a hurry. "It took me twenty-five minutes."

Her eyes darted from me to Mariel and back to me again, as if she thought my sister and I were in on some joke we hadn't shared with her. "But I thought you went back to Chicago this morning."

"No, I'm staying for the wedding, remember?" Mariel was right. She was confused. What was going on?

"Oh, yes." Mom's face fell slack, like a sail that had lost its wind.

"Are you feeling any better? I was so worried when I heard what happened."

"I guess my blood pressure was a little high," she said. "They gave me some medicine. I think it's helping. At least I don't feel dizzy anymore. That was frightening."

Her blood pressure. I glanced at the monitors, the green lines zigging and zagging. "How high was it?"

"I don't know," Mom said, as Mariel raised her head and tried to adjust the pillow. "I hope it's only up a notch or two."

"There. Is that better?" Mariel asked. It was just like my sister to try and score points even as Mom lay sick in a hospital bed. I mean, really. When had she ever lifted a finger to help her before?

Mom moved her head back and forth. "Yes, thanks."

I sat down on the foot of the bed. "Mariel said you were at the farmers' market when this started." I straightened Mom's blanket over her. "What happened?"

"The farmers' market." She seemed to mull that over. "Oh, right. I wanted to get some beefsteak tomatoes."

"Corn, Mom," Mariel said. "We went to get corn."

My mother scratched her head. "Was it corn? I don't know. Maybe it was. I didn't feel right from the minute we got there. It was so hot out. I probably should have stayed home."

"Maybe you have heatstroke," I said, wondering why that hadn't occurred to me before.

"I didn't think of that," Mariel said, a sudden lightness in her voice.

"Heatstroke. I've never had heatstroke, although I think I sang a song about it in that play of Dad's, *The Dalton Sisters.*"

Mariel leaned over and placed a palm against Mom's forehead. "You do feel warm. I think I'll ask them to bring you a glass of ice water." She picked up a cup of water from the table next to the bed. "This doesn't even feel cold."

"Not ice water," I said. "Ginger ale. She needs ginger ale. Remember, Mom? Good for what ails you." She always used to say that to Mariel and me when we were little.

Mom turned to me. "Oh, well, sure," she said. "Okay."

"Maybe she can't have ginger ale," Mariel said.

"And maybe she can't have ice water."

"I'll take anything," Mom said. "You can just hand me that…" She pointed to the table.

"I think you need a blanket," Mariel said. "You've only got one, and it's freezing in here. Sara, can you get her a blanket?"

"I don't need another blanket. I'm fine, sweetie."

"But your feet are always cold. Sara, please?"

Oh, for God's sake. "Yes, I'll get a blanket." I got up.

"A heated one," Mariel said as I stepped outside. "She needs it heated."

Heated. I asked a medical assistant for a blanket, preferably heated, and some ginger ale with ice. When I got back to the cubicle, Mariel was sitting on the edge of the bed holding Mom's hand. "Don't worry about that right now," Mariel told her.

"Yes, but if I don't get out of here soon—"

"What are you talking about?" I asked.

"Nothing," Mariel said.

"Well, it must be something." Obviously, they didn't want me to know.

"It's the closet door in the guest room," Mom said, looking at the blood pressure cuff, turning her arm back and forth as if it were a piece of jewelry. "I can't get it open, and Uncle Jack and Aunt Ann are staying there when they come for the wedding." This was Mom's way of avoiding the real issue, her health.

"I'll call that handyman you use and have it taken care of," Mariel said.

"Would you? And there's a light out in the kitchen ceiling." Mom looked upward as though it might be above her.

"I'll get the electrician to come over," Mariel said.

"But I have a whole list of things. Maybe your sister can help you with it. She's good at organizing."

Mariel patted Mom's shoulder. "I can deal with it. I did stuff like that all the time at YogaBuzz. You know, calling people in to fix things, keeping the place running. I know where your list is. I'll get everything done."

"Oh," Mom said, looking a little surprised.

This was too much. I'd never heard Mariel offer to do anything around the house. When we were growing up, she barely picked up her clothes. I was sure she still didn't.

"We'll divide up the list," I said, unable to keep quiet any longer. "We'll finish it faster that way."

"Thanks." Mom sighed. "You girls are so helpful." The curtain opened and a man in a white coat stepped inside, a stethoscope in his pocket. "Camille Harrington?" He looked at Mom.

"Yes?"

"I'm Paul Sherwood. Leslie Miller's brother."

Leslie Miller was a friend of Mom's who lived in a house on a ten-acre parcel to the right of Mom's property. "You're Leslie's brother?" Mom asked. "I thought you were an orthopedic doctor. I didn't know you worked in the ER."

"I am in orthopedics," he said. "I don't work in the ER. I was in the hospital, and I came by to check on you because Leslie called and told me she'd seen an ambulance pulling out of your driveway. She got worried and asked me to see if you were here."

I liked Dr. Sherwood's soft voice, his long, elegant nose, his silver-gray hair. "I'm Mrs. Harrington's daughter," I said.

Mariel sat up a little straighter. "And I'm her other daughter. The younger one."

Oh, please. Was I the only adult in the room?

"Well, that was awfully nice of Leslie," Mom said. "And nice of you. I'm just waiting for someone to come back and tell me what's going on."

"I understand," Dr. Sherwood said. "There's a lot of waiting in the ER. Is there anything you need? I know my sister would want me to make sure you're comfortable. And, well, I want to as well. I'm familiar with your work."

Mom smiled. "Oh, you're a fan?" She tilted her head coyly.

"I certainly am. I saw you in *Right as Rein* and *Minor Infractions*."

"How nice." Mom tucked a lock of hair behind her ear and the two of them were off in conversation.

"I was wondering," Dr. Sherwood said a few minutes later, "if there's any chance that . . . well, that you might take a selfie with me." He looked almost shy.

He was about to be disappointed. Mom never did selfies. With anyone.

"Of course. We can take it right now if you want."

What?

Dr. Sherwood took out a cell phone and snapped a couple of photos with Mom. "This is great. Thank you." He slipped the phone into his pocket. "It was a pleasure meeting you all." He glanced from me to Mariel to Mom, then walked out.

I was still in shock over the selfie when the cubicle curtain opened again and a dark-haired woman came in. The badge clipped to her white coat said AUDRA FREEMAN, MD. She was followed by a girl of about twenty who carried a laptop.

Dr. Freeman introduced herself. "And this is Meg," she said. "One of our medical scribes."

"Can you please tell us what's going on with our mom?" I asked.

"Your mother's blood pressure was very high when she was admitted," Dr. Freeman said. "Two twenty over one eighteen. We started her on hydralazine to bring it down and she's responding to that."

It had to be the stress of Mariel's wedding that had caused Mom's blood pressure to go that high. She just couldn't say no. But it wasn't fair. Mariel was a grown woman who should have been doing everything herself, not foisting it on our mother.

Dr. Freeman turned to Mom. "We're going to adjust your blood pressure medication. We're switching you from a calcium-channel blocker to an ACE inhibitor. We think that will be more effective."

"Is that the reason why all this happened?" Mom asked. "Because my blood pressure medication wasn't working?"

"It could be the reason," Dr. Freeman said.

Fantastic. It could just be her blood pressure medication. Which was why they were switching it and . . .

Wait. What blood pressure medication? "Hold on. You said *adjust* my mother's blood pressure medication? She's not on any blood pressure medication."

Meg, who'd been taking notes on the conversation on her laptop, looked up.

"Yes, I am, honey," Mom said.

"Since when?"

"Since about three months ago."

I glanced at Mariel. "I didn't know about that. Did you?" If this was Mom's way of not worrying us, it was coming back to haunt her.

Mariel shrugged. "You mean the medicine? Yeah, I knew."

She knew and she'd never thought to mention it to me? This was just like the two of them, to have their little talks and not tell me a thing.

"Mrs. Harrington, we're going to continue the hydralazine until your blood pressure's normal," Dr. Freeman said. "And we'd also like to get a chest X-ray, a CT scan of your head, some additional blood work for troponins, and a D-dimer."

Hold on. X-ray? CT scan? And what were those other things? A cold feeling began to settle in the pit of my stomach.

Mom had gone a little pale. "But I thought it was just my medication."

"Yes, why does she need all those things?" I asked.

Dr. Freeman turned to me. "We want to make sure your mother didn't experience any kind of cardiac event. And we also want to rule out any type of blockage, like a blood clot in the lungs or the brain."

Oh my God. Cardiac event. Blood clot. Did she mean Mom might have had a stroke? Or a heart attack? And what was that all-encompassing *any type of blockage?* She was talking about serious things. Very serious.

"When is she going to have these tests?" Mariel asked.

"We'd like to do them now. We'll have her taken over to radiology and then—"

"Now?" I said as Meg tapped away on her keyboard.

"We'll bring your mother back as soon as she's done," Dr. Freeman said. "But it may take a while, so if you need to leave, you might want to make sure the desk has your number."

"Oh, we're not leaving," I said. "We'll be right here."

A few minutes after Dr. Freeman and Meg walked away, a man in a yellow uniform came in. He had the kind of body that made me suspect he'd once been a bouncer. I saw Mom checking out his name tag.

"Your name is Jay?" she said. "I've always liked that name."

Jay looked pleased. "Yeah?"

As Jay wheeled Mom away, I heard her say, "Did you know it's derived from the Sanskrit word for 'win' or 'victory'?"

"I can't believe this," Mariel said. "Blood clots? A cardiac event?"

"That's a heart attack."

"I know that."

I thought about what Mariel had told me on the phone. "You said Mom ate a hot dog and fries at the farmers' market. You knew she had hypertension. How could you let her have a hot dog? There are a million grams of sodium in one of those things."

"I don't know, Sara. I didn't think about that. And anyway, I can't control what Mom does. She's not a kid, you know."

"You could have controlled a hot dog."

She started to cry.

"I'm sorry. I shouldn't have said that."

"My wedding's in eight days. What if she can't be there?"

"This is about Mom, not you."

"I'm thinking about Mom. What if she's still in the hospital? What if they have to operate on her or something? And what if—I mean, what if something bad happens and she..."

I put up my hand. "Don't even say it. She's going to be fine." I had to stay positive. These were tests, but tests could go either way. You could pass a test as easily as you could fail one. I had to believe Mom would be okay. But what if this was only the beginning of something horrible? What if she did have a blockage in her heart or—I could barely form the thought—a blood clot in her brain?

Three hours later, Mom returned, but Dr. Freeman didn't show up for two more hours. "So far, everything looks good," she said when she finally breezed through the curtains, Meg still in tow. "X-ray, CT scan, urinalysis, blood work. Nothing unusual."

I felt as if I'd started to breathe again. Mariel clapped. Mom smiled and let out a loud sigh of relief.

"But we'd like to admit you for further observation and blood pressure control," Dr. Freeman said.

"Further observation?" Mom asked.

"You may have had a small stroke or a TIA. That's like a stroke, but it lasts only a short time and doesn't cause permanent damage. They're not detected by a CT scan, though. Which is why we want to do an MRI. And repeat the troponin levels."

"Troponin?" I said.

"The blood tests we're doing to rule out a heart attack."

Heart attack wasn't what I wanted to hear. I wanted Mom to come home. Now. More tests meant there could still be bad news. "What do you think, Mom?"

"I guess I need to stay." She looked exhausted. She looked worried. I just wanted to take her home.

A tech came in with a stack of blankets. "Somebody asked for these?" He placed them at the foot of the bed.

I started to complain that we'd asked for them hours ago, but Mom waved me off. "Yes, that's very nice. Thank you, uh, Ed?" She squinted at his name tag.

"Yes, ma'am. You're welcome."

"Are you warm enough?" Mariel asked as Mom reached for the remote control and turned on the TV. "Maybe I should open these a little more." She spread the blankets out, tucked the sides under the mattress, and folded the corners with the precision of a military officer. Trying to score points again. I was amazed she had any idea how to make a bed.

"Oh, that's great," Mom said as she surfed the channels, then stopped at a cooking show.

"What about your feet?" I asked. "Are they cold? I can go to the gift shop downstairs and see if they have socks." Two could play at this game.

"No, honey. My feet are fine."

"Are you hungry?" Mariel said. "Do you want me to see about getting you some food?"

"Thanks, sweetie, but I'm okay right now. And I'm sure once they get me into a room—"

"Mom," I said, "if you don't like what's on TV, I have an iPad in the car. I can run and get it."

"An iPad? But I—"

"She doesn't want an iPad," Mariel said. "She probably wants to listen to some music. Those show tunes on her cell phone." Mariel went rummaging through her handbag. "I've got some earbuds in here. You can use them."

Mom put up a hand. "That's sweet, but it's—"

"She can use my earbuds." I began hunting through my own handbag. "They're better."

"Girls, I really don't need earbuds," Mom said, as Mariel and I shoved our earbuds at her.

A nurse walked in, HAILEY, RN, on her name tag. "How are you feeling, Mrs. Harrington?"

Mom looked dazed, as though she'd just walked onstage and forgotten what play she was in.

Hailey went from monitor to monitor, inspecting the zigzag of each readout. "Hmm. Your blood pressure's gone back up a little."

Mom's forehead crumpled. "It has?"

Hailey nodded. "I wonder what could have caused that."

Oh God. Had *we* done it? Mariel and I?

Mom peered at the two of us. "I wonder."

CHAPTER 13

DOESN'T EVERYBODY LIKE GRILLED CHEESE?

The next day, Mom called to tell us she was being discharged from the hospital that afternoon. The tests showed no sign of a stroke or a heart attack, which was great. Still, the blood pressure medication she'd been on hadn't done what it was supposed to do. I hoped the new medication would work.

While I waited for Mom to let us know what time to pick her up, I grabbed a few of the old photo albums from her bookcase and took them into my room. I sat down in the middle of my bed and chose some photos of Mariel that I knew she wouldn't want the general public to see, including one where she was in her Britney Spears outfit. I snapped pictures of the photos with my cell phone and e-mailed them to Lory Judd at the bakery so she could print them on the cake.

After that I called George Boyd at the country club.

"I hope your mother's all right," he said when I explained why I hadn't been able to meet with him the day before.

I thanked him and told him she was going to be fine. "Maybe

you could e-mail me your catering menu," I said. "And we can do this over the phone."

He told me he'd send it to me in a few minutes. While I waited for the menu, I put in another call to Brian Moran, the keyboardist and contact for Eleventh Hour. This time he answered.

"Sorry I didn't get back to you," he said. "We had a gig out of town and didn't get in until really late last night."

"That's okay. I just wanted to talk to you about some songs my sister wants to add to her playlist for the wedding reception."

"I'm sure we can handle whatever she'd like," he said. "We can do just about anything—pop, rock, R and B, jazz standards."

"Great. Well, she'd like you to play 'Fifty Ways to Leave Your Lover,' 'You're So Vain,' 'Never Really Over,' 'I Still Haven't Found What I'm Looking For,' and 'D-I-V-O-R-C-E.'" I loved that old Tammy Wynette tune. "Oh, and for the first dance, the groom wants 'To All the Girls I've Loved Before.'"

A couple of seconds of silence ticked by, during which I imagined a confused Brian wondering what this wedding was all about. "They want those *in*cluded, not *ex*cluded?"

"Included. It's part of an old joke they've had going on for years."

"Um, okay, sure," he said, sounding anything but.

After we hung up, I checked my e-mail and found the catering menu George Boyd had sent, all six pages, complete with selections for children's parties. After studying it for a few minutes, I wrote some notes in my pad and called George.

"If you want to review the selections and phone me tomorrow, that's fine," he said. "Or we can set up another meeting. Or you can e-mail me your changes."

"I think we can do this right now," I said.

"Sure. That's fine too. I didn't realize you were ready."

"Here's what Mariel's thinking. She's decided to make this reception much more down-to-earth. Much simpler." I scrolled to the children's selections at the bottom of the menu. "So, for the hors d'oeuvres, we'd like to do the mini–grilled cheese sandwiches, those little pig-in-a-blanket hot dogs, the mini-pizzas, and, let's see...oh, here it is, baked tofu fingers for the vegans."

"Sounds like you'll be having a lot of children there," George said. "So those are in addition to the caviar-and-crème-fraîche tartlets, spinach-and-mushroom puffs, lobster toast with—"

"No, no, they're instead of those."

"*Instead* of them." Silence. More silence.

"Doesn't everybody like grilled cheese?" I asked.

"Oh...I...of course," he said.

"And for the entrée, she wants the options to be chicken nuggets, macaroni and cheese, fish sticks, and the rice-and-bean burritos."

"And are those going to be *instead of* the pheasant under glass, Dover sole, filet mignon, and saffron risotto with roasted—"

"Yes, instead of."

"This *is* for a wedding, correct?"

"Oh yes."

I checked off the photos, music, and menu changes on my list, glad to have made some more progress.

"I'm fine," Mom said when Mariel and I went to pick her up at the hospital. "Whatever you do, don't start treating me like an invalid."

Although I understood her point, hypertension was serious, and she didn't have the best diet. Which was why, later that afternoon, I went through all the food in the refrigerator, freezer, and cabinets and tossed out the high-sodium offenders. Cans of soup and frozen pizzas and chicken potpies were just a few of the things that went into the garbage bags.

On the internet I found some good articles about the importance of diet, exercise, and blood pressure monitoring, including one with the catchy title "Blood Pressure Cuff: Does Size Matter?" I printed out the articles and left them on the kitchen counter along with a note telling Mom I'd ordered her two cookbooks for people with hypertension and a blood pressure monitor that worked with a phone app. I also left some yellow sticky notes on her cabinets: *More kale; Say yes to sunflower seeds; Take a pass on pickles.* It couldn't hurt to remind her.

Mariel walked into the kitchen. "What's all this?" she asked, looking around.

"I'm helping Mom with her diet, getting rid of the stuff she shouldn't eat."

"Those two black bags are full of food?" She untied one of them. "Potato chips? And cheese puffs?" She turned to me, horrified. "You're throwing them out?"

"Mom can't eat that."

"She can eat a little of it."

"Nobody eats *a little* of it."

"Don't you think you should ask her first?" Mariel said. "She told us not to treat her like an invalid. Maybe she wants to make her own decisions."

"Don't be silly. I'm doing her a favor. She needs to get a handle on this." I knew Mom wouldn't toe the line without a little push.

"Well, don't blame me if she gets mad." Mariel pulled a big bag of chips from the trash. "I'll just keep these in my room."

"She's not going to get mad." I was about to ask Mariel why she didn't take the cheese puffs as well when her phone rang.

"You're still there, Moo?" She opened the bag of chips. "Oh, I don't know, honey. Can't you just find something nice and buy four of them? We need to get this done."

I started to walk away.

"Wait, Sara. Hold on. Carter's at Hilliard's getting gifts for the groomsmen. Would you please go down there and help him find something for the bridesmaids? I have to wait here and sign for a package that's coming. Besides, you're better at that kind of thing than I am."

Her attempt to butter me up wasn't going to persuade me. Why couldn't *I* stay and sign for the package and *she* go downtown and deal with the gifts? I was about to suggest that, but then I stopped myself. The opportunity to spend some time with Carter had just landed in my lap. And maybe I could do a little more sabotage as well.

On the way to town, Wade, the photographer, called me back. I explained, as delicately as I could, that we were canceling his services. "She wants to go low-key."

"You're not going to have a photographer there at all?" he asked, sounding shocked.

"Oh, we'll have plenty of photographers there. We're going to ask the guests to take pictures with their phones and upload them to a Dropbox link." I'd seen couples make that mistake before. They ended up with a few decent photos, if they were lucky, and hundreds more with heads and shoulders in the way, red-eyed people, blurry images, and pictures that were too light or too dark.

And that's what Wade said before reminding me that the deposit was nonrefundable.

By the time I arrived at Hilliard's, Carter had picked out the gifts for the groomsmen: leather toiletry cases and fancy razors made by some British company.

"Ah, she told me she was sending the chief," he said, looking apologetic. "Sorry to drag you down here."

"Oh, it's fine. I don't mind." If he only knew how happy I was to have a few minutes alone with him.

"I have no idea what to get a bridesmaid," he said. "I didn't even know what to get the guys."

I picked up the razor; its stainless-steel handle was decorated with geometric lines. It was heavy and felt good in my hand. "These gifts are lovely. All you have to do is get some cards, write a nice note to each of them, and you're done."

"What do I do about the bridesmaids?"

I couldn't believe Mariel had roped him into that. The guy who negotiated deals for Hollywood A-listers was hunting for bridesmaids' gifts. I would never have asked him to do that if he were marrying me.

"Come on, there must be something here," I said, leading him through the shop. Hilliard's had always carried an eclectic selection of goods, everything from crystal decanters to neckties to goggles to wear while chopping onions.

We passed nautical-themed glassware, black agate coasters,

porcelain dog bowls, and an inflatable tic-tac-toe game for use in a swimming pool. I'd never seen that before. I picked up the box, which had a cover showing a pink tic-tac-toe grid floating in pale blue water. "This is it. This is what we'll get them."

"Perfect," Carter said, playing along. "But hold on a second. What if they don't have a pool?"

"If they don't have one, they'll just have to *get* one."

"Of course. A problem easily solved. Maybe we could slip in a gift certificate to help out."

"Yes! Great idea. A gift certificate for a pool. Why didn't I think of that?" I laughed and put the box back on the shelf, and we moved along.

"Hey, what about a hat?" Carter said, picking up a white raffia hat with a floppy brim and putting it on my head.

I pulled it down over my eyes, hoping to look seductive. "Hello, dahling."

"Hmm. That actually looks okay on you. But then, you always looked good in hats."

"Do you really think so?" I put the hat back.

He glanced at the scented candles, picked up a crystal vase.

"Hey," I said, "do you remember that store we went into—I think it might have been in San Diego—where they had all those crazy hats upstairs?"

"Crazy hats?" He put the vase down and walked on.

"Yeah. I tried on a hat that looked like a birthday cake, remember? It had candles sticking out of the top. I think it was made of felt. And there was one that looked like a lobster. And you tried on a pirate hat, and we took pictures."

"Oh, yeah. I do remember. That pirate hat wasn't me, though. Maybe I just don't have the pirate personality. Probably because I don't believe in plundering."

I laughed. "No, you're definitely not a plunderer."

We went down another aisle. Cashmere sweaters, silk scarves, fancy soaps. "Oh, here we are. This is it." I held up a loofah sponge that looked like an ice cream cone. "And it comes in such a nice box."

"Packaging is important," Carter said. "But I don't know. I'm not getting the right feeling about it."

At the end of the aisle, he waved his arms. "Search is over. We're done." He picked up a pair of brass bookends, each one a hand with a cigar between the fingers.

"Oh, that's it," I said. "Any woman would want those. Even if she didn't smoke cigars. I mean, they're just…"

"I agree. They *are* just…" He winked at me. My heart melted.

He put the bookends back and took a breath. "All right, what are we really going to get them?"

Ah. The game was over. And we were having so much fun. Soon we'd be finished here and he'd walk out of my life again. "I think I have a few ideas," I said. I led him around the store another time, slowly, pointing out some things I'd noticed that I thought were worth considering.

"I like that," he said when I showed him a silver jewelry dish.

"You do? Do you think Mariel will like it?"

He picked up the dish, turned it over, studied it. "Do you like it?"

I nodded. "Yes, I do."

"Okay, then, it's settled."

At the checkout counter, Carter asked the saleswoman if she had four of the dishes.

"Oh, I'm afraid we only have this one, but I can order more for you. I take it they'll be gifts?"

"Yes, bridesmaid gifts," he said.

"You know, you're the second couple to come in today looking for bridesmaid gifts."

"Oh, we're not a couple," I said. "We're—" What were we? Ex-lovers. About-to-be siblings-in-law. So inconvenient.

"We're old friends," Carter said, putting his arm around my shoulder and giving me a little squeeze. His touch made me want to dissolve into his arms.

"The couple that came in earlier met on vacation in Hawaii," the saleswoman said. "And he proposed to her two weeks later!"

"That's awfully quick," I said, wondering how long that marriage would last.

Carter scratched his head. "Two weeks. It took me longer than that to come up with the *idea* for a proposal."

"What in the world did you do?" I asked, realizing too late it would probably break my heart to hear about it.

He had that little sparkle in his eyes I'd always loved. "I made a movie trailer. With photos and videos of me and Mariel together. And I rented a theater on Sunset and invited...well, a lot of people. She had no idea. She thought she was going to see a movie with a few of her girlfriends. They showed the trailer and brought up the lights and I walked over to her and proposed. She loved it. Everybody went wild."

She must have loved it. "That's really sweet," I said. Maybe it wasn't what I would have liked, but I couldn't imagine how much time and effort had gone into it. And what did it matter what I liked? This wasn't my wedding proposal we were talking about.

The saleswoman clicked some keys on a computer. "I'll need to get your information and a credit card. And then I'll call and find out what the shipping time will be, and we can talk about how you'd like them sent. When do you need these?"

I turned to Carter. "Hey, look. I can handle the details here. You get on with your day and I'll finish up."

"Really? You don't mind?"

"I don't mind. I'm the wedding planner, remember?"

I walked him to the door and watched him cross the street. Then I went back and picked up the brass bookends with the cigar-holding hands.

"We've changed our minds," I told the saleswoman. "Instead of those silver trays, how many more of these can you get?"

CHAPTER 14

LESSONS FROM THE PAST

I spent most of Sunday working on the company sales meeting, the board meeting, and a golf outing the client services' group wanted to hold for some of the firm's most important clients. David had come back after his two days in Manhattan, and at five o'clock he picked me up for our drive to Jeanette's.

"Glad you could leave a little early," he said as I got into the van. "We have to go about fifteen miles out of the way." We were taking a detour so he could look at a piece of property.

"I'm just happy to get out of the house. I've been inside all day."

He drove for a couple of miles, then turned and headed northwest. I squinted at the sun, pulled down the visor, and searched my handbag for my sunglasses.

"There's a pair of shades in the glove box if you want them," David said.

I opened the glove compartment and pulled out a pair of Ray-Bans. "Wayfarers. I've always liked these." I put them on. "They make me think of that old song Don Henley did, 'The Boys of Summer,' and that line about the girl having her Wayfarers on."

"Great song, great line. And those shades look good on you."

We drove for forty minutes, David on business calls most of the time, me happy to gaze out the window. Soon after passing a sign that said ENTERING PUTNEY, SETTLED 1644, we approached a small downtown area where old wooden houses had been primped and painted and turned into businesses. Tranquility Teahouse, Gilded Lily Antiques, Mayflower Grocery. David ended a call, stopped at a traffic light, then answered his phone when it rang again.

"Hey, Doug, what's up?" Across the street, two men deep in conversation leaned against a blue pickup truck. "Yeah, I think that's a good idea," David said after listening for a moment. "I don't want to take a chance on it without getting that additional info. Maybe it's overkill, but I'd rather be safe than sorry." The light turned green and we drove on, leaving the shops behind us. "Sure," David said. "I'm on my way there now to take a look."

He was still talking a couple of minutes later as the road meandered past fields and trees and streams. "We'd have to bulldoze what's there anyway. Take it down. Too expensive to keep the...what? Yeah, exactly. Start fresh." He looked at his GPS. "Hey, listen. I think we're almost there. I'll call you later."

We turned onto a road flanked on both sides by woods, the street sign obscured by vines. The asphalt was cracked and broken and full of potholes that looked big enough to eat a wheel or break an axle. "What's in here?" I asked as he maneuvered the van to avoid the craters and bumps.

"You'll see in a minute."

I couldn't see anything but woods. Then I noticed a few rose-colored spots between the trees. The road swung left and led to a clearing where a long, three-story red-brick building loomed before us. It must have been at least a hundred years old.

The bricks had turned all sorts of colors. Some were burnt orange, some rosy pink. Some looked like they'd been hit with a bucket of whitewash. Vines had scuttled up the walls and died, leaving dried stalks, and the windows were empty of glass and covered with green cyclone fencing to deter vandals. The dark holes that remained peered down at us like disapproving eyes. The roof sagged, and the shingles curled like bits of pencil shavings. I felt as though I'd been transported to an industrial ghost town.

"Wow," I whispered. "What is this?"

David turned off the engine. "It used to be a woolen mill." We stepped outside. Gravel and sand crunched under our feet; birds chattered quietly in the woods behind us. The air seemed hotter there, and stale.

"When I was in high school," I said, "I wrote a paper about the history of Connecticut's textile mills."

David smiled. "You must be an expert, then."

I was hardly an expert. Although I did remember driving with my friend Whitney Reece to one of the abandoned mills to take pictures. The place gave me the creeps. At least at first. But then I began to think about all the people who had gone through the doors and worked there over the years, all the fabric they'd made, how they'd fed their families and scrimped and saved, and maybe a few of them had even sent a child to college on what they'd earned there.

I started to imagine what it had once looked like, how beautiful it must have been, and it made me sad to see it all those years later. Closed. Dead. An eyesore.

"I'm definitely not an expert," I said as I stepped closer to the building. "But I do know a lot of these mills were built in Connecticut in the early 1800s and that people came from all over the world to work in them."

Bricks had fallen from the building in several places and vines clung to the walls like fingers refusing to let go, but I could tell the structure must have been magnificent in its day. I wondered who had set the dozens of arched windows in place and who had laid the thousands of bricks. Where had those masons come from? Were any of their descendants still alive? If so, did they even know this place existed?

I ran my hand over the bricks, which still felt warm from the fading sun. "Don't ask me how I remember this, but the largest thread mill in North America was in Willimantic, Connecticut. The American Thread Company. And here's a fun fact: it was the first factory to install electric lights and the first to give workers coffee breaks."

David peered through a window into the darkness. "And they didn't even have Starbucks. Imagine that."

I gazed into the window as well. I couldn't see anything except rubble and a pile of rusted metal bars. I thought about what David had said on the phone. *We'd have to bulldoze what's there anyway... Start fresh.* They were going to tear the building down. Sad, but not a surprise. I wondered what they would do with the property after that. Build a movie-theater complex? An office park? Anything was possible. I walked along the side of the building, looking into other windows; pools of darkness stared back at me.

"I wonder when this place closed," I said.

"I read it was in the late seventies."

He'd done some research. "That means it operated for a hundred and fifty years," I said. "That's a long time. There's a lot of history here."

We paused near what was once the front door but was now just a frame with a strip of cyclone fencing over it. I gazed at the broken concrete slab leading to the entrance and imagined the workers—men, women, even children—heading into the building carrying their lunch pails, hearing the steam whistle announce the beginning of their shift. I could see them at the carding machines that brushed and straightened the wool fibers, the spinning frame that transformed the fibers into thread or yarn. I pictured them standing at the skein winders and the looms. I wondered what had gone through their minds when they looked out of these windows. What were their hopes and dreams?

I picked up a small piece of concrete from the ground and turned it over. "A whole way of life just vanished when these mills closed. These buildings were beautiful back in their day. And now..."

"That's what happens when buildings are left behind," David said. "Nature takes its course."

But why did we have to let that happen? It seemed negligent to stand by and watch such lovely things be destroyed. I knew the building could be beautiful again if someone cared enough and had enough money to do the work. I also knew it wasn't as easy as it sounded. David and his partners, or whoever bought the place, couldn't be blamed for wanting to tear it down. But that meant this place, with its history and its soul—the collective memories of all the people who had worked there—would be gone forever. I wished he hadn't brought me here. I dropped the piece of concrete, and it splintered on the ground, the chips scattering.

"I realize nature takes its course," I said. "But don't you think old things are worth saving? I mean, just because something's old, does that mean you should just let it—"

"You can't save everything," he said as he began walking again. "Sometimes it's not practical." I hung back, parsing his words, picturing a graph where the costs side outweighed the benefits side. Then I ran to catch up.

He stopped, angling his head. "Do you hear that?"

I listened and heard the faint sound of water rushing, splashing— the river that had once generated the power to run the mill's machinery. We walked around to the back of the building, where the sound was loud, the river running in quick white currents at the bottom of an embankment of dirt and rocks, water racing over boulders, around saplings, twirling into eddies dappled by the waning sunlight. The air was dank and cool. I tossed a stick and watched the current pull it downstream to a patch of white water, where it spun in a manic dance until it was dragged under the froth.

"What will you do with the property?" I asked David.

"*This* property?" He turned around to view the factory again. "I don't know if we'll even buy it. I'm just taking a preliminary look. A lot would depend on what kind of incentives we could get from the state, among others. Tax breaks, grants."

"What kind of grants?"

"Remediation, for one. This will be a huge environmental cleanup job." He glanced at the ground and pushed a little hill of dirt away with his sneaker. "From all those decades of dumping pollutants before it became illegal."

"And you'd try to get the state to pay for some of that?"

"Sure. We're talking millions of dollars. Some states have programs to help developers clean up brownfields like this. Connecticut is one of them. There are other sources, too, like federal grants. But it's not easy. It's the government, you know. And there's only so much money to go around."

Brownfield. I was still stuck on that word. How sad it sounded. And how sad that it was so expensive just to resolve the environmental problems. If David and his partners bought this, I knew they'd be putting up that office park or condo complex. How else would they get back their investment and make a profit? This old building would be gone, and this place would be changed forever.

I thought about Dad and how he used to say we should welcome the future but respect the past. When he and Mom moved from Manhattan to the house in Hampstead, the first thing he did was replace the modern-looking addition a previous owner had grafted onto the farmhouse with one that fit the early-1800s period when the house was built.

"Why do old things always have to be sacrificed to make way for new ones?" I said. "What's so great about new stuff? This place almost feels alive with the memories of the people who were here. The men, the women, the children. It seems like such a shame to wave goodbye to all that, let the wrecking ball come in and—"

"What are you talking about?"

"I'm talking about saving it," I said, eyeing the factory again. "Yes, it's old. Of course it's old. And it needs a lot of work. But it could be beautiful, David." I picked up another stick and took a step to throw it in the river. "And you'd be..." I was about to say *preserving a piece of history* when I felt my feet almost go out from under me.

David grabbed my hand. "Sara, careful!"

My heart raced for a moment before I caught my breath. "Oh my God, it's slippery. Thanks." His hand was tight around mine. It felt nice. His warmth, his strength.

"I don't want you ending up in the water."

I was about to tell him I wasn't worried, that I knew how to swim, but then I realized the currents were strong and I thought maybe that's what he was concerned about. We stepped back, and as he released my hand I had a sudden feeling that I didn't want him to let go.

I tried to sweep away the thought. "Old things are...they're important," I said. "They represent what we once were. Sometimes they're the best examples of what people can create. And they keep getting torn down like they don't matter. But they do. If we lose our history, we lose ourselves. Don't you see?" How could I make him understand? "You've got to save this place."

The sun, barely more than a soft curve on the horizon, cast a faint glow over the bricks, a last-ditch effort to illuminate them. David looked confused. Maybe no one had ever questioned him about what he did in his business. Maybe someone should have.

"Sara, just so you understand, *if* we buy this property—and that's a huge *if*—we won't be tearing down the building."

Now I was the one who was confused. "You won't?"

"No. We'd keep it," he said as we began walking back toward the van. "That's the whole point. We'd probably look at doing a mixed-use design. Apartments, some retail, maybe artist lofts, some office space. It would depend on the community need."

Mixed use. Community need. That all sounded good. Very good. "So you were never going to tear it down?"

"No, it would be a rehab. We've done a number of projects like that." He started to tell me about something they'd just finished in Cincinnati, but I felt so embarrassed, it was hard to concentrate. He'd done this before. He'd renovated old buildings. And I'd been talking to him as though he were a novice.

"I feel like a fool," I said as we got into the van. "Lecturing you about saving this place when that was your plan all along." I wondered how I could have been so wrong, and then I remembered his phone conversation. "But you said something on the phone before about everything needing to be bulldozed."

David started the engine. "Bulldozed?" He gazed into the distance. "Oh wait, you mean when I was..." He nodded. "I did say that, but I was talking about another project, a building damaged in a hurricane. It's mostly rubble."

Another project. I was relieved to know I'd gotten it wrong.

"I can show you photos of some of the other rehabs we've done."

Now I wanted to drop the subject. "It's fine. I—"

"Let me see." He pulled out his cell phone and began tapping the screen. "I have an album that I...oh, here it is." He held the phone between us. I could smell something citrusy and a little spicy on his skin. Aftershave? Soap? Whatever it was, it smelled nice. "This was an old wire mill in upstate New York. We renovated it and turned it into a mixed-use development. Apartments, restaurants, retail. I took these as the project went along. Scroll through and you'll see." He handed the phone to me.

There were photos of the outside of an old red-brick building not unlike the woolen mill—grimy, stained, bricks missing. Inside the factory, the floors were covered with puddles of black water; green paint flaked in sheets off the walls, electrical cords dangled from the ceilings, and broken glass sat like jagged teeth in the window frames.

As I scrolled on, the photos revealed a gradually changing building. The missing bricks were replaced and the façade cleaned. The floors, which I now saw were made of wood, had been refinished and shone with an amber hue. Light poured in through new glass in the oversize windows, and I couldn't believe the dark, dank-looking place in the first photos had become this clean, sunny space.

"We turned that floor into apartments and artist lofts," David said, pointing to a photo I'd enlarged of a renovated studio.

"This is incredible. I can't believe the difference." It seemed like magic.

"Yeah, it came out pretty nice."

He backed up the van. "You know," he said, gazing at the building that must have held a million secrets, "sometimes I think about the people who worked in these places. Decades ago, or a hundred years ago. I wonder about them—who they were, where they came from. How did they get here? Did they cross the ocean? Some of them did. Probably a lot of them. I imagine them at their machines, working. There are places in the floors of some of the factories we've rehabbed where the wood is worn from years of people standing by the machines. Think about that."

I *was* thinking about that. I could see those people. I wondered if he'd read my mind.

CHAPTER 15

INTRUDERS

It was dusk when we made the turn onto the path that led up to Jeanette's house. The woods seemed to have grown thicker since our visit a few days before, and I began to feel as though I'd stepped into the middle of a Grimms' fairy tale. We reached the top of the hill and drove into the clearing. The house was dark.

"Looks like they're not home," I said, a feeling of foreboding edging into my bones.

David parked the van. "Who knows? Maybe they use candles. That would be their kind of thing."

That did sound like them. Still, there should have been some signs of life. I gazed from window to window. The place felt deserted.

"Well, they knew we were coming," David said. "Let's go ring the bell."

We walked to the porch and he yanked the bell's cord; the clang shattered the blue stillness of the evening. Fireflies blinked in the yard, yellow dots rising from the grass. I peeked through the little window in the kitchen door, but it was too dim to see anything inside. I rapped on the glass. The wooden boards of the porch creaked under my feet.

David rang the bell again. "It's eight fifteen. She said to come at eight. Where are they?"

"I don't know." I didn't have a good feeling about this.

David took out his phone. "Do you have her cell number?"

"She never gave it to me," I said, realizing too late we should have asked for it.

"Let's wait in the van. They're probably on their way back now from wherever they went."

I slapped a mosquito on my arm as we headed to the van. Inside, David turned on the radio. John Coltrane was performing magic with his tenor sax, playing an old classic called "Say It."

"Coltrane," I said. "From the *Ballads* album."

"Yeah. Great album. You know, it might not be the one most people would associate with him, but it sure shows how well he could make beautiful music."

It was beautiful music indeed. We sat there and listened as the sky went dark and the song came to an end, Coltrane's final notes hanging in the air like gossamer. I watched the lightning bugs send their mating signals to one another through the night. "Where or When" began to play, Sinatra singing the Rodgers and Hart tune. I sat there, mesmerized.

"You know, you've got a nice voice," David said.

I sat up straight. "What?" Oh my God, I'd been singing. Talk about embarrassing. "Sorry. It's a bad habit. Sometimes I don't realize I'm doing it. I know these songs like the back of my hand."

"No, I mean it. You've got a decent voice. It's soft. It's pretty." He was staring at me, all serious now.

I could feel myself blush. "Oh, no way." He was being polite, that's all.

"If you'd been around during my Jazzmatazz days, I would have had you audition for vocals. We had Pete Rinaldi. He could play guitar, but he sure couldn't sing. You would have been a lot better."

He was looking at me in a funny way. An intense, concentrated way, as though everything had suddenly slowed down. "Just because you played sax in Jazzmatazz doesn't mean you're an expert on vocals," I said.

"Oh, I think you're wrong about that. I'm definitely an expert on vocals. I'm an expert on a lot of things." There was a mischievous tone in his voice.

I laughed, wondering where this was going. "Yeah? Like what?"

"Like what?" He looked through the windshield for a moment as though sizing up the Gwythyrs' house, which was visible now only in silhouette. Then he turned back to me. "Well, like this."

I don't know what I expected, but I wasn't expecting what he did. He leaned in and kissed me, there in the front seat of the van, with Sinatra crooning, and a chorus of crickets and cicadas outside. His lips were warm. His skin smelled like oranges. His kiss was soft.

But it was all wrong.

I was in love with Carter, and David was about to be engaged. What were we doing? This wasn't in the plan at all. We pulled apart.

"Oh God, I'm sorry," he said. "I don't know what I...I didn't mean to..."

I waved my hands like I was trying to clear the air. "Just a mistake. That's all. Let's forget the whole..."

He turned the radio off. "Yeah, yeah. Maybe we'd better, uh, figure out what we're going to do here. I mean, you know, about the hand." I sat there pretending to think about the hand, but all I could think was *What just happened?* and I knew he had to be thinking the exact same thing.

"Yes, the hand," I finally said, but I kept remembering the feeling of his lips on mine. And I hadn't even minded the stubbly beard. Okay, that was enough. I had to stop.

David glanced at his watch. "You know, I don't think the Gwythyrs are coming back."

I didn't think they were coming back either. This night was going sideways. "Maybe we should leave a message on their phone. And a note on the door."

"Good idea. I can come back tomorrow if I know they're going to be here."

I searched through my handbag for paper and found a scrunched-up Sizzling Wok takeout menu. I wrote a note on the back and we stuck it between the front door and the jamb. Then I called their phone. We could hear it ringing inside the kitchen. The answering machine picked up, Jeanette's voice on the recording. The message was new.

Hello there! You've reached Jeanette and Cadwy. We've gone to a psychic fair in New Mexico. We'll be back...uh, Cadwy, when are we coming back? Cadwy? Oh, never mind. In a week, I think. We'll be back in a week. Oh, two? Okay, two. So, leave a message.

And if you need any herbal remedies, tell us and we'll call you when we're back in town. We've got a special going right now on coffee enemas. Buy one, get one free. Be well.

New Mexico? I felt like I was going to crumble. "I can't believe this. They skipped out on us."

David was quietly banging his head against the front door.

"They knew we were coming," I said. "How could they leave without telling us?"

"Maybe they forgot. Maybe Jeanette's *mental calendar* malfunctioned," he said. I could hear the frustration in his voice.

I wanted to dig a hole and hide. "I can't believe this is happening. I never should have trusted her. I should have known she was too flighty. I'm so sorry." We stood by the door, the chorus of nocturnal insects growing louder by the second. "What are we going to do?"

"We're going to leave. We've gone as far as we can. I'll do what I should have done in the beginning—tell Ana and Alex what happened. They'll make an insurance claim, and—well, that's it." He stepped off the porch.

Ana. Her name felt like an intrusion. But I had no right to think that way. She was David's girlfriend, soon to be his fiancée. And my plan was to get Carter back. Carter, the man I loved.

Enough of that. I needed to deal with the immediate problem. The hand had to be inside the house. It was probably finished and ready for us. Were we really going to walk away when we were that close? "I have an idea. We'll go in and get it."

"What do you mean, *go in and get it?* They're away. The house is locked."

"We could see if there's a door or a window they forgot to lock. And if there is, all we need to do is go in, get the hand, and leave them some money."

"You're kidding, right?"

I didn't say anything.

"Sara, that's insane. We're not doing it."

"Hold on, listen. Nobody's around. And you can't even see another house from here. It's all woods. At least let's check. If something's unlocked, then we can decide."

"No way. You're out of your mind. That's too risky. Something bad could happen."

"Or something good could happen. We could get the hand back." I started to walk away. "I'm doing it."

"Oh, for God's sake, I can't have you prowling around here in the dark by yourself."

We walked the perimeter of the house and I tried pushing up windows and opening the back door, but everything was locked. Then we came to the left side, where I found a window sash that moved a little. "Give me a leg up. I might be able to get in here."

"You're not really doing this."

"We'll be in and out in no time. And, let's face it, if we *could* get in touch with the Gwythyrs and we told them we were out here waiting because they'd stood us up and flown to New Mexico, you know they'd tell us to go inside." I was on my tiptoes, trying to push up the sash.

David looked across the yard, into the blackness, and rubbed his temples. "I can't believe I'm doing this." He took a deep breath, then laced his fingers together, and I put my foot in his hands. He gave me a boost and I slid the sash up and wriggled through the window into the living room.

I let my eyes adjust for a few seconds and then went into the kitchen and opened the door. David came inside, turned on his cell phone's flashlight, and led the way down a hall. I could smell linseed oil and turpentine. We peeked through a doorway and saw a small bedroom with a mural of hot-pink radishes on the wall. We moved on.

In the next room, the walls were lined with shelves and cubbies that held chisels, hammers, rasps, and blocks of modeling clay as well as books and pads, brushes, jars of liquids, and tubes of paint. David shone the light on a worktable against the wall. And there it was, Alex Lingon's hand. Every broken finger had been repaired; all stood upright.

"She did it!" I said. We raced to the table and examined the places where Jeanette had mended the fingers, saw the way she had matched the texture of the papier-mâché and the shades of green paint. "It looks fantastic."

David seemed stunned as he ran a hand over the thumb. "I can't believe it."

"I told you she'd do a great job."

He gave me an exasperated look. "A minute ago you said she was flighty. Come on, let's take this and get out of here. How much money do you think we should leave?"

"I don't know. My handbag's in the car."

"Don't worry. I got it."

"No, I can't have you paying. I feel responsible. I'll go out to the van and—"

"For God's sake, Sara. Let's get out of here, okay? I'll leave her a check."

He sounded frustrated. I was only trying to help. He wrote a check for four hundred dollars, scrawled his name on the bottom, and put it on the table. "If that doesn't take care of it, she's got my number. Let's go."

We picked up the hand and carried it down the hall. I wanted to celebrate. Have a party. I couldn't believe I'd done it. Now David could drop the hand at the gallery; it would be in the show and no one would be the wiser.

We stepped into the kitchen. His cell phone's light illuminated something on the counter. It looked like a pie. "Hold on. Let's put the hand down for a second." I walked over and took a look. It was a cherry pie with a lattice crust. They'd gone away and left an entire pie. They must have had to leave in a hurry. It seemed like a shame to waste a good dessert. But there wasn't anything I could do about it.

"Sara, come on, let's go. What are you looking at?"

"Nothing." I went back to the hand and was about to pick up one side when I changed my mind and grabbed the pie.

"What are you doing?"

"I'm taking this."

"You *are* nuts. Do you know that?"

"They're gone. Who's going to eat it?"

"You can't take that pie. It doesn't belong to you." He had that testy sound in his voice.

"But it'll go to waste."

David opened his mouth as if he were going to say something. Then he just shook his head.

We stepped onto the front porch and as I was about to close the door, I heard a voice.

"Eastville Police. Leave that door open and come out here in the yard."

A knot lodged in my throat. Two uniformed officers stood in front of the house, one tall with a shaved head, the other shorter with fiery red hair. They aimed their flashlights at us, voices crackling over their radios. "I'm Officer Madden," the taller one said. "And this is Officer Barnes."

Twenty minutes later, they arrested us for burglary.

CHAPTER 16

THE INTERROGATION

Burglary?" David glared at me as we sat in the back of the police cruiser on a rigid plastic seat. In handcuffs. With our bodies practically shoved up against the Plexiglas divider between the front and back of the car.

I swallowed hard, wishing he weren't mad at me. Who would have guessed the Gwythyrs had a silent alarm? "Don't worry," I whispered. "This is a big mistake. I'll get us out of it."

"I don't need any more of your help. Didn't you hear all that? They read us our Miranda rights. We're criminals."

I did feel like a criminal when Officer Madden told us we had the right to remain silent, the right to a lawyer, and all those other things I'd always heard on TV. And when they took all our stuff—including our cell phones, my handbag and jewelry, David's wallet and keys. But we weren't really criminals, were we? We were just trying to get back what belonged to David. I mean, to Alex.

Officer Madden pulled out of the driveway, the cruiser's head-lights shining into the blue-green night. Officer Barnes followed in another car.

"This is crazy," I said through the partition. "We're not criminals. I told you we tried to get in touch with the owners, but we couldn't reach them."

"As far as the law is concerned, you burglarized their premises."

I knew if they'd been able to reach the Gwythyrs, we wouldn't be sitting in a police car. Especially after all that *Stick it to the man* and *Viva la revolución* stuff. "One of the windows was unlocked," I said.

"It's still burglary." Something came over the police radio. A woman was trapped in her bathroom.

"But I told you we didn't steal anything. We came to get what the owner repaired for David." I looked to David for support. He was silent. "Sorry," I whispered, wishing I could make it all go away, watching the darkness snake past us. A lone car turned onto the road up ahead, sped off, and disappeared into the night.

"We left a check for the work Mrs. Gwythyr did," I said. "Three hundred dollars. It's right there in the house. Why don't you go back and look? Why would we leave a check for something if we were stealing it?" I thought that was a good point, but there was no response from the front of the car. After we'd gone another mile down the road, he made a right turn, and soon I saw lights and a cluster of buildings.

"What about the hand?" David asked. "What's going to happen to the hand?"

"We'll keep it at the station until the homeowners return," Officer Madden said. "They can claim it then."

"Great. That might be two weeks," David mumbled as we pulled into a driveway by a white two-story building with a sign that said EASTVILLE POLICE DEPARTMENT.

Officer Madden shrugged. "Sorry." He pulled the car around the back and drove down a ramp into an underground garage.

"And what about the van?" David asked.

A garage door slammed behind us. I felt my heart plummet. "We're impounding it. We'll give you a receipt. You can pick it up at the impound lot."

"Impound lot." David groaned. "Super." I could feel his icy stare. I blinked away tears. I could hear Dad telling me I had to stop being impulsive. That I had to slow down and use my head and not assume I had the answer to everything. He was right.

Officer Madden led us into the police station, where David and I were put in different rooms. A female officer patted me down, removed my handcuffs, and took my picture in front of a height chart, which I don't think was accurate because it showed me as five foot five and a half and I knew I was five six. I wasn't going to argue about it, though.

I was finally allowed to call Mom, who I knew would rally whatever troops were needed to help me, but my call went straight to voice mail. The night was not going well. I left a message letting her know what happened but trying not to alarm her, which was a challenge. *Can you please get me a lawyer? And pick me up?* And maybe she could bring a tape measure so I could see how tall I really was.

I didn't know if I should wait for Mom to call a lawyer for me or if I should do it. I had no idea where she was or when she'd get my message. I couldn't help thinking, though, that this was just a big misunderstanding and that it would get straightened out. If the police wanted to talk to me about it, that was fine.

The female officer led me down a hall and into a tiny room with bare walls, three chairs, a table, and a large mirror I suspected was two-way. Were they recording this? Videotaping? "Have a seat, Miss Harrington," she said. "Detective Brickle will be here in a minute."

A detective? Maybe this was a good sign. Maybe this was someone with more authority, someone who would let us go. I sat down and began to review what I was going to say, the history leading to the night's event. *It all started when my mother tricked me into coming back to Connecticut...* Well, that might be too much history. I'd start with the car accident at the inn and go from there. I was getting it organized in my mind when a man walked in. He looked to be around fifty and had a square face, gray hair, gray suit, and gray tie. He closed the door.

"Miss Harrington." He took a seat across from me, setting a pad and pen on the table. "I'm Detective Brickle."

I said hello.

He offered me something to eat, something to drink. I declined. I couldn't eat or drink. I wanted to get out of there.

"I see you live in Chicago," he said. "What are you doing in Connecticut?"

I told him I'd grown up in Hampstead and that I was visiting my mother. He asked about my family. He wanted to know how often

I came back to Connecticut. He asked about my personal history, from schools to career to what I'd done since I'd left Hampstead, jotting down notes on his pad.

Then he put down the pen and set his hands on the desk. "Miss Harrington, how long have you known David Cole?"

I hadn't expected that question. "David? I just met him Tuesday. So, I guess five days."

"And what's your relationship with Mr. Cole?"

Why was he asking me about David? "My relationship with him? We're friends."

"I see. And how did you and Mr. Cole come to be at the home of Mr. and Mrs. Gwythyr this evening?"

"Well, David has this hand sculpture," I said, not wanting to get into the complexities about it belonging to Alex Lingon. "And I accidentally damaged it, and a few days ago we took it to Jeanette's— Mrs. Gwythyr's—so she could fix it. She's a sculptor. She told us to come back at eight o'clock tonight to pick it up, but when we got there they weren't home. And then we found out they were away. We didn't think they'd mind if we went in and got it. We left a check. We weren't stealing it."

Detective Brickle continued scribbling notes. After a moment, he stood up, leaned against the wall near my chair, and crossed his arms. "Tell me about the pie."

"The *pie?*" Was he trying to catch me off guard? I couldn't believe he was asking about that.

"Was it in the house when you arrived?"

Why was he asking me about the pie? "I don't know. I suppose so. I mean, it was there when we were leaving."

"And where was it, exactly?"

"It was in the kitchen. On the counter." He hadn't asked where the hand was, but he wanted to know about the pie.

He flipped over a page of his pad. "What kind of pie was it?"

I looked around the room, then peered into the two-way mirror. Who was back there? Was this all a reality-show prank?

"Miss Harrington? The type of pie?"

He was serious. "It looked like cherry."

"Cherry," he muttered, writing it down.

"With a lattice crust," I added. He wrote that down too. What was going on?

"And why did you decide to take the pie?"

Why would anyone take a pie? "To eat it," I said. "It would have gone bad sitting on the counter. I didn't want it to go to waste."

More jotting of notes.

"Can I ask why you're so interested in the pie?"

He ignored me. "Ever take a pie or some kind of baked goods from someone's home without their permission?"

What? He thought I'd done this before? "No, of course not."

"Mm-hm."

Why did he sound like he didn't believe me?

"Are you aware that we've had other recent burglaries in the area?"

Other burglaries? They thought I'd committed *other* burglaries? "No, I wasn't aware. What are you talking about?"

Detective Brickle sat down again, leaned across the table, and gave me a long, sharp stare. "I'll tell you what I'm talking about. Angela Calabrese. Eighty-five years old."

"Who?"

"Maybe you don't know her name. But you'd remember her house. Little white farmhouse? Route 465? Two loaves of banana bread. Stolen right out of her kitchen a week ago. She's so rattled she hasn't been able to bake so much as a cupcake since."

I couldn't have heard that right. "Banana bread? You think I took somebody's banana bread?"

"You and your partner. Mr. Cole."

"My *partner?* You really think..." I looked at the two-way mirror again. "David had nothing to do with this. He was there, but he didn't want to go into the house. It was all my idea."

Detective Brickle sat back and clicked the button on the end of his pen. "Let me ask you another question. Apple strudel. Taken from the home of Louise and Dusty Wilmott on Orchard Lane. Know anything about that?"

"Louise and Dusty who?" What would I want with an apple strudel? I didn't even like it.

"Or the poppyseed cake that was stolen from Willie and Beth McGregor's house on Pasture Way last Sunday?"

"You're asking me about the disappearance of a *poppyseed cake?* I wasn't even in the state until six days ago. And believe me, if I were a thief—which I'm not—I'd never take a poppyseed cake."

Detective Brickle narrowed his eyes. "You've got something against poppyseed cakes?"

"No, they're perfectly fine. I just don't like getting those seeds stuck in my teeth."

"Uh-huh." He threw the pen on the table. "Well, within the past week, all those things and a few others were taken. Some from right here. Some from other towns." He clasped his hands. "And I'd like to catch whoever is committing these crimes. We've had about enough of it."

"Look, I don't know anything about these thefts, and I'm sure David doesn't either. I'm not saying another word unless I have a lawyer here." Where the hell was Mom anyway?

There was a knock on the door, and Officer Barnes walked in. "I need to talk to you," he told the detective, and they stepped outside.

I didn't like the serious tone of Officer Barnes's voice. Were there other crimes they were going to try to pin on us? The plastic chair felt so hard; the two-way mirror seemed to glow. I wanted to get out of there and get David out as well. Finally, Officer Barnes walked back in.

"Miss Harrington, there's, uh, been a mistake."

I heard a phone ring down the hall and the clicking of keys from a nearby computer. "What do you mean?"

"You're not under arrest."

"I'm not?" At last, some good news.

"We finally got a hold of the homeowners and they said you did have permission to be in their house and take the sculpture. And the pie."

I took a deep breath. We were getting out of there. With the hand. I followed Officer Barnes into the hallway. "What about David? Where is he?"

"He's coming." Officer Barnes's badge flashed green under the fluorescent lights. "We'll give Mr. Cole a receipt for the van so he can get it out of impound tomorrow."

I'd forgotten about the impound lot. "Tomorrow?" David wouldn't be happy about that. "Why can't he get it tonight?"

"It's too late. The lot's closed."

He couldn't get the hand back to the inn without the van. I didn't think he'd be too pleased about leaving the sculpture at the police station, but it looked as if that's what was going to happen.

In a room off the lobby, a female officer handed me a plastic bag with my belongings in it, everything they'd taken from me at the Gwythyrs' house. I was signing a receipt when I heard Mom's voice.

"Well, of course it's a mistake," she bellowed. "Anyone who knows my daughter could tell you she's not a criminal. I'm glad you finally figured that out. Now, where is she?"

I walked into the lobby. Mom was standing at the reception window talking to the person on the other side, her pink dress a bright spot against the gray interior of the station. I rushed to her and she opened her arms. "Sweetheart. Sorry I didn't get here sooner."

"That's okay. I'm just glad you're here now. It was horrible. The police thought David and I were stealing pies and poppyseed cakes from people."

Mom took a step back, her hands on my shoulders. "What? You must be kidding."

"I'm not. I'll explain later. Let's just get out of here."

"They told me they'd made some kind of mistake. Thank God they got it straightened out. I had Frank Stoddard lined up to deal with it," Mom said, shooting the woman behind the counter an angry glance. "He's a fabulous criminal attorney, even if he *has* been through four wives. I don't hold that against him. Anyway, better that we don't need him."

Officer Madden was walking toward us, David behind him. "We're free!" I said, running up to David. But he didn't look at me. He stared beyond me at the wall where a large round clock ticked loudly. "My mother's here," I told him. "She'll give us a ride back to Hampstead. We can drop you off at the inn."

He looked at me then, his jaw set, his eyes cool. "I have a ride. I've got a taxi coming."

A taxi? He was going back in a taxi? I wanted him to drive back with us. We'd gone through this experience together. We had a special bond because of it. We should be celebrating. But he was going back by himself in a cab. I felt as though some part of me had come loose and was being left behind. "David, please come with us. Let us give you a ride."

He shook his head. "No, thanks. And I'd like my sunglasses back." He held out his hand.

His sunglasses. His Wayfarers. The ones he'd said looked good on me. "Of course." I pulled them out of the plastic bag and held them for a few seconds. Then I handed them over. "Thanks for loaning them to me."

My mother clapped her hands like a schoolteacher signaling her charges that it was time to move. "Well, whoever is going, let's go now. *Mistakes have been made, but we will not let ourselves be defined by them,* as my character Eda Vernon said in *The Sirens of Summer.*"

"It's just me going with you, Mom." I felt empty and sad. I looked back at David, but he'd turned away.

My mother linked her arm through mine. "All right, then. On we forge."

I found my watch and ring in the plastic bag and put them on as we walked to the doors. Just before they opened, Mom stopped and turned to Officer Barnes, who was talking to the woman behind the reception window.

"A poppyseed cake? Really? Why would my daughter want to steal that? The seeds get stuck in your teeth."

CHAPTER 17

THE HANDOFF

All Sunday night I had terrible dreams. In one I was running down dark streets, dim alleyways, carrying a coconut cake with raspberry filling, Detective Brickle chasing me. I could hear his shoes hitting the pavement as he got closer and closer. And then he yelled, *Stop! Drop that cake!* I awoke in a cold sweat, my heart skittering in my chest as I pulled myself from sleep, relaxing only when the landmarks of my bedroom came into focus.

I let out a breath. They'd arrested us but they'd let us go. It was over. I could put it behind me. I had to put it behind me. I had a much more important matter to get back to: Carter. The wedding was only five days away, and although he'd been very sweet to me and we'd had a few laughs, I knew I needed to up the ante to really get his attention. New hair, new makeup, new wardrobe, new me. I had to make myself irresistible.

I grabbed my phone from the bedside table and called Harmony Day Spa, the place where Mom had been going for years. They loved her there, which was good for me, because it usually took several days to get an appointment, but when I explained that I had a hair emergency and added that I was Camille Harrington's daughter, the receptionist figured out a way to squeeze me in the next morning. Wow. The power of Mom.

Sitting on the banquette with my personal planner, I made a list of the stores I wanted to look in for new clothes. I'd just put down the planner when a text message came through on my cell phone. David.

Eastville PD needs us both to sign something to release the hand.

I texted back: They need me too? It's not even mine.

Well, it's not mine either. And don't forget who got us into this mess in the first place.

How could I forget? From the tone of the text, I could tell he hadn't thawed since last night. I offered to drive, since I figured the van was still sitting in an impound lot somewhere, but David said he'd already picked it up and that he'd meet me at the police station. Things were still chilly. Monday wasn't starting well.

At eleven a.m., I pulled into the parking lot of the Eastville Police Department. The building didn't look nearly as intimidating in the daylight. Maybe the fact that I wasn't arriving in handcuffs also had something to do with it. I spotted the white van and parked next to it. David got out.

"Hello," I said.

He gave me a prickly "Hello" and we walked inside.

"You need to go to the property room," the officer at the front desk said. "All the way down the hall."

I'd just mumbled that they'd probably never had a giant hand in the property room before when someone called my name. I turned. Detective Brickle stood in the hallway, dressed in an all-gray ensemble, like last night's. I felt the air around me harden.

"So, Miss Harrington, we meet again. And I presume this is Mr. Cole." He looked at David, who gave him a perfunctory nod. "Can I talk to you two in my office for a minute?"

What was there to talk about? I wanted to get the hand and leave.

"We're here to pick something up," David said.

"Yes, I know what you're here for. This won't take long."

We followed Detective Brickle into his office and sat down in a couple of metal chairs by his desk. "I just wanted to mention that although the homeowners told us you had permission to go into their house and take the sculpture, as far as the other crimes go, we don't consider the matter closed." He picked up a coffee mug, the words I'M A DETECTIVE. WHAT'S YOUR SUPERPOWER? printed on the side. He took a sip of whatever was in it.

"What other crimes?" David said. "I came here because I was told we needed to sign something so we could pick up the sculpture."

He didn't know? "Didn't they ask you about this last night?" I said. "The banana bread and the cake? Somebody's stealing desserts from people's houses and they think it's us because I took that pie from Jeanette's."

He laughed. "You're kidding, right?" He looked from me to Detective Brickle and then realized we were serious. "Nobody talked to me about anything. I said I wanted to see my lawyer and the next thing I knew, I was let go. Told it was a mistake."

"We didn't have the evidence to detain you," Detective Brickle said, putting his arms behind his head. "At least, not at that moment, but we still have an open case here." He leaned back in his chair, which pressed against a bulletin board and a poster announcing a fifty-thousand-dollar reward for information leading to the arrest of a man who looked a little bit like our old piano tuner.

"I was informed this morning that the scope of the investigation has widened," he went on. "Similar occurrences in other towns in the county. We think they're related. And I just got word about an incident right across the border. A little town called Turnbridge, New York. Sound familiar? Ever been there? My money says you have. Two trays of cinnamon buns. Same MO."

"Oh, for God's sake," David said. "Are you seriously accusing us of taking food?"

"I'm not accusing anybody of anything. I'm just telling you we're not letting this rest. Good people have gone out of their way to make good food, and somebody out there thinks it's fun to steal it. We don't find that amusing."

"Okay, for the record," David said, "we didn't take any of your cookies or pies or whatever it is you're looking for. I can't believe you people spend your time on this kind of stuff. Aren't there enough real crimes out there for you to solve?"

Detective Brickle stiffened and leaned toward us. "Oh, you don't think these are real crimes? Let me tell you something. These *are* real. Today a pie, tomorrow a car. That's how it goes. And that's why we're going to put an end to it. We have a nice, quiet little town here with people who like to bake, and we want to keep it that way. We don't want trouble. So take this as a warning—we've got our eyes on you."

"Okay, that's it," David said. "If there's anything else you want to say, you can call my lawyer. And the same goes for Sara." He put his hand on my arm. "Don't say a word. I'm not letting these people push you around. Let's go."

He stood up. I stood up. He led me out of the room, and the tight feeling in my chest subsided. We were a team again.

We decided to deliver the hand together—after all, this was the big send-off. David followed me back to Hampstead, to the Brookside Gallery, which was in a large, red, contemporary-barn type of building with oversize windows on the street side. We walked through the door and into a huge rectangular room with a cathedral ceiling and lots of natural light. Workers in black clothes, some wearing gloves, were busy moving paintings, pushing sculptures on dollies.

"Oh, I'm sorry, we're closed." A man in creased blue jeans, an orange tabby cat on his shoulder, strode toward us. "That door is supposed to be locked. We're getting ready for a show." He tapped his black-framed glasses, straightening them on his nose.

"I understand," David said. "But I need to speak to the owner, please. It's important."

"That would be me," the man said, glancing back at two workers moving a giant feather made of silvery metal. "One second." He raised an index finger, spun around, walked to the men, and issued some instructions I couldn't hear, the cat sitting still the whole time.

"As I was saying," he continued when he returned, "I'm the owner. Kingsley Pellinger." His mouth twitched into a smile that lasted barely long enough to see.

David introduced us and explained that we knew about the up-coming show. "My girlfriend, Anastasia Ellsworth, is Alex Lingon's assistant and she asked me to do her a favor—"

"That's lovely," Kingsley said, presenting his little flick of a smile again. "But I do have my hands full right now with—"

"Yes, I know," David said. "The show. That's what this is about."

Kingsley turned away again and eyed two men who were moving an eight-foot-tall blue ampersand sign. "Make sure that gets to Doris Gables *today*. They've called at least six times." He turned back to David. "Sorry. You were saying?"

"I have a piece of Alex Lingon's work that's supposed to be in the show."

"I don't understand." Kingsley's broad forehead wrinkled; the cat stretched a paw. "We took delivery of everything last week. It's all here. We're about to start setting it up."

"This piece wasn't with the others," David said. "It never made it onto the truck. I drove it here from Alex's studio. It's in a van outside."

"Another piece. Hmm." Kingsley scratched the jowl under his chin.

I didn't like the sound of that *Hmm* or the way he was looking at us. I hoped he wasn't going to start making phone calls, asking questions we didn't want asked. Or answered. The thought of him calling Ana or, God forbid, Alex made me shiver.

Kingsley's eyeglasses slipped a millimeter down the bridge of his nose. He took them off. He stared at them. He twirled them. Finally, he said, "Well, let's see what it is you've got." He walked us to the door, then turned to the workers once more, snapping his fingers. "People! Let's keep this locked. I can't have the whole town walking in here right now." He gave David a placid look. "Where are you parked?"

"Down the street."

"Drive around to the back, then. There's a buzzer. I'll open the door."

David and I walked to the van. "Interesting character," he said, imitating Kingsley's smile. I couldn't laugh. We'd come this far, and now I was worried something was going to go wrong. Maybe Kingsley would figure out the piece had been damaged, and he'd start asking questions. Or he'd call Alex to talk about the mix-up with delivery. What would we do then?

We drove around to the back of the gallery, and I pressed the buzzer. A moment later Kingsley appeared, without the cat this time, and he and David brought the bubble-wrapped hand inside and put it on a table in a room where artwork was being stored.

As David and Kingsley unwrapped the hand, I thought again what a fantastic job Jeanette had done. The fingers shimmered under the ceiling light, a hundred shades of green vibrating like rippling water. I almost felt a little sad about giving it up.

Kingsley stared at the sculpture, stepped back, stared some more, and walked around the table. "It's lovely. Quite lovely." He pressed the tips of his fingers together, resting his chin on top. "Alex certainly has a consummate grasp of form and tactility."

"Yes, he does," David said.

"He told me he'd begun experimenting, that he was heading in a new direction," Kingsley added. "But it's not at all what I expected. It's a bit more, uh, primitive than what I'd imagined." He flicked his smile again. "But then, Alex does like to surprise us, doesn't he?" He took a closer look at one of the knuckles, the tip of the pinkie. He examined the other side again. Then he clasped his hands. "Quite remarkable, really. Yes, I like this new direction. I like it very much."

We'd done it. The hand was home.

"Do you need a lift to your car?" David asked as we stood by the back door of the gallery.

I didn't know if he was serious or joking. My car was only a block away. "No, thanks. I have some shopping to do in town." New clothes, new makeup. The Carter plan.

"I'm heading back to Manhattan," he said as we walked toward the van.

That shouldn't have surprised me. He lived there. It made sense he'd go back. He'd gone back last week for a few days. But this was different. We'd accomplished our mission to get the hand to the gallery, and David was leaving for good. The disaster with Alex Lingon's sculpture had been a major thorn in my side, but now that we'd had it repaired and left it at the gallery, I felt a heavy sense of loss.

"Well, I guess that's it, then," he said, opening the driver's side door.

"Yeah, I guess it is."

The moment that spun out between us felt awkward. We'd been through a lot together. Trying to fix the hand ourselves, getting it fixed but getting arrested, being blamed for thefts all over the county—even in New York. But most of all, there was that kiss. I knew I had to forget about it, though. I loved Carter, and David loved Ana.

David broke the spell, pulling me toward him and wrapping his arms around me. "Thanks. I'll see you Friday."

"Friday?"

"The opening." He looked at me as though he couldn't believe I'd forgotten. "You're coming, aren't you? I'll be there. With Ana. You can meet her."

The opening. "Yes, of course I'll be there."

I felt better knowing I'd get to see him one more time. But the comment about Ana bothered me. I wasn't sure I wanted to meet her.

CHAPTER 18

IDENTITY CRISIS

Harmony Day Spa was downtown on Main Street in a white house with light blue shutters and a hedge of pink hydrangeas out front. Stepping into the reception area, with its green and white décor, and inhaling the fresh scent of mint and eucalyptus, I felt confident this was where I'd find the new me.

"We've got you with Danielle for your color and Jen for your cut," the girl behind the counter told me, adding that Danielle was Mom's colorist.

I sat down, silently thanking my mother, and was greeted a few minutes later by a tiny woman no older than thirty. Her short, pale pink hair was tucked behind her ears. "I *love* your mother," she said, her voice an octave higher than most people's.

I thanked her, although I'd never been quite sure about the correct response to that. She led me into a room where several clients were having their hair colored, the salon employees brushing dye over squares of foil, dabbing at roots with paintbrushes.

"So, what can I do for you?"

I took a seat in Danielle's chair, wishing I could tell her the truth the way I would have with my colorist in Chicago: that I wanted to win back my former beau and I needed to look spectacular to do it. But she knew Mom, so I couldn't go there. "I need a new identity," I told her. "I want to look different, become someone else."

She raised the chair a few inches and draped a plastic cape over me. "A new you. Okay, I can handle that."

I liked her smile, her confidence.

"Is this for something special, like an event? Or are you just tired of what you've got?"

"Honestly," I said, "it's more a matter of necessity. It's complicated."

She ran her hands through my hair, revealing a rose tattoo on the underside of her arm. "Well, I see you've got highlights, but they look a little faded."

I nodded. I didn't want to look faded.

Danielle pulled a lock of hair between her fingers. "Your natural color is light brown. Which is pretty..."

Her voice trailed off. My natural color wasn't pretty. I knew that. It was the reason why I'd been highlighting it all these years.

"But you could do with a little more spark."

Ah, now we were talking. "Yes, spark sounds good."

"Have you got anything in mind?"

I did have something in mind. I scrolled through my cell phone and found the photo of Carter and Mariel. "I like this style, with the layers and everything, but I don't want my hair this short or this blond. Could you do something not quite as light? Maybe just a shade lighter than what I have now?" I'd be going in the direction of something Carter liked.

Danielle looked at the picture and then studied my reflection in the mirror. "Sure, I think that would look good on you."

She went to mix the colors and I skimmed through some e-mails. Change orders to supplier contracts for the fall directors' meeting. A reminder from Accounts Payable that I'd neglected to attach the hotel receipt to my last travel voucher. A chain letter (were people still sending those?) for single women, which I deleted.

Danielle returned with two plastic bowls of acrid white dye and a couple of paintbrushes. "So what's it like, having Camille Harrington as your mom?" she asked as she began brushing the dye on my hair. "Oh God, I'm sorry." She let out a nervous laugh. "Everybody must ask you that. You must hate it."

"No, it's fine," I said, although she was right—lots of people asked. "She's pretty much the same as any other mother. She made my sister and me do our homework, do chores, keep our rooms clean."

Except that she wasn't like any other mother. Living with Mom could sometimes be like living with a tornado. She could suck all the air right out of a room with her energy and her theatrics. And she didn't always understand how to treat children. She thought nothing of asking one of my friends where she saw herself in ten years. When the girl was seven. She took Mariel and me to see *Cabaret* when we were in grammar school. All those musicians and dancers in their bawdy costumes, Mom trying to explain what cross-dressers were. I used to tell my friends I was adopted.

"I guess my mother's been coming to you for a while," I said.

Danielle dipped her paintbrush into one of the bowls. "Four or five years. She's a lot of fun. I could listen to her stories all day."

Her stories were all the same to me. Or maybe they'd just blended together over the years. The writers and directors, the actors and composers. The places she'd been. I'd tuned the tales out ages ago. Or maybe she'd stopped telling them to me. I picked up a copy of *Travel and Leisure* and began to page through it, stopping to glance at an article about young, up-and-coming architects.

"I love to hear about all the stuff she's done," Danielle said, dabbing at my hair. "Being in all those plays. Meeting so many cool people. And when she talks about who she hung out with...wow. Bernadette Peters, Diane Keaton, Jeff Bridges. She told me your dad even knew Frank Sinatra."

"Well, he met him a few times," I said as I flipped ahead to a piece about a newly refurbished hotel in St. Barts. "They weren't really friends."

"Yeah, but Frank Sinatra. I mean, you know..."

She seemed young to be so familiar with that generation of entertainers. But maybe her parents got her interested in them, like mine had.

"Danny?" A woman walked toward us, her dark hair in a twist. "Can I see you for a minute?"

The owner, Danielle mouthed. She disappeared for a few minutes, and when she returned, she brought another bowl of dye. I read the article about the hotel and studied the before-and-after photos as Danielle continued to cover my hair with white paste. I was well into an article about luxury barge trips when her assistant told me it was time for a shampoo.

I closed my eyes and relaxed at the sink while she washed away the bitter-smelling dye and massaged my head. With my hair clean and in a towel, she escorted me into the next room, where stylists were snipping away with scissors and hoisting blow-dryers to new cuts.

"This is Jen," she said, introducing me to a girl with bright red lipstick.

"I hear you want a different look," Jen said in a hushed voice as I took a seat.

Was this supposed to be a secret? "Yes, I need a new image." I showed her the photo of Mariel. "I want this style, but I don't want it this short. I'd like it a couple of inches below my chin."

Jen looked at the photo and back at me. "I think it's a good place to start. With your situation, though, I'd suggest going a little shorter."

"My situation?"

Her eyes swept the room. "I just thought, because you said you needed to look different…"

That was true. I did need to reinvent myself. T minus four days and counting until the wedding. I was wasting time debating this. "Okay, I guess I could go a little bit shorter. If you think it would look good."

"Oh, I do." When she took the towel off my head, I was disappointed. My hair was wet, but I should have been able to see some difference in the color. It didn't look much lighter than before. Maybe Danielle had been too conservative. I hoped not. I needed Carter to really notice me.

I flipped ahead in *Travel and Leisure* to an article on the Greek isles. Brilliant white buildings with white roofs and blue domes were pressed into hillsides, the ocean swirling in the background. I was mesmerized by a story about the five hundred and eighty-eight steps people climbed to reach the village of Fira on Santorini when I heard the blow-dryer go on and felt a blast of heat against my scalp. I looked up.

Inches of my hair were gone, lying in tufted puddles on the floor. What remained was much shorter than what I'd expected and layered like the steps on Santorini. And now I saw that Danielle had been anything but conservative with the color. I'd gone from light brown with faded highlights to three shades of blond: light, lighter, and platinum. It was Mariel's exact hairstyle. I'd turned into my sister.

"Oh my God." I stood up, barely recognizing the image in the mirror.

Jen was biting her nail. "What's wrong? You don't like it?"

For a moment I couldn't form the words. "I didn't want it this blond or this short. I told you."

"I think it looks great," Jen gushed, but what could she say? She had to defend herself—and Danielle, who was quickly walking toward us. They exchanged nervous glances.

"You told me you needed a new identity," Danielle said. "And you showed us the picture."

"But that was a picture of my—" I kept touching my hair, still not believing what I was seeing. "I told you what I wanted. I didn't want this."

"We, uh, we thought you needed more."

"More *what?*" A few of the other clients had turned to look at us.

"Well," Danielle said, "when Alena, the owner, showed me the picture of you, I put two and two together and realized—"

"What picture of me?"

"In the *Review.*"

There was a picture of me in the *Review*? I felt a prickling sensation at the back of my neck.

"You haven't seen it?" Danielle walked to a table of magazines and returned with the *Hampstead Review*. In the top right corner of the front page, the place reserved for the most important story of the day, the headline read: "Suspected Baked-Goods Bandits Freed—for Now." Underneath were the photos from the Eastville Police Station, the mug shots of David and me. My mouth went dry.

Suspected Baked-Goods Bandits Questioned at Eastville PD; Hampstead Connection Confirmed
By Trey Simson, Staff Reporter

Two people suspected of being the Baked-Goods Bandits were seen leaving the Eastville Police Station late Sunday night after being questioned by detectives, according to an anonymous source. At least one of the suspects has ties to Hampstead. David Cole, of New York City, and Sara Harrington, originally from Hampstead and now living in Chicago, were interrogated by Eastville detectives about the rash of baked-goods thefts affecting Eastville that has recently spread to several other towns in the county, including Hampstead.

The source confirmed, however, that no arrests had been made. "They were questioned but released. We didn't have enough evidence to hold them." The source noted that the Eastville Police Department is committed to protecting the safety and property of all residents within its borders and that these criminals will be caught and brought to justice.

So now I had my sister's hairstyle, and my mug shot was in the paper. I squeezed my eyes shut and moaned.

"Uh, are you okay?" Jen said. "You look a little—"

"I could use a drink."

"We have coffee."

"Something stronger."

"Espresso?"

"Forget it."

"I'm so sorry," Danielle said. "I thought you wanted a disguise because you were arrested. And you said you needed a new identity. I just assumed..."

What would Mom say? And, oh Lord, *Carter*. All that nonsense about stealing food. I couldn't imagine what his reaction would be. At least David was in Manhattan. He'd be furious if he saw this.

I pulled off the cape. "I've got to go."

"Wait," Danielle said, wringing her hands. "I'll fix it."

"She'll fix it," Jen said. "Don't go."

Everyone was staring. "No, no. I need to leave. I have to get out of here." I dropped the newspaper and dashed toward the lobby, my mind disintegrating. How could this have happened? How did the *Review* get those photos and our names? The cloying sounds of a flute and a waterfall emanated from speakers in the lobby. I slapped my credit card on the counter and scrawled a signature on the receipt.

I had to get a hold of myself. This was a crisis, but I could handle it. I'd figure out a way through. I just had to stay calm and come up with a plan. Maybe hire an attorney. Or maybe not. It might be better to let the thing die a natural death. Once tomorrow's news came out, today's news would be old. Nobody would care anymore. That's what I'd remind Mom. And Carter. Oh, Carter. He had to know I wasn't a thief. That I could afford to buy my own cookies. Four days to the wedding and I'd become the joke of the town. It couldn't get any worse.

Except it did.

I ran outside and saw that almost every store on Main Street had the same poster in the window, white with blue lettering and a graphic underneath. They might have been for an upcoming event, like the high-school summer-theater production of *Into the Woods* or the Lyme Disease Symposium or the Garden Club's plant sale. But when I looked at the poster in the window of Harmony Day Spa, I saw it wasn't for any of those things. The words printed in blue said FREE THE BAKED-GOODS BANDITS! LET THEM EAT CAKE! And beneath that were blowups of the mug shots of David and me.

CHAPTER 19

THE EXIT IN THE BACK

Someone was squeezing the air from my lungs. That's how it felt. The posters seemed to multiply before my eyes. On the windows of the First Trust Bank and Stryker and O'Toole, Accountants. On the bike rack in front of Déjà Vu, the vintage clothing store. Everywhere, people were looking at the photos. Wasn't there a constitutional right to a decent mug shot?

I put on my sunglasses. Maybe Danielle and Jen were correct. Good or bad, my hair looked different. I had a disguise. Racing up the street, I kept my head down as I passed poster after poster. When my phone rang, I grabbed it out of my handbag and saw Mom on the screen. She must have seen the newspaper. Of course she had. I sent her to voice mail, knowing I'd have to deal with her later, and I continued up the street. When the phone rang again, David's name showed up. I pressed DECLINE once more, so grateful he wasn't in town.

I turned off the ringer and stopped to catch my breath by a

telephone pole plastered with leaflets: GARAGE SALE, 127 ORCHARD LANE, EVERYTHING MUST GO! REWARD FOR MISSING LLAMA, ANSWERS TO "RICKY." ERIC DUBOWSKI, ELECTRICIAN, LICENSED AND BONDED. HAVE YOU SEEN THIS PIE? Wait, what was that? I stepped closer. There was a color photo of a pie with a crumbly topping and below it the owner's phone number and e-mail address.

I looked to the right. REWARD FOR SAFE RETURN OF OUR OLIVE BREAD—TWO LOAVES! announced another leaflet. Several phone numbers followed a photo of two crusty loaves of bread on a cooling rack. LOOKING FOR OUR MISSING SIX-LAYER CHOCOLATE CAKE another leaflet said; below that was one photo showing a lofty cake drenched in swirls of dark chocolate icing and another depicting a faded, deflated-looking version, generated, according to a footnote, with age-progression software.

I turned away, unable to read any more of them. I'd become the center of a maelstrom, the butt of a town-wide—rather, county-wide—joke. Carter would never speak to me again. And what would Mom say? And the most innocent victim of all—David. How could he avoid seeing these when he returned?

Either my head was spinning or the rest of the world was whizzing around me. Maybe both. I wrapped my arm around the pole but couldn't shake that dizzy feeling. I lowered myself to the sidewalk and sat with my head down, the sun beating against my back.

"Are you okay?"

I looked up and saw a teenage girl staring at me, FIREFLY MUSIC FESTIVAL printed on her black crop top. "Thanks. I think I will be in a second." At least I hoped so.

"Maybe you should go inside somewhere, like in the

air-conditioning," Firefly said, pushing a lock of wavy hair from her face. "Maybe the Rolling Pin." She pointed to the bakery.

"Good idea," I said. A minute or two of air-conditioning and I'd be fine. I got up; my legs were shaky, but as soon as I stepped inside the shop I felt a rejuvenating rush of cool air. A middle-aged man and woman sat at one of the tables drinking coffee, part of a muffin on a plate between them. Behind the counter, Alice, the owner, was putting cookies in a display cabinet, her red hair back in a barrette.

Alice. She knew Mom. And even though I hadn't been in there in a few years, she knew me. What was I thinking? Then I remembered my disguise.

"Sit anywhere you want, miss," she said, then went back to singing along to the Eagles' "Hotel California."

I took a seat at a table, closed my eyes, and tilted back my head to let the air from the ceiling vent cascade over me.

A moment later, Alice asked, "You all right there? You look a little peaked."

I opened my eyes and saw her standing over me in her yellow apron. "I think I'm okay, thanks. I just need a minute to cool off." I leaned back again, luxuriating in the cool breeze, and heard the muffin man say, "Well, it's better than stealing cars. That's what they used to do in Jersey when I was growing up. Nobody there would bother with a cake."

There it was. People talking about it. I couldn't escape.

"But who put up all the posters?" the woman asked.

"I don't know," Alice said from behind the counter. "But I bet you whoever did it had a connection at the newspaper. That would explain how they got a copy of the photos and made the posters so fast." She picked up an empty coffee carafe and put it in the sink. "Anyway, I don't see the harm in having a few posters up around here. People seem to think the whole baked-goods-bandit thing is fun. Whoever's doing it isn't causing any trouble. I mean, it's just food. And I figure it can only help my business." She glanced my way. "You want some water?"

I think I might have jumped. "Me? No, no. I'm fine." People thought the food thefts were a *good* thing? That was crazy. I just wanted all of it to go away.

The muffin woman put down her mug. "Everybody's trying to figure out what they're doing with the food. Are they giving it away, like Robin Hood? Or are they eating it themselves? And where are they going next?"

"Nobody knows," Alice said as she took some cookies from the display case and put them in a box. "Although some folks are placing bets. Steve Francisconi, over at the firehouse, has a pool going. Point spreads and the whole thing."

Point spreads? I'd heard enough. I got up to leave.

"Hold on there. Take these with you," Alice said, setting the open box on the counter. I walked over and saw a half a dozen cookies in it. "Orange chocolate chunk," she said. "Three kinds of chocolate in that recipe. Good for a little energy boost."

I took out my wallet.

"No, no. This is on the house."

"But I—"

"Don't worry about it. I know your mom." She closed the little box and handed it to me. "And besides, you're a celebrity."

"Excuse me?" I said, putting the box in my handbag.

"Oh, honey," she said, her voice hushed. "I knew it was you. From the minute you walked in. Even with the new hair..." She wiggled a hand above her head. Then she picked up a copy of the *Hampstead Review* from behind the counter. "I've been looking at your face all morning."

I froze. I'd been busted by the bakery lady. I opened my mouth, but nothing came out. For once I didn't know what to say. I stepped outside, nearly colliding with a man walking a dachshund, and hurried down Main Street, my mug shot following me again. I'd become my own *Mona Lisa.* Everyone was staring at me as if they knew I was the one on the poster. At least, that's how I felt.

I walked faster, passing a man carrying a potted fern, a woman pushing a stroller. I swear they were giving me the eye. Picking up the pace, I decided I'd cut through one of the stores and use their back exit to get to the parking lot where I'd left my car. When I came to Then Again Antiques and saw that they didn't have a poster in the window, I figured it might be a safe place. Opening the door, I ducked inside.

A bell jingled as the door closed, and my eyes adjusted to the dim light. I stared at a mountain of furniture before me, the pieces piled so high on top of one another I couldn't see the back of the shop. The place smelled of old wood and stale, dry air. I walked to the left, down a narrow aisle like a footpath, past huge armoires and hutches, Hepplewhite chests and Chippendale sofas, tables piled with brass lamps, wineglasses, clocks, and candelabra.

"I'll be right with you." A man's voice came from somewhere in the back. Deep, with an accent that had me imagining Christopher Plummer.

"Oh, I'm okay," I said, moving past a carved headboard, a steamer trunk, a large wooden bucket.

"Ah, there you are."

The man with the accent, about two hundred fifty pounds of him, blocked my way in the aisle. His large face sagged beneath a head of jet-black hair that didn't look real. A gold crest adorned the pocket of his blazer. "Albert Cuttleworth, proprietor," he said, his chin raised slightly, as if he needed to fit something underneath. "Are you hunting for anything in particular?"

I should have admitted I was hunting for the back door, but I told him I was browsing. Hoping he'd let me squeeze by, I feigned interest in a copper weather vane with a trotting horse on it.

"That's a rather lovely one, don't you think? Circa 1919. British."

I looked up. "Oh, yes. Very nice."

"It's in wonderful condition. Are you looking for a weather vane?"

"Not exactly." I pictured my apartment in Chicago. The thirteenth floor. I didn't exactly have a roof.

"That one is an excellent value."

I nodded, looking at the price tag of seventeen hundred dollars. "Yes, well, I'll think about it."

"Ah, maybe you're not in the market for a weather vane. Well, no matter. Would you like to see a few things that just arrived?" He turned and began walking toward the back. I followed, happy to at least be going in the right direction. "Look at this lovely piece." He stopped in front of a huge wooden wheel. "A ship's wheel, of course. Late nineteenth century. Oak and mahogany. Beauty, isn't she?"

I wondered if he'd let me leave if I bought it. "Yes, she is. I'm just not sure I have a place for her."

"No place for a ship's wheel? You don't have *walls?*" He sounded a little put out.

"Yes, I have walls. I just mean it won't really go—"

"Ah, what a pity. Well, browse away," he said, his arms outstretched. "I've got hundreds of gems."

I had to get out of there. I looked at my watch. "Oh, my. Time flies, doesn't it? I need to be somewhere. Else. Is there a back door I can use? I'm parked behind the stores."

"Back door? Yes, just follow this aisle until you—oh, here, I'll show you."

I followed him the rest of the way down the aisle into a small room. I could see red letters glowing on an EXIT sign. A woman was in there, her back to me as she looked at a folding Japanese screen with gold pagodas and trees and dragons on it. She turned, saw me, and the smile on her face vanished in a second. Mariel.

"What did you do to your *hair?*" She took a step closer, examining me, scowling.

"What are you doing here?"

"I asked you first."

"I had it done. A cut and some highlights."

"You had it done to look *exactly like me.*" She was fuming.

"I just added a little spark, that's all."

"You added *my* spark. It's my hair."

"Nobody owns spark, Mariel. Or a hairstyle." I turned to Albert, whose eyes darted between Mariel and me. "I'm her sister."

"Yes, I see the resemblance."

"She's my *much older* sister," Mariel huffed. "Of course he can see the resemblance. You're trying to be my twin."

"Only three years older, and I'm definitely not trying to be your twin." I casually picked up a brass candlestick.

"That's one of a pair," Albert said. "Circa 1840, I believe. Stellar condition." He paused. "In case you have room for them."

I put the candlestick down. Albert raised his eyebrows and walked away. "What are you doing here?" I asked Mariel again.

"I'm checking the registry to see if anything's been bought."

She had to be kidding. "You're registered here?"

She shrugged. "Sure. Why not?"

"Isn't it a little…" I lowered my voice. "Pricey?"

"I'm not forcing anybody to buy anything here, Sara. People can get something if they want. Or not."

"Right. Like that Japanese screen? I'm sure they'll be fighting over that. It's probably fifteen thousand dollars."

"Don't be silly. It's only ten."

A steal at that.

"I want to know what's going on here," Mariel said. "You had more than a cut and some highlights." She crossed her arms. "What are you trying to do? Destroy my life?"

She'd lost me. "What are you talking about?"

"Your hair. Hello. Look in the mirror." She pushed me toward an oval mirror with a gilt frame. "See?" She jabbed a finger at the glass. "You're totally copying me with those layers. And look how short it is. And how…blond. Ugh."

She was right, of course. I already knew it.

"And you've turned into some kind of a criminal," she went on.

"Your picture's all over town. And in the paper. You and that guy. Mom's seen it too, you know."

Mariel had seen it. Mom had seen it. I was sure Carter must have seen it. My heart was unraveling.

"Hold on. I'm not a—"

"What's wrong with you? Stealing food from people. During the week of my wedding. You're doing this on purpose. You're trying to embarrass me. And now you're making yourself look like me. People will think I'm involved in it. They'll think I'm a thief too."

"Oh, for God's sake, Mariel. No, they won't. Get over yourself."

"Ladies, ladies." Albert was back, his face looking strained. "There are other customers in the shop. Perhaps you could keep it down."

"I'm leaving," I said.

"Excuse me, yoo-hoo!" a woman called to Albert. "Can I get some help, please?"

He gave us a stern look before stepping away. I headed toward the door.

"You need to change your hair back to the way it was!" Mariel stomped after me, her Louboutin heels clicking against the floor. I heard the tinkling of glass, and when I turned, I saw she'd bumped into a low-hanging chandelier from which forty crystal teardrops dangled and swayed.

Albert scurried back and steadied the crystals, beads of perspiration glinting on his forehead. "This is Baccarat. Nineteenth century. Let's do be careful."

"Yes. Sorry," Mariel said, flashing him a smile that was gone as soon as he turned around. "I refuse to have you going all over the place trying to look like me."

"Oh, stop. I'm not trying to look like you. Why would I want to look like you?"

"To get Carter back."

Oh my God. She was so close to the truth, I think I stopped breathing. "Give me a break," I said, trying to put the right amount of denial and outrage in my voice. "That's ridiculous. I wouldn't even want him back. And I'm keeping my hair the way it is."

"You're not going to get away with it, Sara."

An older couple turned and stared at us. I picked up a porcelain jug. One side had a chip in it. "Away with what?"

"With ruining the week of my wedding. The way you ruined so many other things in my life."

Albert had scurried back again. He laid a hand on Mariel's shoulder. "I know how stressful it can get before a wedding, but I'm sure you and your sister can work this out. Somewhere else. Shall I call you with any updates on your registry?" He was smiling, but his eyes were the eyes of a lion. I thought I saw points on a couple of his teeth.

"Just for the record," I said, "I never ruined anything of yours."

Albert lifted the jug from my hands. "I'll just put this back here. I'm assuming you don't have room for—"

"Are you kidding? You were horrible to me. You always resented me for being prettier than you."

"I did not."

"Yes, you did. And you never gave me credit for anything I could do besides look good. If I won a ribbon at a horse show, you said it was because I was pretty, not because I was a good rider. If I got an A on a paper, you said the teacher had a crush on me. You hated that I was pretty. And you couldn't stand it when I did something besides be pretty. I'm not as smart as you, Sara, and most of the time it *is* the way I look that gets me places, but once in a while I can pull something off using my head, and it would be nice if you could recognize that."

I bristled. Could I have been as bad as she claimed? Had I failed to see who she really was? I hoped not. She had to be blowing it out of proportion. And what about the way she'd always copied me?

"You weren't exactly blameless yourself," I said, my elbow bumping a large wooden birdcage. "Always imitating me, wanting to do whatever I was doing. Horses, tennis, the violin, the school paper. All you ever did was try to get in the way and compete for attention, especially from Mom and Dad. You ruined my college graduation. You told Mom you were too sick to get out of bed, knowing she'd go stay with you rather than see me get my diploma. And then you went out that night and partied."

"You should have been happy I recovered so fast," Mariel said.

"You weren't sick to begin with!"

She glared at me. "You wrecked my chance to get that job at the Getty."

"How could I have known some offhand comment I made at a cocktail party would get back to the hiring manager?"

"The guy you were talking to was on their board, Sara. You did know that. Didn't you think telling him I wouldn't know the difference between a Monet and a Manet was something that might get around?"

She was right. I should never have said it. I'd been angry with her about something, but now I couldn't remember what it was.

"You're such a bitch!" Mariel said.

"I'm the bitch? You're the bitch! I could name ten really rotten things you've done to me, starting with Carter."

"Enough!" Albert said, grabbing our wrists as if we were misbehaving children. He pulled us the final few yards toward the door, Mariel knocking over a brass coatrack on the way. He shooed us out, and I heard the clunk of a deadbolt after he closed the door behind us.

Mariel strutted on ahead of me. I watched her go and then saw her stop in a dead freeze in the middle of the parking lot. She stared at her phone, and she kept staring. Then she wheeled around to me, her face white. Something was up. Maybe it was Mom. Was she back in the hospital? Oh God, I hoped not.

"What's going on?" I said. "What's wrong?"

"I think you've done enough for one day." Her eyes were so cold, I shivered in the July heat.

And I knew. She'd found out about my plan. Someone had talked. Maybe the photographer or the guy from the band. Or that opera singer. I should have known Britney Spears was too much of a stretch.

CHAPTER 20

KIND OF VIRAL

I heard the siren before I noticed the blue and red lights flashing in my rearview mirror. Was I speeding? Had I forgotten to put on my turn signal? Maybe there was a mechanical problem; maybe the brake lights weren't working. I hoped they wouldn't give me a ticket for that. It was a rental.

I pulled over to the curb, still frazzled from the argument with Mariel. How had she discovered my plan? In the side mirror, I watched the police officer walk to the car. "Do you know why I stopped you?" He leaned in my open window.

"Are the brake lights out or something? It's a rental. I don't own it."

"There was a stop sign back there at Canoe Hill. You slowed down, but you didn't stop."

"I didn't?" That wasn't like me. I was a good driver. It was all because of Mariel.

"I need to see your license and registration, please."

I pulled my driver's license from my wallet and found the

registration in the glove compartment. "I didn't mean to run a stop sign," I said. "My sister and I just had a big fight and..." I realized it wouldn't matter to him. "Never mind."

There would be an expensive ticket at the end of this. And my insurance company would raise my rates. And maybe I'd get points on my license. This was Connecticut and I lived in Illinois, but their computers probably talked. Mom was right—I had to be nicer to Siri.

The policeman went to run my license. David phoned again and I let the call go to voice mail, then sat there biting my lip and worrying about what Mom was going to say when Mariel told her I'd planned to ruin her wedding. Points on my license paled in comparison.

But I got some good news when the officer returned several minutes later. "I'm going to let you off with a verbal warning," he said.

Oh, happy day. The traffic gods were smiling on me. "You mean no ticket?"

"No ticket. But you need to be more careful."

"I will. I will. I promise." I gave him a little salute and then remembered they didn't do that on the police force.

He handed me the license and registration. "Okay, Miss Harrington—you, uh..." He glanced at the passenger seat, where I'd put the little white box with THE ROLLING PIN printed on the top. Should I offer him one of the cookies? Would he consider that a bribe? I didn't think so. He'd already let me off.

Something sparked in his eyes. "I just realized who you are. You're one of the baked-goods bandits."

I needed a better disguise. "We didn't do it. The Eastville Police let us go. It was a mistake."

He straightened up, peering down at me. "Do you have a receipt for those cookies?"

Gulp.

It took a phone call to Alice at the Rolling Pin to convince the policeman that the orange chocolate chunk cookies were a gift. After straightening that out, I drove to the house, tearing off cookie pieces and nervously stuffing them in my mouth. Alice's three varieties of chocolate, along with the brown sugar and orange zest and whatever else was in there, oozed onto my fingers.

"Your mother's upstairs," Martha said, giving me a sideways glance as I walked into the kitchen. "I know she wants to talk to you." The *Review* was facedown on the table, the back page visible. I could see an ad for the Alex Lingon show at the Brookside Gallery. I knew what else was in there, and I was sure Mom had seen it. I was also sure Mariel had called her and told her what I'd done.

I walked up the stairs and stopped in the doorway of Mom's bedroom. The normally tranquil room, decorated in pale blue and white, looked as though someone had ransacked it. The bed was strewn with clothes; scarves and belts had been thrown over the back of an armchair, and shoeboxes were stacked like skyscrapers on the writing table. She was cleaning her closet, something she did in times of high stress.

As I studied the carnage, Mom walked out of the closet, a blouse draped over her arm. She did a little double take. "I've been trying to reach you."

I put the box containing the four remaining cookies on the

table and waited for the bomb to drop, for her to tell me how disappointed she was with me.

"What's going on with your sister?"

There it was. The bomb had been released.

"She called me," Mom said, "sounding very distraught. She was on her way to see Suzie McEntyre. I asked her to come home, but she said she wasn't ready to do that. I guess she needed a friend." Mom was nudging me with her eyes, giving me a look like she thought I might have some information to impart. I held my breath. "She's upset with Carter about something, but she wouldn't tell me what it was."

"She's upset with *Carter?*" That's what was happening?

The little line that emerged between Mom's eyebrows when she was worried had made its appearance. "Do you have any idea what's going on, Sara?"

"I don't. But knowing Mariel, she's probably making a mountain out of a molehill. You know how she can get."

"I'm worried. She sounded really upset."

"Whatever it is, I'm sure they'll figure it out."

Mom laid the blouse on the bed. "I hope so. I've always said she and Carter are perfectly suited for each other."

"Hold on—you once said the same thing about *me* and Carter."

"Well, I didn't really mean it about you."

"What?"

She gave an exasperated shrug. "You two never would have lasted. Carter needs to help people. And he loves the idea that he can do things for Mariel. Loves that she leans on him. Needs him. Ever since your dad died, she's become more fragile, more in need of emotional security. You know she's not as independent as you. Not as self-sufficient. And she's happy being the pretty girl on Carter's arm at the parties, the dinners, the fund-raisers. She doesn't need to be more than that." Mom picked up a cocktail dress from the bed, folded it, and dropped it into a carton on the floor. "Maybe you should call her. Maybe she'd talk to you."

"I don't think so. We had a fight this afternoon, downtown."

"What about?"

"My hair."

"I was about to ask you what in God's name you'd done with it."

I ran my hand through what was left. "I had it cut. And high-lighted. I went to your place, Harmony."

"Hmm. Turn around." She motioned with her hand and I turned. "You look like your sister. Were you *trying* to copy her?"

"I really don't want to talk about this."

Mom took one of the belts from the armchair and tried it on. "*Imitatus.* Past participle of *imitari.* 'To copy.'"

I sighed; I didn't need the Latin lesson. I asked her what she was doing with all the clothes.

"I'm taking some things to the church thrift shop. And dropping off a couple of old costumes at the playhouse." She took off the belt and put it in the carton. "By the way, did you happen to see the paper this morning?"

I stiffened. Now it was coming. "Uh, yes."

"What in the world is going on with this whole baked-goods-bandit situation? I looked at the *Review* and there you were on the front page, larger than life. You didn't tell me they took your mug shot the night I picked you up at the police station."

"They arrested me," I said, collapsing into Mom's armchair. "That's part of getting arrested."

"But why did the police think you were stealing desserts from people? You can afford to buy whatever you want." She glanced at me, a gentle look in her eyes. "Can't you? Because, sweetie, if you can't..."

"Of course I can. I told you that night, the whole thing was a mistake. It's because we took a pie from the art teacher's house."

"I thought you went to get a sculpture."

"We took that too. The pie was a last-minute thing. I saw it on the kitchen counter, and I knew the owners weren't coming back for a couple of weeks."

She seemed to mull that over. "I guess there's no sense wasting a good pie."

"That's what I thought."

"I saw those posters too."

The nail in the coffin.

"I'd already seen the paper, and then Lydia Harper called. She told me she was coming out of her eye doctor's office and her pupils were dilated, but even with her bad vision, she knew it was you on those posters. You and that David fellow. FREE THE BAKED-GOODS BANDITS. I didn't believe her. Thought she might have started drinking during the day again. So I drove to town to see for myself."

I cringed. But then I realized she didn't seem all that angry. What was going on? "I'm sorry," I said. "I know it's embarrassing."

"Well, it's embarrassing for you. Honestly, couldn't the police have taken a better picture? One where you were at least smiling?" She plucked another cocktail dress from the bed and folded it.

"Were the police in *that* much of a hurry that they couldn't take another photo?"

I glanced across the room at the pink baby sneakers and silver teething ring on one of the shelves. The shoes were mine, the teething ring Mariel's. "It's not like when that photographer used to come and take our picture for the Christmas card. They don't take thirty and give you a choice."

"I would have gotten them to retake it."

I'm sure she would have.

"I always say, if you're going to have your picture spread around, make it a good one. Oh, I know, in this age of Instagram and Facebook and Twitter and who knows what's next, everybody's snapping photos and putting them online. But that's the problem. There's no discretion. Frankly, I'd rather have one great picture of myself out there for the world to see than a thousand horrible little shots." She looked around. "Did you notice a pair of black heels anywhere? I just had them a minute ago."

"So your only concern is that the picture could have been better?"

"What other concern should I have?" She walked around in search of the shoes. "It doesn't look like it's done you any harm. There was a piece about it on TV this morning, the local news. It looks like people around here love the whole dessert-thief idea. So ride the wave, honey."

The local news? Ride the wave? Even for Mom, whose publicist was the first one on her favorites list, she seemed way too blasé.

"Maybe you can use it to your advantage when you go out on your own. With your event planning." She grabbed a jacket from the floor, revealing a pair of black heels underneath. "Here they are."

"I'll probably never go out on my own."

She held the heels in midair, stood perfectly still, and stared at me. "And why in the world not?"

"Because I need money to get started. And contacts. I don't have enough contacts in Chicago."

"I have contacts."

"Not out there."

"No, but I have them here. And in Manhattan."

"Well, even I have some contacts here. But if I was going to start my own business, I wouldn't start it on the East Coast."

Mom looked as though I'd insulted her. "Why not?"

"I don't know. I guess because my life's not here." The possibility of coming back east wasn't on my radar screen. "I never considered it."

"I think you should. I could connect you with lots of people."

I knew that was true, but it didn't matter. Moving back, finding a place to live, trying to make ends meet while launching a business—the idea was daunting. "It's too risky right now. I'd need to pad my bank account like crazy before I'd even think about it."

"I could help you. I could give you some money to get started."

Give me some money. All I could think about was Mariel. She'd be happy to take money from Mom to start a business. In fact, she'd done it. A dog-walking business, a gift-basket business, a vegan-soap business. All failures. "Thanks, Mom, but I don't need your money."

"Then I could loan you the money at a very low interest rate. Or you could make me a silent partner with a tiny share of the business. I could talk to a lawyer about it."

"I appreciate the offer, but it's not something I'm going to do." I took a framed photo from the table next to me and studied it. Mom, Dad, me, and Mariel, my freshman year at UCLA. How happy I'd been to be on the other side of the country, on my own. And then in my senior year, Mariel arrived in town to attend Cal State.

"You know, it wouldn't hurt if you occasionally let someone help you. Did you ever consider the idea that people might want to?"

"Why would I need help? I'm fine. Really."

She took the heels into the closet. "At least try to be open to it," she said when she came out. "I do have a few good thoughts now and then."

I knew she meant well. "Yes, okay. You do. Although the idea that this publicity might be a good thing for me is a little crazy. No offense, but I live in Chicago."

"Meaning?"

"Meaning no one there will even hear about this."

There was a suffocating silence before she said, "Hmm. I wouldn't be so sure."

Something in the *uh-oh* section of my brain switched on, and an uneasy feeling began to skitter up the back of my legs. "What do you—"

"It's on the internet. And it's gone kind of viral."

"What?" I stood up. "There's no *kind of* viral."

"Viral, then. Just plain viral." Mom looked at me like I was overreacting. "Oh, don't worry. *I* know you're not a pastry thief."

"But the rest of the world doesn't know it. My boss doesn't know it. Ca—" I almost said, *Carter doesn't know it,* but I caught myself.

"It says *suspected.* It doesn't say *convicted.*"

"But I'm not even a suspect." I looked at the floor. "Oh God, I think I need an attorney."

"Don't be silly." She flapped a hand at me. "You just need a publicist."

By the time I'd convinced my mother that I wasn't going to hire a publicist, that I just wanted all of this to go away, we were standing in her closet together. She held up two dresses and asked me which one she should wear to the wedding.

"I like the lacy one better. And that taupe color will look beautiful on you."

"All right. That's what I'll wear. Glad I've got that settled." Somewhere in the bedroom, her cell phone rang, and she went to answer it. When she came back, she was beaming, her smile so wide she could barely speak. "I got the part!"

"What part?" I didn't know she'd auditioned for anything. It had been years since she'd worked as an actor.

"An HBO series."

"Mom, that's fantastic!" I hugged her. I was so proud.

"I'm going to play a psychiatrist. It's only a small part—three episodes. But it's a good role. I'm really excited about it."

"We should celebrate."

She stepped back. Her smile disappeared. "Oh, no, no, I shouldn't even be talking about it. My agent doesn't have the contract yet. I don't want to jinx things. Don't say a word to anyone. Please?"

I'd forgotten how superstitious she was about that. "I won't. Cross my heart." I made the gesture.

She gave me a thumbs-up. Then she pulled out an ivory cocktail dress and hung it on a valet rod.

"Ooh, that's pretty."

"Do you like it? I just got it the other day. Thought I'd wear it tonight." There was a lilt in her voice I hadn't noticed before, even when she'd told me about the HBO part.

"What's tonight?"

"Oh, nothing." She brushed an invisible piece of lint off the dress. "I have a little date, that's all."

A date. That was not what I'd expected to hear. Was it the guy from the acting class? I hoped not. He was closer to my age than hers. "Who is it with?"

"Do you remember Paul—I mean, Dr. Sherwood? The one who popped in to say hello when I was in the ER? My neighbor Leslie's brother?"

The orthopedic doctor. The good-looking guy with the silver-gray hair. Yes, I remembered him. "He asked you out? How did that happen?" I wondered why the conversation was beginning to bother me.

"He called Leslie and asked her for my phone number." She giggled. She was acting like a child.

"Where is he taking you?"

"We're having dinner at the Corner Table."

Expensive and romantic. I was liking this less and less. "The Corner Table. He's not holding back. Going all out."

"Honey, it's just a dinner." She stroked my cheek. "What's wrong? You're the one who always said I should date."

"I know, I know." She was right. I had said that. And over the past few years she'd had a few dates here and there. She'd told me about them, but she'd never been too excited about the men. This seemed different. I thought back to Mom and Dr. Sherwood in that little curtained-off cubicle in the emergency room, about how he'd asked if he could take a selfie with her and she'd agreed. Actually *agreed*. I should have known then.

Okay, I was getting carried away. She'd just met the man and it was only a dinner. It might not lead to anything. But what if it did? Was I worried that she'd forget Dad? That someone would try to take his place? Or did it bother me because it seemed like everyone was moving on with their lives except me? Maybe it was a little of both.

"Hey, would this fit you?" Mom pulled out an emerald-green silk dress on a hanger. It was a simple slip dress, but the color and the deep V-neck made it especially elegant and sexy.

"Where'd you get that?"

"I don't remember. I've never worn it. It's too young for me, but I'll bet it would look good on you. You should try it and take it if it fits." She hung the dress on a pullout rod. "You know, I'm glad you decided to help your sister with the wedding. She's been a lot more relaxed about things since you took over. And it's better for you. It's time you got on with your own life and stopped dwelling on the past."

That was easy for Mom to say when even she was *getting on* with things. I pulled a burgundy velvet evening gown from a hanger. Red feathers adorned its sweetheart neckline. The skirt had rows of ruffles and layers of fabric. It looked like one of Scarlett O'Hara's dresses from *Gone with the Wind*. "What's this?"

"That's a costume. I wore it in *View from the Top*," Mom said, running her hand over the feathers. She looked at me. "Lots of good things are going to happen to you, honey. You're only thirty-eight."

"I feel old," I mumbled as I held the dress up in front of me and peered in the mirror.

"You're not old."

"I want to get married and have children."

"Children are overrated."

"Excuse me?" I turned and stared at her.

"Well, I didn't mean *you*. I meant in general."

"Right. In general."

"Things will fall into place, honey. You just need to move ahead with your life. It doesn't do any good to be bitter about things. You know, I was in a play years ago with a man named Stuart Greer. He was so talented. A wonderful actor. But not long after the show closed, his wife ran off with her periodontist." Mom looked as though it pained her to remember this. "I think Stuart had suspected it for a while. She was getting too many gum treatments. Poor man. The bitterness just destroyed him. A year later, he was dead."

"Wait. You're saying he *died* from bitterness?"

"Well, they said he died of cancer." Mom hung the Scarlett O'Hara dress back up. "But I know that wasn't the real reason. Honestly, anybody with half a brain could have figured out the truth."

I didn't think *bitterness* was a valid medical diagnosis, but I stayed silent.

"I just want you and your sister to be close again. The way you used to be."

We were never going to be the way we used to be. Not to

mention that the way we used to be wasn't half as close as Mom, in her Broadway-storied mind, imagined we were. How could I have been close to someone who was always trying to be a replica of me? Trying to chase me from my own life? *I hear your sister's a writer for the* Meridian, somebody told me a month after Mariel began high school. I'd been a photographer on the school paper for three years. Within two weeks of hearing that, I quit.

"I don't know all the ins and outs of your relationship with Carter," Mom said. "And I don't need to know. But I do remember there were problems. And if there were problems…" Her voice trailed off.

I felt something cold lodge in my spine. I didn't want to talk about it. "I should go."

"Oh, sweetie. I'm sorry. I'm just trying to get you to see…come on, don't leave like that."

I was about to walk out when I noticed the midnight-blue Dior gown Mom had worn the night Dad and his partners got the Tony for *Rough Seas*. I touched the fabric, and it felt like I was greeting an old friend. "I remember this."

Mom stood beside me and ran her hand over the dress, a dreamy look in her eyes. "I can still see your dad walking up to that stage with Joe and Charlie," she said. "They were so excited. And they all looked so handsome in their tuxedos, especially your dad."

I could see him walking to that stage as well; Mariel and I, teenagers then, were watching at home on TV. I remember how silvery Dad's hair seemed that night. Maybe it was just the lights. Or maybe it was the first time I realized he was getting older. He was only fifty, but that seemed old to me then. He'd worn his black-framed glasses, the ones he thought looked best with a tux, the ones that were still in the top drawer of his bureau. He had looked so handsome.

I opened that drawer, the one that held his watches and cuff links. Everything was there, exactly where it had always been. I ran my hand over the watches, the bezels shiny, the bands sparkling. I picked up a pair of gold cuff links, replicas of an Austin-Healey 3000 Mark III, the same car he had restored. Three pair of glasses were in the drawer, including Dad's tuxedo glasses. I lifted them from their place; the frame was cool and smooth in my hand.

"I know I've told you this before," Mom said, watching me, "but I want you to remember that your father was the love of my life. No one can ever replace him."

I nodded, put the glasses back, and closed the drawer. He had been gone for five years. I guessed she deserved some happiness.

After Mom left to bring the clothes to the thrift shop, I went back into the closet to take another look at the green silk dress. The color of the fabric was so deep and lush, it looked like something that should be worn only by royalty. I undressed and slipped the garment over my head. It shimmered under the light. I turned; I twirled. The silk rippled and the V-neck plunged. The dress looked as though it had been made for me.

I was still twirling when I heard the doorbell chime. Mom must have forgotten something. "Coming," I yelled, heading down the hall in my bare feet, silk flowing around me. The bell rang again as I ran down the stairs. "I'm coming, hold on."

But when I opened the door, it wasn't my mother standing there. It was Carter.

241

CHAPTER 21

CHANGE OF PLANS

Sara." He gave a quick shake of his head. "For a second I thought you were..." He stepped into the foyer, a shopping bag in his hand. "I thought you were Mariel. Your hair looks—what did you do to it?"

His eyes, which were usually as blue as a piece of the sky, had a gray cast to them. He disapproved. That's what his look meant. He didn't like my hair. He hated it. "I went to my mom's...to get...but it didn't come out..." I clasped my hands. Put them behind me. Dropped them to my sides.

"It looks great."

Oh my God, he liked it.

"And that dress." His eyes went up and down, over the dress, over me. "It's, uh, wow. I mean, you look really nice. Are you going somewhere?"

"Me? No. I was just trying on some things in my mom's closet."

Carter put his shopping bag on the table. "Sara, are you okay? I saw those posters downtown. Your picture. What's going on?" His tone was full of concern.

He'd seen them. Of course he had. Everyone had. "It's a big mistake. Someone's going around stealing pies and things, and the police in Eastville thought a friend of mine and I were doing it."

"Why would they think that?"

"It's a long story. Trust me, I'm not stealing anybody's food."

"But they arrested you. Why didn't you call me? I would have found you a lawyer."

He would have. I was sure of that. It's what he did—he rescued people. "That's okay. It's over now. I just want to forget about it."

He closed the front door. "You know, I still care. About what happens to you. Just because we're not—"

"Thanks, Carter." I knew what he was going to say, that he cared even though we weren't together anymore, and I couldn't bear to hear it. A piece of me was breaking off, slipping down some river like driftwood.

He glanced at the shopping bag he'd put on the table. "Is your mom here?"

"No, she went to take some clothes to the thrift shop. I think she has a meeting at the playhouse after that. She should be back in a couple of hours."

"Oh." He looked disappointed. "Well, I'll leave that for her. It's just something I saw in town I thought she'd like."

"Why don't you give it to her later?"

He shook his head. "I won't be here later. I just came to pack."

"What do you mean? Where are you guys going?"

"*I'm* going. Checking into a hotel. The Duncan Arms. And then I'm heading back to LA."

I couldn't have heard that right. "But...the wedding. It's in four days. When are you coming back?"

He didn't speak for a moment. The only sound was the brass pendulum swinging in the grandfather clock down the hall, a heavy clunk marking each second. "I'm not coming back. Mariel's called off the wedding. It's over."

I froze, my mouth half-open. The thing I'd dreamed about for so long had happened. "What's going on?"

Carter glanced around; his gaze traveled up the stairs as though he were hunting for an escape route. "Look, Sara, I feel awkward talking to you about this. You and I never really discussed our own, uh, situation, our...I mean, after Mariel and I got together."

"We should have talked back then," I said, wanting to ease the pained expression on his face. "It was my fault we didn't." I thought about the texts, the voice mails, the notes slipped under my door. The attempts he made to reach out to me, all of which I ignored. "You tried."

I glimpsed our reflections in the mirror, and it startled me to see an image of the two of us together again. "Why don't we sit down? You can tell me what happened."

"I don't want to do that to you. You don't need to hear about this."

"Carter, come on. What are friends for?"

This time he didn't refuse. We went down the hall to the sunporch, where a warm patch of light blazed on the sofa. "So tell me," I said as we sat down. "What's going on?"

A housefly looking for an exit buzzed against the inside of the window. Carter took a breath. "We had a bachelor party a couple of weeks ago in Palm Springs, at the Desert Palm—do you know that resort?"

I nodded. I'd done some events there.

"Anyway, I drank too much. I shouldn't have, but I did. And things got a little crazy. Around two in the morning, somebody came up with the idea that we should decorate the big fountain out front with toilet paper and shaving cream. So we bought a lot of shaving cream. It was stupid. Crazy. Like a college prank, except I never even did that stuff in college. But at the time it suddenly seemed like a great idea. And then somehow three of us ended up *in* the fountain. Which might not have been so bad, except we were, well, pretty much naked. Although we did have shaving cream covering our…" He looked down and grimaced.

"Shaving cream? That's all you were wearing?"

"Yeah. If you can call it *wearing*. The whole thing was nuts. Completely nuts. I can't believe I did it."

I laughed, trying to picture the scene. "Carter, that's so unlike you. You're lucky you didn't get arrested."

"That would have been better than what did happen. Somebody took a couple of photos and figured out who I was. I still don't know how. Anyway, the pictures got onto the internet—social media sites, blogs, you name it. Now they're everywhere. And the comments are…well, they're not good. *Boys gone wild. Guys behaving badly. What's wrong with men today?* That kind of thing."

"That's awful. I'm sure you just want it all to go away." I knew that feeling.

"Yeah, no kidding. This afternoon one of Mariel's friends sent her the photos and told her to check the internet. Mariel did and she went nuts. She told me she couldn't marry me. She said she couldn't be with a man who acted like that. She said I wasn't dependable."

That seemed like an overreaction, even for Mariel. Maybe it wasn't Carter's finest hour, and maybe it was embarrassing, but that wasn't the way he typically behaved, and I didn't think she should be that hard on him. "I'm sorry she's so upset with you," I said. And I meant it. I did feel sorry for him. But what was I thinking? Mariel being hard on him only helped me.

"You know how she gets when things don't go the way she expects," Carter said.

I did know. She got angry and turned inward and refused to talk to anyone.

"And she doesn't have your fortitude, Sara, your flexibility."

I knew that as well. And I liked having him think about how different I was from my sister.

The housefly buzzed again, batting its wings against the glass. Carter got up, opened the window, and shooed the creature out with his hand. "Before you took over the wedding, she was almost impossible to deal with."

"Impossible? How?"

"She said I hadn't been involved enough with the wedding plans." He lowered the window sash. "Which is crazy, because I did a lot. I listened to every idea she had. About the vows and the music, the linen colors, the table settings, you name it. And I've got clients to handle, a law practice to run. The world doesn't stop just because you're getting married. For a few days, sure. But she expected me to be as excited as she was about the filling for the cake and what song the band was going to play for our first dance. She said they should play our song. We don't *have* a song because she kept changing her mind about what it should be."

Carter and I never had a song. Not an official one, although my choice would have been "Come Away with Me" by Norah Jones, because that's what was playing the night I fell in love with him. I remembered the party in Laurel Canyon, the terrace where we stood, the lights of the city blinking below us, how magical it felt. How magical I felt when he came over and put his arms around me and kissed me. And Norah Jones was singing.

"I told her in the beginning to hire a wedding planner," Carter went on. "But she wouldn't do it. It's almost like she wanted to prove that she *could* do it. To me. Or to herself. Or maybe to you."

Me? "I'm sure she didn't want to prove anything to me."

"You know she changed the seating chart seventeen times? Seventeen. And every time, she asked me to review it. How would I know if your eighty-eight-year-old aunt Bootie—"

I almost laughed. "Aunt Bootsie."

"Aunt Bootsie, then. How would I know if she'd rather sit with Mrs. Duff or Robert Maze? I don't know either of them."

"She'd definitely want to sit with Bob Maze. He's an old friend of Mom's. Very handsome. And Aunt Bootsie's a huge flirt."

"Well, there, you see? You can answer that, but I couldn't. So why did she keep asking me these things? I finally told her, *I don't care where anyone sits. Throw away the damned chart and let them sit wherever the hell they want.* That would have solved it." He dug his hands into his pockets and stared out the window at the paddocks, where Jubilee was cantering along the fence line like a young colt.

"Yeah, it would have."

"You think so?" He turned to me and flashed a smile, looking relieved. Then the smile disappeared. "Well, *she* didn't. She had to have everything the way she wanted it. It couldn't be any other way. And now, with these photos…" He collapsed back and sank deep into the sofa, as though he might never get up. "Yeah, they're out there for the world to see. Yeah, it's stressful. But it's more stress for me than her. I'm the one in them. And you know what? If this is how she wants to be, then I don't want to marry her either." He crossed his arms and looked away.

"My mother said Mariel was upset but she didn't know why. Mariel hasn't told her."

"She's going to tell her. And then I'll talk to her. I'm not looking forward to that conversation."

I wouldn't have been either, but Carter was always ready to face the music; he was never one to run away, which I respected him for. "It'll be okay," I said, although I knew Mom would be crushed. "It's Mariel's decision. It's not as though you're leaving her at the altar."

The late-afternoon sun had moved across the sofa, and the patch of light had slipped onto the floor. "Yes, but from her perspective, I've let her down. It's hard to believe this is where we are."

It *was* hard to believe. Even for me, and I'd wished for their breakup for more than a year. "I'm sorry," I said, laying my hand on his shoulder, the feel of him so familiar. And I *was* sorry for him, but I couldn't stop thinking that given another chance, I could make him happy.

"Thanks, Sara. I appreciate your listening to me. I know this is awkward." He stood up. I stood up. Outside, Anthem let out a little whinny. "I guess I'd better grab my stuff and head over to the hotel, the inn, whatever it is."

"The Duncan Arms." I followed him out of the room. "Do you need a ride?"

"I've got a car coming."

I was disappointed. I wanted more time with him. "What are you doing for dinner?" I asked as we walked down the hall. "You shouldn't eat alone. We could get a bite together at the Duncan Arms."

"Thanks, Sara. You're nice to offer, but I'm not hungry." He nodded toward the stairs. "I'll just go up and get my stuff."

I watched him go, and I waited in the foyer until he came back down, his suitcase in his hand. "Come on," I said. "Have something to eat with me later, even if it's just a bowl of soup. You need to eat."

His hand rested on the doorknob. "Soup? Yeah, I guess. Okay."

Maybe he was placating me, but I didn't care. A horn beeped outside. "I'll make a reservation at the Tree House," I said. "Seven o'clock?"

"Yeah, sure." He was about to open the door, but he stopped and turned to me. He looked like he'd remembered something he'd been struggling to recall. Something in the wall creaked, the sound of the house settling. The air-conditioner fan turned on with a quiet whir. The muscles in Carter's face relaxed, and he smiled. "Those photos wouldn't have scared you away, Sara."

Ten points for me. I was going to get him back.

CHAPTER 22

ADVICE FROM A FRIEND

On the porch of the Duncan Arms, people were sitting at tables drinking cocktails, reading books, and looking at their cell phones in the soft light that settles just before seven o'clock. I walked to the front steps in the emerald-green dress, wearing the makeup I'd bought after David and I dropped the hand off at the gallery— everything from the Starry Night eye-shadow palette to the Rose Dream blush to the Pink Impulse lipstick. I'd called the Tree House and preordered dinner, including the seafood paella, one of Carter's favorites. Everything was set.

Halfway up the steps, I heard my name, and when I turned, I saw David sitting alone at one of the tables. He was supposed to be in Manhattan until Friday. This was Tuesday.

"I almost didn't recognize you," he said when I walked over. "You look so different."

"Oh. Right." I frowned and touched the back of my head, still shocked to feel how little hair was left. "A mistake."

"No, I mean you look different *good*," he added, standing and eyeing my dress.

"Really? Well, thanks."

"I've been trying to get a hold of you," he said.

I remembered then that he'd called me a couple of times earlier, when I was dealing with the shock of discovering our mug shots were all over town. "I'm sorry. I should have called you back. Things have been a little, uh, busy." He pulled out a chair. I looked at my watch. It was six fifty-five. I had only a minute or two, but I sat down. "I thought you were going to be in New York until Friday. Did you just get back here?" I hoped he'd say yes. I hoped he hadn't been downtown. If I could just explain, warn him before he saw the posters...

But it was too late. He pulled something from his briefcase. Today's *Hampstead Review* and *Eastville Chronicle*, our mug shots on the front pages of both papers. I shifted in my chair. He'd seen them. Of course he had. What fairy godmother did I expect would rescue me from that? "I guess you saw the posters as well?"

"The posters, the newspapers, the internet."

A muscle in my neck tightened. "I'm sorry, David. I really am incredibly sorry. I wish I'd never insisted that we break—I mean go into Jeanette's house. Then none of this would have happened—the mug shots, the newspapers, the posters."

"The internet," he reminded me.

I could never utter enough *sorry*s for the screwups I'd caused. "I didn't mean to complicate your life, but it seems like that's all I've done. You're a good person and I feel terrible that I've dragged you through the mud." I hoped he believed me. I did feel awful about it.

And he was a nice guy. There was something charming about him. The way he was going to propose to Ana. So sweet. How he looked when he stood up at the Gwythyrs' and said *¡Viva la revolución!* So funny. That he wanted to save the textile mill. So wise.

"I was pretty mad," he said. "Those pictures. The article. I couldn't believe it. All I could think was *Here's my professional reputation ruined.*"

I hadn't even thought about that. The idea that I might have damaged his career, his business, made me cringe. What an idiot I was. I wanted to turn back the clock to before I'd made that ridiculous decision to go into Jeanette's house. Or farther back, to before I'd crushed Alex Lingon's hand with the car. Then none of this would have happened. Although maybe that was going back too far, because if I hadn't crushed the hand, I never would have met David. And I wasn't sorry about that.

"Anyway, I thought this was going to be the end of everything," he said. "I figured people would think I was some petty criminal or that I'd end up a joke. Either way, it wouldn't be good. And then something odd happened." He leaned back in his chair. "Ever since this morning when the papers and the posters came out, people have been stopping me on the street, asking for selfies, telling me how they love the story and how they're following it to see what the Baked-Goods Bandits are going to do next. The old guy who owns the dry cleaner's gave me a twenty-five-dollar gift certificate."

"Mr. Penny? The one with the striped suspenders?"

"Yeah, he's a riot. And a lady who has a clothing store told me she'd be happy to bail me out if I ever got arrested again. Gave me her card." He pulled a card from his wallet and handed it to me.

GIFFORD'S SMALL AND TALL. "By the way, why don't they carry any regular sizes?"

I handed the card back. "Patty Gifford. Her son's five foot three and her husband's six six. You should watch out for her, though. I heard she's looking for another husband. The first four didn't work out."

He dropped the card like it was a burning ember. "I'm not tall enough anyway. Look, what I'm trying to say is that the whole thing began to be kind of, sort of, well...fun."

Fun. He thought it was fun. People stopping him, talking about his mug shot, asking for selfies. "Really?" He couldn't be serious.

"Yeah. Really. And it might even help my business. The reason I didn't go back to Manhattan on Monday is that I was able to schedule a meeting with some people on the textile-mill property, so I ended up staying. I've got another meeting tomorrow."

"You're making progress. That's great."

"Well, here's the thing. This afternoon a guy called from the state community development agency, and they're interested in getting a proposal on the project. He said my celebrity status might even make it move through the works a little faster. Of course, that's not official. And who knows what will happen. These things take forever. There'll be a million meetings, documents to submit. Governments move slowly. But I think it's a good sign."

As he spoke, something warmed inside me. I couldn't help feeling I'd played a little part in the mill project, given that I was at the site with David when he first saw the property. More than anything, though, I felt proud of him. "I hope it works out. I hope you'll be able to buy the mill and fix it up. I'd love to see it when it's done."

"I'd love to have you see it." On the lawn, birds hopped in the grass, and a mourning dove sent a plaintive *coo* into the air. "So tell me, why are you all dressed up? Is there something special going on tonight? Something to do with the wedding?"

Yes, it had to do with the wedding, but not in the way he might have been thinking. "The wedding's off. They're canceling it."

"They're canceling it?" He looked stunned.

I told him about the photos and all the negative publicity. "My sister's very concerned about having a man she can depend on a hundred and twenty percent. And those photos have really shaken her."

"I can understand that," David said.

"I can too. But this situation has given me a chance. To get Carter back. I'm about to have dinner with him. That's why I'm here." I looked at my watch. It was a couple of minutes after seven. "And the really good thing is I don't even need to use the sabotage plan."

He gave me a quizzical look. "What sabotage plan?"

I remembered I'd never told him about that. "I had this plan worked out to...well, I was going to do a few little things to mess up my sister's wedding. I re-pinned her gown to make it too small. I changed some of the music for the wedding and reception. I revised the menu and the seating arrangement..." As I rattled off the parts of my sabotage plan, I began to feel a little uncomfortable about having done them.

I waited for David to speak. Four men at a table behind us talked about a golf bet, and farther down the porch, a group sang "Happy Birthday."

"I can't believe you did that," he finally said. "Things with Carter didn't work the first time. What convinced you it would work a second time? And don't you think you might be catching him at a vulnerable point in his life? He tells you his marriage to your sister is off, and you're going in for the kill."

"I'm not going in for the kill," I said, feeling uneasy, wishing he hadn't used those words. "I just thought we could make it work if Carter was available again and we both knew the pitfalls from before and—"

"What about your sister? Didn't you give any thought to how she would have felt if you'd ruined her wedding? And do you think she'll be happy about you running off with her fiancé?"

Why was he lecturing me? It wasn't any of his business. "Hold on," I said, hearing my voice rise, sensing people were looking at us. "For one thing, he's her *ex*-fiancé. And for another, this whole thing started when she took him from me, remember? Carter and I were very…we were happy…until Mariel got involved."

David shook his head and gave me a look that told me he wasn't buying it. "Oh, come on, Sara. You're a smart girl. You really believe that? How happy could the two of you have been if he went off with your sister? I didn't hear you say she tied him up and kidnapped him, which means he went willingly. And that means something wasn't working between the two of you. He needed something that you couldn't give him and she could. Maybe you should admit that and move on. Or are you so competitive with her that you can't stand to lose no matter what damage you cause?"

I got up. It was after seven, I was late, and I didn't want to hear anything else he had to say. He could think whatever he wanted to. I didn't care. "What you said about me being competitive is ridiculous."

"Oh, is it? You really think so? I wonder. Maybe it's time for you and your sister to start acting your ages. At least *you* ought to. You're the older one." His forehead was full of furrows. "You ought to be glad you have a sister. Be a grown-up for a change. Maybe if you act like one, she will too."

Be a grown-up. He thought I wasn't being a grown-up. What right did he have to say that? What right did he have to say anything? "I thought we were friends." I blinked back tears. "But I can see I was wrong."

He called out to me just before I walked inside. "Real friends can be honest with each other."

I kept going.

CHAPTER 23

DINNER

I stopped in front of a mirror to dab at my mascara, which was running, then walked into the Tree House. I hadn't been there since the family dinner we'd had on the evening of my high-school graduation. I remembered running into Deedee Huffman and Bridget Kay, two of my friends, and going into the ladies' room to down airline-size bottles of Captain Morgan Spiced Rum they'd snuck in. The good old days.

The décor looked a lot more modern now, with white chairs and tablecloths and lime-green wallpaper printed with clusters of plump white trees. The place was full of people and buzzing with conversation.

"The other member of your party is here," the hostess told me. Tingles went up my arms. It felt like a first date and that was exciting. But something bothered me. David's words lingered in the air: *What about your sister?*

The hostess led me to a table in a little nook in the back, just what

I'd hoped for when I'd requested something private. A single candle glowed like a beacon in a small hurricane lamp, and a vase held the large blossom of a pink cabbage rose. Carter sat on a banquette, looking handsome in his white shirt and blue blazer, the light of the candle illuminating his face.

"Sara." He stood up. "You're wearing that dress. You look great."

He liked it. He really liked it. I felt my knees rattle as I took a seat across the table. "You look nice too."

A waiter approached and asked if he could start us off with cocktails. Yes, he certainly could. I ordered a Long Island iced tea, and Carter ordered a martini.

"You know, you never told me about your job," he said. "How's it going? Do you like it?"

I told him what I was doing, what I liked and what I didn't, and he listened patiently. "It keeps me busy, which is good," I said. "But I'm still undecided about Chicago. I don't feel I fit in there. Not yet, anyway. What about you? What's going on these days at Bingham Keith?"

He shrugged. "The same. You know, different day, different crisis."

I did know. There was always a crisis. I never understood how he handled his job, his clients. So many big egos to deal with. So many problems.

"Toby Keith's son joined the firm," he said as the waiter returned with our drinks. He removed his martini olive from the toothpick and let it drop to the bottom of the glass. "And we had a big shake-up in the employment law department. Six attorneys left. Started their own firm. Took a couple of paralegals with them too."

"Yikes," I said, knowing that was pretty much the whole department.

He took a drink. I took a drink. We glanced around. We were out of small talk. My foot bounced under the table. "I hope you don't mind," I said, "but I already ordered for us. I looked at their menu online and saw a couple of things I thought you'd like."

"I really didn't want you to go to any trouble."

"It wasn't any trouble. Honestly. I couldn't let you skip dinner. That's the whole point."

As if on cue, the waiter arrived with our salads—red and orange slices of tomato, chunky croutons, and pale yellow champagne vinaigrette dressing drizzled on top. *"Bon appétit,"* he said, setting the plates in front of us.

Carter had always appreciated good food, and I hoped the old saying that food was the way to a man's heart would hold true. "Yes, *bon appétit,*" I said. I cut off a piece of tomato, savored its sweetness, the tangy taste of the dressing. We ate in silence while I built up the courage to shift gears in the conversation.

"Are you really leaving tomorrow?" I asked.

He looked up. "I don't know. It depends on when I can talk to your mother. I don't want to leave until I can see her."

"So I guess you weren't able to do that today."

"I wanted to, but I haven't heard that Mariel's talked to her yet."

"I know Mom is going to be disappointed. She's always really cared about you. Ever since the days when you and I..." I looked away. I didn't bother finishing my thought.

*   *   *

Carter seemed pleased with the seafood paella. And the pinot noir. He poured more wine into our glasses, squinting at the label.

"We went to that winery," I reminded him. "The time we were in Sonoma. A hundred and five degrees, tasting wine all morning." I could have added that we'd made love all afternoon, but I didn't. *He tells you his marriage to your sister is off, and you're going in for the kill.*

"I remember," Carter said. "That little hotel we stayed in was beautiful."

"Yes, the hills, those olive groves…the whole place was straight out of a movie."

He put the bottle on the table, sat back, and gave me an appraising glance. "I can't believe you did all this."

"Did all what?"

"Ordered everything." He gestured toward the dishes. "Planned this whole thing. But then, you were always the planner, Sara." He picked up his wineglass. "Here's to great plans."

"To great plans," I said, and we toasted.

A group of musicians arrived and began tuning up, playing keys, plucking strings, rattling drums. A few minutes later they opened with "Witchcraft."

"My father loved this song. Especially when Sinatra sang it." I picked up my wineglass and twirled the stem. I'd heard the song a million times, but one particular occasion came to mind. "Do you remember that opening we went to? I think it might have been a Johnny Depp film. Where that crazy guy was singing 'Witchcraft' and trying to walk down the red carpet?"

"He was drunk."

"You told him to leave. I was afraid he was going to punch you. I couldn't believe you did that."

"I probably shouldn't have. Anyway, it didn't do much good. It was the cops who got him out of there, not me."

I remembered when the police came. "Yes, but you did get him off the carpet. You were pretty cool about the whole thing."

He sat back, gazed across the room for a while. "You hated those things."

"What things?"

"Premieres. Award shows. All of that. I was just thinking about how you hated them."

"I never hated them." I knew they were things Carter had to do. *We* had to do. Go to movie openings, to parties, make small talk, mostly with people I didn't want to be around. And nobody really wanted to talk to me anyway. Nobody cared what I had to say. I was just an extension of Carter. "Okay, I hated them."

I poured us some more wine and we listened to the music, the band moving on to "Let's Fall in Love." My head felt light, wispy, as if it weren't fully attached to the rest of me. But there was a leaden feeling in my stomach, and I wondered if the food wasn't settling right.

"You knew how to make decisions," Carter said. "I never realized what an asset that is in a partner. Being decisive. Looking back, I think part of the reason I fell for Mariel was that she seemed a little unsure of herself. And I liked being the person she looked to for advice. It made me feel as if she needed me. I think that's what I was attracted to. Her need for me."

"Wait a minute. You think *I* didn't need you?" It felt like a slap in the face.

"Well, kind of. Yeah."

"But that's crazy. Of course I did."

He raised his hands. "Okay, maybe that's not exactly what I meant. I meant you didn't need me *as much*. That Mariel never had your confidence."

How could he say that? Mariel was so beautiful that when she walked into a room, everyone noticed her. She was like the sun and we were all planets in orbit around her.

"She depended on me for things," he said. "Things you would never need to depend on anyone for. She called me her anchor." A wistful little smile crossed his face, and there was a tender look in his eyes.

Her anchor. She called him her anchor the same way I'd called him my rock. But now she didn't think of him that way. He wasn't her solid, dependable guy, the one who made her feel secure.

"She said she could always count on me," Carter went on. "And that made me feel…" He looked as though the word he was searching for might be written on the tablecloth. "I don't know. Important, I guess."

"Are you saying I never made you feel important?" This was a revelation. I couldn't believe that's how he felt. "Why didn't you ever tell me?" I could have done something. I could have changed. Been different. Let him do more for me. Done less for myself. "Of course I needed you. Of course I thought you were important. We should have talked about this. We could have straightened it out."

"Yeah, I guess we should have," Carter said. "Maybe we missed an opportunity there. I don't know. Everything's so confusing right now. I'm trying to get my head around what happened today, put it in perspective." He stared at the candle as it flickered. "Maybe Mariel was never meant for me. Long term, it probably wouldn't have worked out." I couldn't tell if he was serious or if he was trying to talk himself into the idea.

He tilted back his glass and finished his wine. Then he pushed the glass to the side. "You and I *were* good together, weren't we, Sara?"

He reached across the table and put his hand on mine, looked into my eyes. The band was still playing, people were talking and laughing, servers were moving around. But all that stopped for me. It was just Carter. He'd opened a little door, one I could push open further. I didn't know if he really believed his relationship with Mariel wouldn't have lasted or if he was just saying that. But if I took this as an invitation for something more to happen, who knew where it could lead? It might lead to the two of us being a couple again.

I thought about that, but as I sat there, my mother's words and David's words kept running through my head, reminding me that when Carter and Mariel became a couple it hadn't been all Mariel's fault, telling me what I'd been determined to ignore. And now I had to face the truth. The things that hadn't worked the first time Carter and I were together wouldn't work the second time. I couldn't change the basic chemistry that existed between us. In a few months or maybe even a few weeks, we'd be back to dealing with the same issues that had split us up before. The events I didn't want to attend, the small talk I didn't want to make, the crisis calls at two and three in the morning, the canceled vacations. I realized I didn't want to go back to Carter.

But I also knew there was another reason I wouldn't pursue him, a more important one: my sister. The heavy feeling in my stomach had more to do with her than anything else. She needed him. And he needed her. And everything I'd done to try to get between them and ruin their wedding had been selfish and childish and awful. David was right about something else as well. My sister and I did need to start acting our ages—or anyway, I had to start acting mine. I could set an example and hope she'd follow. And even if she didn't, at least I'd be able to get my own house in order.

I pulled my hand away.

CHAPTER 24

FATHER-DAUGHTER TIME

It was sunny and warm the following afternoon as I drove past the Spencers' farm. Three horses were in the field, their fly masks on, and I remembered that day I'd gone to Carl's with David and he'd said he'd never ridden a horse. That seemed like a hundred years ago.

I turned onto Coventry Road and a couple of miles later took the right onto Sugar Hill. The road cut a steep track upward past woods and fields. At the top, a wall and two pillars marked the entrance, and I turned there onto a narrow road. It could have been a park inside that entrance, all that green, the grass neatly trimmed, the ancient elms and maples providing shade with their graceful, leafy branches.

When I saw the giant cross with GRANT on it, I slowed the car. That monument had always been my landmark, my way to find Dad. I pulled over to the side and stepped out of the car. The scent of something sweet blew by on a warm breeze. Honeysuckle, maybe.

I could see the valley below and the top of the next ridge in the distance, a patchwork of green.

Walking between the rows, I gazed at the headstones and crosses, the obelisks and pillars. Granite, marble, limestone. Slate and red sandstone for the older graves, the ones from the Civil War, the Revolutionary War. Some of the stones were so worn, the names and dates had faded, evaporated, leaving only ghostly traces.

I found my father's grave, the arch-shaped slab of rose granite shining in the sun.

BELOVED

JOHN HARRINGTON

I ran my hand over the stone, tracing the words, then I touched the birth and death dates inscribed below his name and the space between them. Such a small space for such a large life.

"Hi, Dad," I said, sitting down in the grass.

I stared at the letters, the numbers, grooves carved into granite. I pictured us dancing around the sunporch when I was a child, Sinatra playing, my little feet on Dad's shoes, my small hands in his.

"You used to tell me how proud of me you were," I said. A bee droned; a bird warbled a three-note call. "I remember the first time I took grand champion at a horse show. The time I raised five hundred and twenty-two dollars for the animal rescue league. The day I got an A on a chemistry test. You were so proud of me."

I plucked a piece of grass from the ground and twirled it between my fingers. "You wouldn't be proud of me now, though. I've done some really bad things. I wanted to get Carter away from Mariel.

To ruin their wedding. And now the wedding's off because of these photos that have gone around—Carter in a fountain with shaving cream and..."

I gazed at the hills across the valley, purple in the distance. "Dad, I know I've gotten off track the past year and a half. Especially the past couple of weeks. A friend told me I was acting like a selfish child. And he's right. I have been. But I'm trying to make amends. I'm trying to do the right thing.

"Last night I called a guy I know in LA, J. P. List. He's got a big public relations firm there. I thought he might be able to figure out a way to put a positive spin on the photos. If anybody can work miracles, J.P. can. He checked out the pictures and said, 'Three almost-naked guys, a fountain, and a whole lot of shaving cream looks like fun to me. What's the big deal?' I'm really hoping he can help, Dad."

The breeze blew against my face, ruffled the grass, shifted the silhouette of branches on a nearby oak. "I wish you were here. I wish I could talk to you." I wondered what he'd say. And then I realized I already knew. He'd say what he'd said many times: That people make mistakes. That it's impossible not to, because we're human. That the key is to take responsibility, pick up the pieces, do everything you can to make things better, and move on, smarter for the experience.

"I have to rescue the wedding, Dad. That's what I need to do. Talk to Carter, talk to Mariel, convince them they should get married, remind them how much they love each other." They needed to get beyond the momentary distraction of the photos and think about why they'd wanted to get married in the first place. "I've got some work to do."

I took a deep breath. The air was sweet, as if the memories of the people buried there had bestowed some magic. As I inhaled the scent of summer, I began to feel a little lighter, more optimistic, almost happy. Maybe the right man for me wasn't going to come along for a while. Or maybe he was never going to come along. But whether he did or didn't, as Mom would say, *The show must go on.* Besides, I wasn't alone in the world. I had Mom and maybe I'd have Mariel and Carter if I could straighten things out with them.

I stood up and brushed the grass from my pants. "Dad, I've got to go. I've got stuff I need to do. But thanks for the talk." I touched the top of the gravestone, the rose granite warm from the sun. A tiny pair of iridescent wings flickered toward me, and I heard a soft buzz as the dragonfly veered away at the last second. It touched down briefly on the headstone where my hand had rested. Then it took off into the sky.

CHAPTER 25

SHAVING SHOULD BE FUN

I stood in the doorway of Mariel's room on Thursday morning, watching in silence as she flung clothes into an open suitcase on the bed. Dresses and sweaters, skirts and pants, went zinging across the room. "What are you doing?"

Her eyes were red and puffy, her cheeks mottled. "What does it look like I'm doing?" She sent a lacy bra winging by me and then retreated into the closet. I heard the jangle of hangers.

"Where are you going?"

She reappeared in the closet doorway, a pair of black jeans in her hand. "Back to LA. Where else would I go?"

"I don't think you should leave."

"I don't care what you think. Or what anybody thinks. I'm going to see if I can get my old job back at YogaBuzz." She pitched the jeans toward the bed. They landed on the floor.

"You shouldn't leave," I repeated, picking up the jeans and folding them. I set them on the bed, away from the suitcase. "You should stay and marry Carter on Saturday."

"I'm not going to marry Carter."

"Mariel, listen to me. He was just having a little fun with the guys, letting off some steam. Something he never does. So cut him some slack. Don't let those stupid photos get in the way of the rest of your life. The rest of your lives together."

"Having fun is one thing. Ruining your career is another. What if he loses his job, Sara? What'll happen to us? We'll end up living in a tent on the street somewhere. I need a man I can depend on."

"You're not going to be living in a tent. Carter's not going to lose his job. He's a very successful partner at the firm."

"You don't know that. Maybe his clients will fire him because of those pictures. It was such a stupid thing to do." She opened a drawer and pulled out a sweater. "Maybe it's good it happened. I mean, how can two people get along for a whole lifetime? Carter and I proved this week that we can't."

"Hold on. You're jumping to conclusions. Everybody gets frazzled the week before a wedding, even without something like those photos coming along. You're looking at a very stressful time and trying to predict everything based on that. You're not being fair."

She held the sweater over the suitcase and let it fall. "But shouldn't that be the test? If you can make it in stressful times? Otherwise, why bother?"

She had a point. God, she was irritating me, sounding so rational. "I really think you guys can work this out."

"There's nothing to work out. He doesn't love me. If he did, he wouldn't have acted like such a jerk."

"Yes, he does love you. Just talk to him, please? I'm sure you two could straighten everything out. I know how much he cares about you."

"Oh, and how would you know?"

"Because I saw him."

"You saw him." She planted her hands on her hips. "Do you think I need you running interference for me? I know you wanted to get him back all along. You couldn't believe he was in love with me. Me, the pretty one without the brains, instead of you, the brainy one…"

Without the looks. She didn't say it, but I knew that's what she was thinking. I let it pass. I needed to defuse, not escalate.

"You can have him," Mariel went on. "He's all yours." She threw a pair of black heels toward the suitcase; one of them narrowly missed my head.

"Okay, okay." I raised my hands. "You're right. I admit it. I did want him back. I did want to take him away from you." There. I'd said it. I waited for the world to come crashing down around me.

Mariel shoved a canvas tote into the suitcase. "I know that. How do you think it made me feel? Sure, I get it. I knew I wasn't going to be nominated for the sister-of-the-year award when Carter and I got together. Even though it wasn't my fault. He swore things had already gone way south between you two. That it was over."

She was right. He was right. It was over. I'd been trying to keep our relationship on life support, but it was over. I thought about the ill-fated trip we'd taken to Montecito that fall. How we'd just arrived at Rich and Margo's house when Carter got the call. His new client, twenty-two, superstar singer, arrested for cocaine possession.

We drove right back to LA so he could take command and save the day. It didn't matter that she had a criminal lawyer, a therapist, a publicist, a life coach, and parents who lived an hour away. Was that when it began to fall apart? Was that when I realized our relationship had worn thin? Or had it already been unraveling bit by bit, death by a thousand cuts?

"It *was* over," I said. "I shouldn't have blamed you. But I was jealous. And hurt."

"What happened between us just *happened,* Sara. You always made it seem like it was personal."

"Well, it *was* personal. You're my sister."

"And I wish I weren't. I wish I were a stranger so you would have left it alone, accepted the way things were and gone on. Mom kept telling me I had to reach out to you and make things right, that if I didn't do that, I'd never really be happy. I tried to, but you wouldn't talk to me."

She slammed the top of the suitcase down and tried to zip it up, but the sleeve of a dress was sticking out and the suitcase wouldn't close. "I've got to get out of here."

"You're not going anywhere."

Mariel and I turned. Mom stood in the doorway. I had the feeling she'd been standing there for a while. "Not until you and Carter and I can sit down and talk about this together, rationally. I just want a few minutes with the two of you. Before you go off and ruin your lives."

"What is this? An intervention?" Mariel tried to close the suitcase again, then gave up.

"You owe it to Mom to talk to her," I said.

Mariel wheeled around. "Since when did you become Mom's BFF?"

That was laughable. "Me? Are you kidding? I'm the odd man out here. You two are the BFFs, in your own little bubble. I'm floating way off to the side by myself."

"What are you talking about?" Mom asked. "What bubble?"

"I mean you've always favored Mariel. And don't deny it. I have a whole lifetime of proof that you love her more than me."

Little lines I'd never seen before appeared on my mother's face. "Sara, that's not true. I love you girls equally."

"No, you don't. You've always given her more attention."

Mariel raised her hands. "How can you say that? Half the time I talk to Mom, she's telling me I need to be more like you. 'Make goals for yourself. Plan your future. Figure out how to do things on your own.'"

That was news.

"Well, you two share secrets," I said, glancing from Mariel to Mom. "Things you don't talk about with me."

"Like what?" Mariel asked.

"You want an example? Okay, here's one. Mom's high blood pressure. You guys never told me about that."

"Maybe there are things Mom doesn't tell you because she's afraid you'll be a pain in the ass about them."

"A pain in the ass? When am I a pain in the ass?"

Mariel let out a shriek of laughter.

"That's not how I'd put it," Mom said, giving Mariel a look that silenced her. She turned back to me. "But your sister has a point, honey. Sometimes I don't mention things to you because you try to take over, as if no one else can do as good a job as you. When I found out I had hypertension, I didn't tell you because, well, for one thing, I didn't think it was a big deal. Lots of people have it. They take their medicine and they're fine. How could I know that the medicine wouldn't work for me?

"But the other reason was that I was afraid if I did tell you, you'd drop whatever you were doing and come flying back here wanting to take over, fix everything. Which was what you did. You threw out my food, you left me dozens of articles to read, you put notes all over the kitchen about what I should and shouldn't eat, you got me a blood pressure cuff and two cookbooks. I could have done all that myself."

Maybe she could have, but I wasn't so sure she would have. "I was trying to make things easier. And I was worried you wouldn't do it yourself." She would never have gotten rid of those frozen pizzas. "I don't want anything to happen to you."

Mom's eyes softened. "Sweetheart, you've got to let me make my own decisions, do things my own way. I appreciate the help. I know it comes from a place of love." She touched my cheek. "But let *me* work on that. I promise I will. You need to work on loosening the reins a little. You can't control everything."

Was I really that controlling? Did I make people think they were incapable of doing things themselves? I didn't want to be that way. Still, Mom had her own issues about control. "You can't control everything either. You still support Mariel. If you didn't, she wouldn't be able to keep her apartment and put food in the fridge. She's never been independent. And that's because you've always enabled her."

"You're right. I do help your sister. I've probably helped her too much. She could take some lessons from you about being more self-reliant. Of course, I'd help you too, if you asked. Except you don't. You want to be completely independent."

"You could have asked me if I needed help. But I don't want to be like Mariel. She has no idea what the real world is about. Her life has been so easy."

"My life has *not* been so easy," my sister said, surprising me when her voice cracked. "How would you like to be the one with the perfect sister? The sister who's so great at everything? I'm sorry I can't be just like you. You think I don't try, but I do. I've tried my whole life to do what you do, but you always do everything better."

How could she not see that the real problem was that by copying me, she made me crazy? "That's the whole issue. You drove me away from things I loved because you were copying me, getting into my territory, my space. I couldn't stand it."

"I didn't mean to copy you. I just thought if I did what you did, people would like me the way they liked you."

"People did like you," I said. "You always got attention, lots of attention."

"Because of how I looked, Sara. Do you know how hard that is? People never say, *Oh, there's Mariel. She's so talented, so clever, so smart.* No, they say, *She's so beautiful.* Everybody thinks that's great, to be beautiful. But that's all I've got."

"That's not all you've got. You just don't stick with things long enough. You don't persevere. If you want to be good at something, you've got to put time and effort into it. I've told you that since we were kids. You could have been a great rider. Much better than me. You *were* better than me. But you gave up too fast."

Mom sat down on the edge of the bed. "That's true, Mariel. I used to tell you the same thing. Maybe I didn't say it enough. Or maybe I should have pushed you more. Maybe I let you give up too easily." She looked at me. "You're right, Sara, about me giving your sister more attention." She ran her hand over the jeans I'd folded. "Maybe that was easier for me than being tough. I never had to worry about you being independent, Sara. You knew what you wanted, knew how to get there. Mariel always seemed a little lost."

I sat down next to Mom; Mariel sat on the other side of her. "I'm sorry," Mom said, her eyes misty. "I'm sorry I've let you down." Mom grasped our hands and we became a chain, like something forged of steel. She pulled us in tight. I could smell the freesia on her cheek as we sat there, jigsaw-puzzle pieces that hadn't always seemed to fit together. But we were getting closer.

I heard the doorbell ring. "I'll get it," Mom said. A minute later she called up the stairs, "Mariel, Kellie's here."

"Kellie," Mariel muttered. "She wasn't supposed to come until..."

She headed for the door and I followed her. Downstairs, in the foyer, Mom was fussing over Kellie, one of Mariel's friends from LA. Mariel and Kellie hugged and squealed as if they hadn't seen each other in years, although I knew it had probably been a matter of days.

"What are you doing here?" Mariel said. "I thought you were coming tomorrow."

Kellie adjusted the scarf around her neck. "Listen, babe, when I saw what was going on with those photos and then you told me you were going to call off the wedding, I dashed over to LAX and got on the redeye. I couldn't let you handle all that on your own."

Mom put her hand over her heart. "A *verus amicus*. A true friend."

"I'm so glad you're here," Mariel said, taking Kellie's hand.

"Oh, I am too. But I guess I didn't have to rush to your side after all."

"What do you mean?" Mom asked.

"You haven't seen what's going on with Carter's photos?" She grabbed Mariel's arm. "There's been this whole backlash to that 'boys behaving badly' thing. Somebody posted one of the photos of Carter and the guys and put 'Shaving Should Be Fun!' over it, and it started going around. And now hashtag-shavingshouldbefun is trending, and people are posting pictures of themselves doing crazy things while they're shaving." She took out her phone and began tapping the screen while Mariel and Mom looked on.

I took out my own phone and went to Twitter. There it was— #shavingshouldbefun. I scrolled through and saw that people had retweeted the photos of Carter and his friends and added comments like *Come on, let them have a little fun* and *Gillette should use this in a PR campaign!* There were even some copycat photos where guys had gone into fountains and shaving-creamed themselves. A couple of them were actually shaving.

"Thank God," Mom said. "What a relief." She put her arm around Mariel. "I don't think you have to worry about this anymore, honey. It looks like the problem's taken care of itself."

I silently thanked J. P. List.

Mom said, "Maybe you and Carter can get married now," just as the front door opened and Carter walked in. He stood there for a second looking at Mom and Kellie and me, then he turned to Mariel. "That's exactly what I think. We can get married now. My

Saturday is completely open and I'd really like to get our wedding back on track. What do you say?"

Mariel smiled, her bottom lip trembling. "Yes!" she said, running into his arms.

Mom looked at me and Kellie. "Exit stage left, girls," she said, and the three of us quietly walked away.

CHAPTER 26

THE RESCUE

I had only that afternoon and the following day to put the wedding back together. I got into the car and raced over to Marcello's, wondering how I was going to tell Bella that the wedding gown she'd thought she fixed needed to be fixed again. When I got there and she brought out the gown and hung it on a rod by the counter, I broke out in a cold sweat.

"This was a *very big job*," she said. "But it came out perfect. Take a look."

I did. And I cringed, because it was perfect. Except, of course, the waist was two inches too small. This was the moment of truth. I had no choice but to come clean.

There was an awkward moment of silence after I told her what I'd done. She looked at me like I was a criminal, which I guess to her I was, having vandalized a Valentino. "You re-pinned this so it wouldn't fit?"

I gave a sheepish nod. "But we made up, and now I want to fix everything. I want her to walk down the aisle in this dress. You've got to help me. *Please?*"

"But the wedding is Saturday, and it's already Thursday. That would only give me tonight and tomorrow. This isn't like doing a hem or shortening sleeves. This is hours and hours of work."

I knew that. I couldn't imagine how long it would take, how many stitches.

Bella looked at the gown and shook her head. "I don't see any way I can do it. We're backed up already. And we're closed next week for vacation. On top of all that, I need to finish getting ready for my father's party on Sunday. He's turning eighty. I've told all our customers that anything we take in now won't be ready until at least the week after next."

The week after next? "But Mariel has to wear this on Saturday," I said. "I'll pay you whatever you want. Double, triple, you name it. I can't sew, but I'll do anything else you need if you can just put those two inches back in there."

"If you can't sew," she said, "what could you possibly do to help me?"

I thought about that as I gazed at the counter, where someone had etched the word EUREKA in small letters in the wood. And then it came to me. "What do you need to do for your dad's party?"

It turned out to be a long list. Food, liquor, drinks, decorations, party favors. I'd have to bounce around three or four towns to get it all done while making calls and going to various places to put the wedding back together. But what choice did I have? I had to get that gown fixed. "I'll do it," I said.

"Then so will I," Bella said, and we shook on it.

On my way to the car I called Wade, the photographer I'd canceled just days before. He sounded a little bit smug when he told me he'd taken another job for Saturday. I couldn't really blame him, not for taking the job or for sounding smug. I sat in the car and called every photographer I could find within a hundred miles. The ones who answered told me they were already booked, and I wasn't optimistic about getting calls back from the others. We were in the middle of the summer, prime wedding season. I put the phone down. It was a lost cause. I couldn't possibly conjure up a photographer at this late date. Unless...

I drove to the Duncan Arms, walked into the Pub Room, and asked the hostess for Jerome's phone number. I wasn't surprised when she said she couldn't give it to me, but she called him while I was there and left a message for him to get in touch with me. Twenty minutes later, while I was on my way to the Hampstead Country Club, he phoned.

"Saturday?" he said after I'd explained everything. "*This* Saturday?"

"Yes. I know it's last minute, but—"

"I thought you two weren't speaking. I thought you weren't going to the wedding."

"I know. I wasn't. But it's all changed. We've made up. And I need a photographer. I canceled the one we had and now...well, I need one. Bad." I crossed my fingers. "Can you do it?" *Please say yes, please say yes.*

"I'd love to help you, hon, I really would, but I work Saturday night. I'd switch shifts with somebody if I could, but I already know I can't because I asked a few days ago—I wanted to go to a big party on the Cape this weekend—and all the other bartenders have plans. I'm sorry."

"I understand," I said, feeling a sharp stab of disappointment.

"I wish I could help. I really do."

I put on my blinker as I approached a turn. "Thanks. I appreciate it. I guess I'm paying the price for what I did—blaming my sister for things she didn't do, refusing to admit my own part in what happened with my ex. Worst of all, sabotaging her wedding. I'm trying to put it back together now, but…" I glanced out the car window and willed myself not to cry. "Anyway, you don't need to hear all that. Thanks for listening."

We hung up and I wondered if I could find my old Nikon camera at the house. Maybe I could take some pictures and…oh, stop. Who was I kidding? I wasn't a wedding photographer. Besides, I was a bridesmaid. Was I going to walk down the aisle with a camera slung over my shoulder? Maybe I'd have to. Maybe I'd have to ask some of the guests to take pictures as well. What a mess.

I drove on to the club, my stomach twisting. When I got there, I sat down with George Boyd in his office and gave him the final seating chart for the reception. I'd put all the guests back where they were supposed to be. At least I knew that would be correct. Then I told George I wanted to return to the original menu.

"So," he said as he pulled up the file on his computer, "you're saying you want the filet mignon instead of the burritos, the Dover sole instead of the fish sticks, the—"

"Yes, yes, yes," I said. "The pigs in blankets are out, the grilled cheese is gone. We want all the food that was originally chosen."

"Hmm." He squinted at the monitor. "That might be a problem."

I froze. "What do you mean?" The food had to work. It just had to.

"Your original menu included pheasant. Seventy people chose it as an entrée. I can't get pheasant for seventy people overnight. It has to be fresh, and that's not nearly enough lead time."

No pheasant. I had a vision of my sister's face as a server set a plate of chicken nuggets and fries in front of her. I told myself to stay calm. "Okay, we can't do pheasant. Let's replace it with something else. What can we do? How about Cornish game hens? Can you get those in time?"

He thought about that for a moment. "I can get them, yes."

I let out the breath I'd been holding. "Fabulous. Great."

"You, uh, understand the overnight delivery is going to be expensive."

I nodded. I certainly did. I'd be the one footing the bill. I couldn't foist that on my mother. This wasn't her fault. Thank God he could get the hens. I couldn't believe it, but I was shaking. I'd been in these situations before, but this time was different. This was for my sister.

Sitting in the car in the club parking lot, I tried to reach Cecelia Russo. She wasn't in, but I spoke to her assistant and explained that Mariel had decided to go with a strictly classical program after all. "Which means the Britney Spears is out."

"Pity" was all her assistant said. I couldn't tell if she was serious or not. I asked her to make sure Cecelia called me.

I did reach Brian Moran, the band's keyboardist. "We're not going to use those songs I called you about," I told him. "You know, 'Fifty Ways to Leave Your Lover,' 'D-I-V-O-R-C-E,' and those other ones."

He assured me he'd remove them from the playlist. "I think that's probably for the best," he said. "They might be a little bit of a downer."

A downer indeed.

I checked the band off the list, glad to have accomplished some-thing else. Then I drove into town. At Hilliard's, I returned the brass bookends with the cigar-holding hands and found some sterling-silver picture frames I hoped the bridesmaids would like. I thought about the day I was there with Carter and how much had changed since then. I also wondered what David was doing. I hoped I'd have a chance to tell him I'd done the right thing after all.

At St. John's, the gray stone church my family had attended for years, Mrs. Bukes, who coordinated the weddings, welcomed me into a little office. I was relieved when we went over the timetable and final details for the ceremony. Everything seemed to be in order. That was, of course, after I crossed off "...Baby One More Time" in the wedding program and asked her to please reprint it.

I went to Cakewalk and left strict instructions with Annette, Lory Judd's assistant, that they were *not* to put any of the photos I'd e-mailed on the wedding cake. "Just plain icing," I told her.

"Aww, but that picture of your sister with the spaghetti in her hair is so cute," Annette said, looking disappointed.

I repeated, "Just plain icing."

At Hall's Florist, I found Ginny working on an arrangement of pink roses and peonies. "You want to go back to the original plan?" She sounded a little gruff. "With the orchids? For Saturday?" She shook her head and frowned as she snipped a stem. "Nope. Sorry, but it's too late. I can't get them and do all the arrangements in time. We've got three other weddings this weekend. You'll have to use what you ordered."

What I'd ordered? Oh God. Hello, mums. Hello, Benadryl.

CHAPTER 27

THE OPENING

I spent Friday tying up the final loose ends for the wedding and running all over the county picking everything up for Marcello's birthday party. George called me from the club at eleven o'clock to assure me that he had the hens. I was in a pharmacy at the time, buying two dozen travel-size packets of Benadryl that would be stuffed into tiny organza bags, one for Mariel and the others for any of the guests who might need them.

That evening I went to Marcello's and dropped off the party supplies with Bella, who was thrilled I'd gotten everything done. She presented me with Mariel's wedding gown, and we settled up on what she owed me for the supplies and what I owed her for the gown. On my way to the rehearsal at the church, my phone rang. It was a Connecticut number but not one I recognized.

"Is this Sara?"

The man's voice didn't sound familiar. "Yes?"

"Hey, it's Jerome, from the Pub Room."

"Jerome?"

"Yes, hi. I was calling to tell you I can do the wedding."

"What? You're kidding!"

"No. Willow's husband got called into work at the last minute, so they couldn't go away. She said she'd take my shift tomorrow. If you still need me."

"Yes, I do. But you're not going to the Cape?"

"No. I'd like to do the wedding."

"Thank you, Jerome. You're a lifesaver. And please thank Willow for me." Whoever she was, I was grateful. I gave him the details and told him I'd e-mail the schedule to him when I got to the church. By the time I arrived at St. John's, I was so happy I was singing.

The rehearsal went smoothly, and when it was over the group went on to drinks and dinner, but I had somewhere else I needed to go first. My plan was to make a quick tour of Alex Lingon's show at the Brookside and then head to the restaurant.

A good-size crowd had gathered at the gallery by the time I arrived, about two hundred people, probably the result of all the publicity, including a huge banner hanging downtown (it was right above the one that said SAVE THE BAKED-GOODS BANDITS!). The place was buzzing with art patrons, local business owners and politicians, media people with press badges, some of them with video operators in tow, and folks who were curious to see what all the fuss was about. Something Cole Porter–ish was playing from the speakers, and the muted lighting cast a warm glow over the room, making the large space feel cozy.

I glanced around, wondering if David had arrived, hoping I'd get a chance to talk to him so I could tell him he was right about what he'd said the other night and let him know that I was trying to work things out with my sister.

"Grilled scallop wrapped in prosciutto?" A server approached me with a tray.

"No, thanks. But can you tell me where the bar is?"

"It's in the back, over there." He pointed across the room.

I began walking, taking in the art as I headed toward the bar. I paused by a group of people looking at *Evolution Number 52,* a giant box covered in blue fabric and surrounded by red, arterial-looking tubes. I walked on, then stopped at a place where the floor had been taped off in a ten-foot-by-ten-foot square. Inside the space, large pieces of corrugated cardboard shaped like arms and legs dangled from the ceiling and lay on the floor.

"Chicken skewer," someone to my right said.

I stared at the objects on the floor. "Umm, they do look a little like that," I said. Then I saw the server at my elbow. "Oh, no, thanks." Embarrassed, I dashed off, passing two rectangular objects that might have been giant hay bales except they were orange and made of plastic.

The bar was in sight, and I navigated around people huddled in groups, snippets of conversation falling around me. A daughter's internship, a husband's knee surgery, a house being remodeled, the new gourmet shop opening next week, the antiques store that had closed after thirty years. I recognized a few of Mom's friends, and I noticed Link Overstreet was there. He was a billionaire art collector from Manhattan who flew to Hampstead in his helicopter on weekends.

As I got closer to the bar, something caught my eye: Alex Lingon's hand, positioned on a large black block. It looked majestic, those shades of green shimmering under the light, the fingers stretching upward, the cracks and dents and damage relegated to the past. A warm feeling stirred inside me, a proprietary feeling, the kind of feeling I suspected a mother got when her child accomplished something great. I felt like I had mothered that sculpture through quite a lot over the past two weeks. No one else in the room would ever know about that connection. But I would always remember.

I walked on, skirting around servers with trays of wine and champagne and canapés. I stepped in line behind a dozen other people at the bar. And that's when I spotted David. Dressed in gray pants, a light gray T-shirt, and a blue jacket, he stood with a small group halfway across the room. How handsome he looked. I watched him as he greeted another man. Watched him laugh at something an older woman said. Watched him nod his head. Watched him...oh God, what was I doing? Everything inside me was bubbling over, my heart pounding. And there was only one explanation: I liked him. As more than a friend. A lot more than a friend. But what was the point? I was wasting my energy. Not only was he in love with someone else, but he was about to become engaged. I couldn't make that mistake again.

A tall blonde appeared beside him, her sleeveless white shift showing off her bronzed limbs, her chin-length hair setting off her high cheekbones. Silver corkscrew earrings dangled from her ears. Ana. The photo hadn't done her justice. She was striking. I watched her say something to David; I saw him reply. They leaned toward each other, so close, so intimate. I stared. My heart was ripping apart, but I couldn't look away. And then they were gone, swept up in the crowd.

"Miss? Miss? Do you want a drink?"

I turned. The bartender was looking at me, waiting. I couldn't think. What was he saying? A drink? "Oh, uh, no. No, thanks."

I walked away and almost collided with a server holding a tray of shrimp toast. He stopped to offer one to me. I waved him off. I didn't want shrimp toast. What I wanted was David. I wanted him to wrap his arms around me, to hold me and kiss me the way I imagined he did with Ana.

The music coming from the speakers now was another old tune, Duke Ellington's "I Didn't Know About You." Ella Fitzgerald was singing, giving every syllable of that torch song its due, asking how she could have known about love when she didn't know about him.

What was wrong with me? Was I going to spend the rest of my life falling for men I couldn't have? Was there some Freudian thing going on that would take decades of head-shrinking to figure out? I didn't want to spend decades doing that. And I didn't want to spend any more time at the gallery.

As I looked across the room to make my exit, someone turned down the music and Kingsley Pellinger, dressed in a slim-fitting paisley suit, asked everyone to gather around. The next thing I knew, I was in a swarm headed in Kingsley's direction. I ended up near the front of the crowd, where I caught sight of David and Ana again.

"Isn't this just fun?" Kingsley said. "Well, of course it is." He grinned. "I see a lot of familiar faces tonight. But for those of you who may not know me—although I don't see how that would be possible if you live here—I'm Kingsley Pellinger, owner of the Brookside, and I want to welcome everyone." He made a little bow. So theatrical. Mom would have loved it.

"I don't usually make speeches," he went on, "but tonight I'm going to say a few words. I'm so glad you could all be here at the opening of this *wonderful* exhibit, this collection of diverse works by the incomparable Alex Lingon." He paused. Some people applauded. "And of course, we have Alex himself here with us." The applause grew louder, and a few people whistled. "I've known this man for ten years. And do you think I can ever predict where this genius is going? No, I cannot. He's constantly a surprise, as you can see by the work on display tonight. And he's standing right here, so without further ado, as they say, I present to you Alex Lingon."

There was loud applause as a wiry man in jeans and a black shirt appeared next to Kingsley. Alex looked a little older than in the pictures I'd seen. Early fifties, maybe. His dark eyes scanned the crowd.

"Thanks, Kingsley. And thanks for coming, everybody. Brookside's a great gallery. I've known Kingsley a long time and I'm glad to have my work here." He paused and squinted. It looked like he was studying something across the room. "These pieces represent some of my..." He thrust his head forward, staring. Then he pointed. "What the hell is that?"

The room went silent. Everyone looked to see what Alex was pointing at. The hand.

"What's *that* doing here?" He turned on Kingsley, who drew back with a mixture of confusion and fear in his eyes.

"I don't understand. Are you talking about the, the *hand?* It's your work. It's part of the show."

"*My* work? Are you crazy? That's not mine. Why is it here?"

Kingsley's neck and face had turned the color of a ripe peach. "But it was delivered as part of your exhibit. It says *Lingon* on the bottom."

"I don't care what it says on the bottom. It's not my work. That *thing* was made by my twelve-year-old nephew—in his art class."

I gasped. Everyone gasped. Kingsley shrieked, his face turning from peach to plum. How could we have spent all that time, money, and effort—not to mention gotten arrested—over a twelve-year-old's art project? I felt sick. I turned to look for David, but I didn't see him anywhere.

"How could you do this?" Alex was inches away from Kingsley. "How can you call yourself a gallerist, an art expert, if you don't even know the difference between an Alex Lingon and a Larry Lingon?"

I could feel an undercurrent of panic in the crowd. Kingsley looked as though he wanted to run and hide. "This is h-highly unusual." He clasped his hands. "A mistake. It was all a mistake. I'm, it's—" He began to sway. Then his legs buckled like a marionette's; his body went limp, and he fell to the floor. A woman screamed, and several people rushed to help.

"Is anyone here a doctor?" someone called out.

I pulled out my spritzer of Poison. "I'm not a doctor, but I've got something like smelling salts," I said, spraying the perfume near Kingsley. He began to come around and two men helped him sit up. A woman brought him a glass of water. I looked for David again, wondering if he was still here and if he'd seen what had happened.

Things had begun to quiet down when someone in the back shouted, "I'd like to buy the Larry Lingon. What's the price?" I heard a collective gasp as people turned to see who it was. Link Overstreet.

"The price?" Kingsley had now regained full control of himself and, with the help of the two men, was standing up. "Is that Mr. Overstreet?" Kingsley brushed off his suit. "Ah, well, I'm not sure of the, uh, the price. So I guess I'd have to—"

"*I* want to buy it," another man said.

He was standing to the right of me, in the front. Tall, shaved head, large red-framed eyeglasses. I realized it was Gil Rosenthal. He'd made a killing selling a tech company a few years back. I'd heard there was bad blood between him and Link Overstreet— something about a piece of art they'd both wanted. Or a woman. I couldn't remember which.

"I'll give you ten thousand for it," Rosenthal said. "Cash."

Ten thousand dollars cash? Who walked around with that kind of money?

"Ah, Mr. Rosenthal. Nice to see you," Kingsley said. "You want to pay...ten thousand dollars?" Kingsley took a swig of water from a bottle. He looked like he might faint again. "Well, I'm sure we can work something—"

"Twelve," Overstreet shouted. "Twelve thousand."

"Fifteen," Rosenthal said, craning his neck to see where his competition was located.

Then a new voice entered the fray, a woman's. British. "I'll pay twenty-five thousand quid—I mean dollars—for the hand."

"Twenty-five thou—" Kingsley took a little step back, then righted himself.

"Thirty," Overstreet said.

Kingsley's head swiveled as he tracked the bids. A man on my left held up his cell phone. "I've got a friend on the line from China who will pay forty."

"The latest bid is forty thousand," Kingsley said, looking pleased and eager for more.

But off to the side, Alex Lingon didn't look pleased. He looked as though he was barely containing his rage as the spotlight continued to move away from him and toward his nephew.

"Oh, bollocks," the British woman said. "Forty-five, then."

"Pounds?" Kingsley asked.

"Dollars, pounds, whatever you like."

Link Overstreet raised his hand. "Fifty thousand."

"Pounds?" Kingsley asked.

"No, for God's sake. Dollars," Overstreet said. Then he scratched his head. "Wait, am I going against pounds?"

Photographers were snapping pictures so fast, it sounded like machine-gun fire. Everyone was waiting for the next bid, and the one after that. The bidding finally stalled at seventy-five thousand pounds, Gil Rosenthal's offer. The room felt like it was vibrating.

"We have seventy-five thousand pounds from Mr. Rosenthal," Kingsley said. "Anyone care to make it eighty?" I looked around, but I didn't see any signs of another bid. "Eighty?" Kingsley asked again. Then he paused. "All right, then. Going once, going twice." He waited a beat or two, then tapped the top of the microphone a couple of times. "Sold for seventy-five thousand pounds to Mr. Rosenthal." Gil Rosenthal threw his hands in the air and, to the sound of applause, walked toward Kingsley.

"Wait a minute. Hold on here." Link Overstreet strode toward the two men. "That sale's not valid. I was trying to make another bid."

"Well, you didn't make it," Rosenthal said.

"I had my arm up, but Kingsley didn't see."

"Then you should have spoken up. That hand belongs to me."

Overstreet pointed to Kingsley. "He doesn't even know how to run an auction. He should have seen me. That sale's not valid. We need to do it over."

"Nobody's doing anything over, Lincoln." Rosenthal, who had a good twenty-five pounds on Overstreet, took a step closer to him.

The temperature in the room jumped several degrees. The place was so quiet, you could have heard a thread land on the floor. "That sale is invalid," Overstreet repeated, standing so close to Rosenthal I was sure the other man felt his breath.

"You don't think it's valid?" Rosenthal thrust a finger at Overstreet. "I'll show you what's valid."

"Please, please." Kingsley's voice quavered. "This is an art gallery. I think we'll leave the Larry Lingon right here for now and discuss it more civilly in the morning. I'm certain we can come to—"

"This is supposed to be an art-show opening," Alex said, looking furious. "*My* art-show opening. I think we should all forget about the hand and have a drink. I'm ready for one."

I thought that was a great idea, but Overstreet didn't agree. "I'm not discussing this in the morning," he said. "And I'm not leaving until we redo the auction. That's the only way to settle it."

Rosenthal tugged the front of Overstreet's shirt. "No, that's *not* the only way to settle it." He drew back his arm and sent his fist flying into Overstreet's cheek; it landed with a thud. People screamed, some edging closer to see what was going on. Overstreet staggered for a moment, and I thought he was going to fall. But he managed to right himself, and before Rosenthal realized what was happening, Overstreet punched him in the stomach, which caused him to wobble back a few steps, double over like a jack-knife, then collapse onto one of the giant orange bales of hay, plastic stalks breaking as the sculpture absorbed the impact of the body.

"Get out of there!" Alex ran to the block of hay, his hands in the air. "You're ruining it! Get out!"

Ana, who seemed to have appeared out of nowhere, was at Alex's side screaming for someone to help.

"Please!" Kingsley yelled. "Get off that! Off! Off! This is terrible! Isn't this terrible?"

It was terrible.

Kingsley and two other men pulled Rosenthal out of the plastic hay bale, where he'd left a large indentation in the shape of a body. Ana was trying to calm Alex, but it wasn't working. I could see a vessel throbbing in his neck, and I worried another fight would start.

I also worried about David. What would Alex do if he discovered David was the one who'd brought the sculpture here? I never learned the answer to that question because the next thing I knew, the police had arrived. Four officers rushed inside and began talking to Kingsley, Overstreet, Rosenthal, and Alex.

I looked for David a final time, then headed toward the door.

"Miss Harrington?"

A man approached me. Something about him looked familiar. He wasn't in uniform, so it took me a moment to realize it was Officer

Madden from the Eastville Police Department. Uh-oh. What did he think I'd done now? "Yes?"

"Hey, good to run into you. Timing couldn't be better."

Good to run into me?

He was smiling. "What a show, huh?" He glanced around, and I thought about making a run for it. "I love this guy's work. Lucky thing I'm off tonight. Heard I just missed an altercation, though. Two art collectors getting into it? What's this world coming to?"

"I don't know," I said, still wary.

"Hey, let me tell you what's going on. We just made an arrest an hour ago. The Baked-Goods Bandit."

It took a few seconds for that to register. "You arrested the Baked-Goods Bandit?" I felt such relief picturing the culprit in a jail cell, imagining a thug from a street gang, somebody who dealt drugs to children when he wasn't stealing their cookies.

Officer Madden nodded. "Yeah. Sure did. You're not going to believe this. It's the guy who owns the house. The house where we arrested you."

He'd lost me. "What guy?"

"The homeowner. The husband. Cadwy Gwythyr."

He might as well have told me it was my mother. "Cadwy Gwythyr? That's impossible. He's just a little guy who...I mean, he sells herbal remedies and drives a car that runs on cow dung. It can't be him."

"He confessed. Apparently, he goes all over the county making deliveries for a healing business they have. He was taking the food from his customers. Said he couldn't help himself. His wife doesn't let him eat sweets."

I couldn't believe Jeanette's refusal to let her husband eat sweets had pushed him into a life of crime. Poor Cadwy. "What's going to happen to him? I know he stole some food, but aren't there more serious crimes to worry about?"

Officer Madden hooked his thumbs in his belt loops. "Yes, Miss Harrington, there are. We've already let him go. Nobody wanted to press charges."

I was glad to hear it.

Officer Madden grabbed a crab cake from a passing server. "You know, if you hadn't taken that pie from their house, we never would have solved it so fast. His prints were all over the pie plate, which isn't surprising. But so were the pie owner's. We were able to connect the dots."

I remembered the Gwythyrs were supposed to be in New Mexico. "But I thought they were away. How did you arrest Cadwy?"

"They were away, but New Mexico authorities extradited him." Officer Madden glanced across the room and nodded. "Yeah, they take their desserts pretty seriously down there."

They certainly did.

CHAPTER 28

THE CONFESSION

I left the gallery and headed straight to the Kitchen, where the rehearsal dinner was going on. The maître d' ushered me into the private room where the wedding party was seated: Mariel and Carter; Mom; her brother, my uncle Jack, who was going to walk Mariel down the aisle; Jack's wife, my aunt Ann; my mother's sister, Aunt Beth; Carter's parents, Jim and Sandy; the bridesmaids; and the groomsmen, one of whom was Carter's older brother.

I'd known Carter's family since we began dating, and I must have wondered a thousand times what it would be like to run into them again. At one point it would have mattered; I would have been embarrassed. Now, as I took a seat, I realized I didn't feel that way at all. Like water seeking its own level, they'd settled into the right place in my life.

"It's only a small part," I overheard Mom say, "but I think it's going to be fun."

The word was out. She must have gotten the contract. I was happy for her.

"Wow, Mom, what a surprise," Mariel said. "I didn't know you'd auditioned for anything."

"Let's toast to Mom," I said. "To a successful show."

We raised our glasses and I sipped my Riesling. As I sat there, half listening to the conversations around me, I couldn't stop wondering what David was doing. He and Ana would be leaving soon for France. Maybe next week.

I pictured them at Le Jules Verne, crisp linens on the table, gleaming silver, Paris glowing through the windows, little buttons of light against a velvet sky. The server bringing Ana a dessert plate with David's proposal written on its rim and, in the middle, the box with the ring inside. What would he say? Something about how much he loved her, how happy she made him, and how he wanted to be with her forever. Something traditional like that. He'd said she was traditional. She'd say yes, of course. Then he'd slip the ring on her finger. Happy tears from her, big smiles from him. Hugs. Kisses. And on to a lifetime together.

Uncle Jack turned to me and asked how I liked Chicago. I pasted a smile on my face and proceeded to give him my pat answer.

I got home and took Mariel's wedding gown out of the back of my car. As I was going down the hall, I heard voices in the kitchen, water running in the sink, ice being dropped into glasses, a champagne cork popping. Aunt Ann and Uncle Jack were laughing. "I never did that!" Mom said, but she was laughing too. I didn't hear Mariel's or Carter's voice. I headed up the back stairs and into my room, took the wedding gown from the garment bag, and laid it on the bed.

Mariel was in her bathroom, sitting in front of the vanity. She leaned into the mirror, reapplying her mascara.

"I need to show you something." I stood in the doorway.

She ran the tiny brush over her lashes. "Hold on a sec. Let me just get this…" Another go with the brush. "There." She turned to me. "What's up?"

"It's in my room."

"Give me a hint. Animal, vegetable, or mineral?"

I smiled. It was something we used to say as kids, and I hadn't heard it in a long time. The question was a tough one. Where did fabric fall? It didn't really fit into any of those categories, although some fabrics came from animals and some were grown, of course. Silk, though, came from silkworms. So was *animal* the right choice? "I can't. You'll just have to come see. But I need to explain something first."

"Okay." She picked up an eyebrow pencil and dabbed at her brows.

"Your wedding gown isn't exactly the same gown it was. I mean, it's close. It's definitely close, but…" How could I say this? There was no good way. "Okay, I had Bella alter your gown to make it smaller so it wouldn't fit you."

Mariel dropped the eyebrow pencil. "You did what?" I felt the heat from her eyes as she stared at me.

"I was angry with you. About Carter. About the wedding. And then you asked me to be a bridesmaid, to take the place of that girl who broke her leg. I didn't want to be in your wedding to begin with, and there I was, being asked to sub for someone else at the last minute. That put me over the top. And that's when I decided I'd be a bridesmaid and be your wedding planner, but my real motive was to sabotage the wedding."

Mariel sat bolt upright. "Sabotage my wedding?"

I wanted to evaporate into the air, disappear through the mirror, but I knew the only way I could ever have a clean slate was to keep telling her the truth, get it all out there. "The day we were at Marcello's, I re-pinned your gown so it would be too small."

"My Valentino! Sara, how could you?"

I held up a hand to stop her. "Bella fixed it, though. She did a really good job. She took some fabric from the train and added it in a couple of places. And she covered the seams with lace. I don't think you can tell at all."

Silence filled the bathroom like toxic gas. I stared at the vanity, at a swirly gray spot in the marble that looked like the vortex of a tornado. I wished I were in a tornado. One that would pick me up and plunk me down somewhere miles away. Another continent might be good.

"There's more," I said. "I did some other things too."

"*Other* things?"

"The seating arrangements, the music, the food—"

"Oh my God, Sara. How could you do that?" Her voice broke. She covered her face with her hands.

"I know. It was terrible of me. Horrible. I'm so sorry. I didn't want you and Carter to get married then, but I do now. I want that more than anything for you. And for him. I tried to fix everything, to put all the arrangements back the way they were. And I have. Well, all except for the flowers." I paused. "Do you like mums?"

"I think I'd like to kill you," she said, the words coming out in a convulsive-sounding whisper.

"I know. But you'd get jail time. Although you'd have a good excuse for the murder."

"It would be worth it."

"Maybe. But think about those orange jumpsuits. That's all you'd ever get to wear."

There was a long stretch of silence while I waited for her to scream and yell and chase me from the room. But she didn't.

"Wow," she said finally. "You really hated me." There was something in her eyes I hadn't seen in a while. Something that looked like empathy. "I'm sorry I made you so miserable, that I pushed you that far. I'm sorry I've been so selfish."

"I'm sorry too. For the mean things I've done. For not listening to you, not understanding you, not realizing what you've been going through. I'm going to be a better sister."

I took her hand and tugged her off the vanity, and we hugged for a long time. I could feel her tears on my cheek. Maybe she felt mine on hers.

CHAPTER 29

WITH THIS RING

The wedding took place at four on Saturday. Looking handsome in his tux, Carter stood at the altar waiting for Mariel. He winked when he caught my eye, and I gave him a thumbs-up. Mariel looked gorgeous in the Valentino gown, and I don't think anyone suspected a single stitch had been changed. No wedding rings were lost or swallowed.

Mom cried during the ceremony. Then she said she felt old. I wasn't sure if she was crying because of the wedding or because she felt old or both. I didn't ask. I was concentrating on the words my sister and Carter were saying to each other. Words like *forever* and *love* and *understanding*. Words like *forgiveness* and *patience*. Words like *together* and *always*. I wasn't envious of her. I was happy for her. I just wished someone would say those words to me.

The weather was a sunny eighty degrees, perfect for an outdoor reception at the club. The tables on the slate patio looked lovely with their white linens, and although I'm sure the orchid arrangements Mariel had chosen would have been spectacular, Ginny Hall had done a nice job on the daisy-sunflower-mum centerpieces. And Mariel had taken the Benadryl.

Tate sat next to me with his plus-one—Amy, the new vet in his practice. He confessed to me he wasn't sure it was a good idea to mix business with pleasure, but I told him you only live once and wished him luck. I was the last person to be critiquing relationships.

During dinner (I had the Dover sole, by the way, which was excellent), Carter's best man, Tim Rucci, got up to give a toast, which included a story about how Carter had had to break into Tim's Jeep one night when they were in college because Tim had locked the keys in the car. I'd never heard that story before and it made me wonder if Carter *could* have blasted open that elevator door the day I met him.

After dinner, I walked over to Mariel and Carter's table and set a small box in front of my sister. "It's not your wedding gift," I said. "I actually got you that Japanese screen you wanted, but they couldn't figure out how to wrap it."

Mariel laughed. Carter looked perplexed.

"An old joke," I said. I tapped the box. "This reminded me of when we were little."

She opened it and held up the snow globe with the two horses inside. "I can't believe it. They look exactly like Crackerjack and Two's Company. The bay even has the same star Two had," she said, giving the globe a shake. White flakes swirled, floating over the ponies and the red barn, collecting in a little drift at the bottom. "I love it. I really love it. Thanks, Sara." She threw her arms around me.

The band began to play "Signed, Sealed, Delivered, I'm Yours," an old Stevie Wonder song. As I headed back to my seat, I saw someone come through the French doors onto the patio and I stopped. It was David. In a suit and tie.

"David?" I scurried toward him, wondering why he was here. Something bad must have happened, probably something to do with the hand. "What's going on?"

"Ah, there you are," he said, looking relieved to see me. "I'm sorry to show up unannounced. I'm not trying to crash your sister's wedding. It's just that I'm on my way back to Manhattan and I needed to talk to you."

I didn't like his serious tone. In his eyes, things swirled and pitched, but I couldn't tell what he was thinking. "What's wrong?"

"I want to apologize for the way I treated you the other night. For what I said, how I said it. I was rude, and I never should have criticized you like that. I had no right to make judgments about you or your sister. I'm sorry."

That's what this was about? An apology? "I thought something bad had happened to you. Maybe something with the hand. That you were in trouble."

He smiled, and I remembered what a lovely smile he had, how it lit up his whole face. "No, I'm not in trouble."

"David, you don't need to apologize for anything. You were right about what you said. About my sister and me acting like children. We *were* acting like children. The two of us have been working at cross-purposes for a while, but I think we're starting to straighten things out."

"That's great, Sara. I'm glad."

"And you were also right about me and Carter. He belongs with my sister."

I gazed across the patio. People were talking and dancing. Someone tapped a spoon against a glass and others followed, the ringing prompting Carter and Mariel to kiss. I watched their embrace, a bittersweet feeling in my heart.

A server walked up to us. "May I get you something?"

I shook my head.

"No, thanks," David said. He watched the server walk away. "You know, I'm not usually so reckless about what I say to people. I just felt you were making a big mistake with Carter. It didn't seem right for a lot of reasons."

"You weren't reckless. You were being honest. Friends should feel they can be honest with one another. That's what you said, and you were right." *Friends*. It wasn't what I wanted, but at least I had that.

"Yeah, well, you're an interesting friend to have. You know, I had a crazy couple of weeks here. I can't believe I did half the stuff I did with you. Tried to fix what I thought was an Alex Lingon sculpture, broke into a house, got arrested, had my mug shot plastered all over town and on the internet. Did I leave anything out? Oh yeah—*¡viva la revolución!* Almost forgot that. And I learned you set the art room on fire in high school."

I winced. "Yes, but honestly that was—"

He waved his hand. "I know, an accident."

"You're right, though. I guess it's been a crazy time."

"I don't normally do the kinds of things I've been doing. But you know what? I wouldn't trade one minute of the past couple of weeks for anything. I've had the most fun ever. I wanted the chance to tell you that." He seemed to be studying my dress. "And now I get to see what you look like as a bridesmaid."

"It's not really my color, but I didn't—"

"I think it looks nice on you."

I felt myself blush. "Oh, well, thanks. You look nice too. I don't think I've ever seen you in a suit before."

"Really?" He glanced at his sleeve as though he'd forgotten what he was wearing. "Well, I couldn't very well show up here in jeans. Even for a few minutes."

A few minutes. That's all the time he had? I wished I could stretch those minutes into hours, into days. But we'd be going our separate ways, and all I could do was be happy for him.

"Well, I'm glad you came," I said. "And I'm glad you survived the two weeks with me. Maybe you can think of it as boot camp. Now you can go back to New York and look forward to something a little more relaxing. Like Paris." I pressed a smile onto my face, but it was hard to keep it there.

David looked across the patio, past the tables and chairs, past the dance floor and the band, to where the blue hills dipped and rose again, and the sun sat like a caramel candy low on the horizon. "I'm not going to Paris."

There was only one thing I could think of that would delay his trip. "Has something come up with your work?"

He continued to stare into the distance. Finally, he turned to me. "I talked to Ana last night. We barely spoke when she was away. We just traded voice mails and texts. I figured she was so busy that...anyway, last night at the gallery, I took her outside and told her everything. About the hand. About what happened to it. About Jeanette. Getting arrested. Everything."

"You must have been relieved to finally come clean about—"

"And then I told her it was over between us."

Over. I looked at him and felt the patio shift under me. "What happened?"

His shoulders rose and fell. "I just realized Ana wasn't what I wanted. That a lifetime with her might not be the right thing for me."

"But I thought...I mean, you were all set to propose. The words on the dessert plate—"

"I know. I was all set. Until I wasn't. I realized my heart wasn't in it. That I was making a mistake. That maybe I needed to be with somebody a little different from Ana."

They weren't getting married. He'd broken it off. He needed somebody a little different. The moment hung there like honey dripping from a spoon. On the putting green behind the patio, children were running and laughing; people were taking selfies. At the bar, servers in black suits were mixing up pitchers of something frothy and pink. On the dance floor, Dr. Sherwood was twirling my mother.

"So, yeah, I was giving Ana this big speech," David went on. "And all of a sudden she stopped me and told me she and Alex had eloped."

I went numb for a minute. And then, maybe because the whole situation seemed so ridiculous, I started to laugh. "What?" And he'd thought she was traditional?

"They got married in Aspen. Crazy, isn't it? She realized she didn't love me; I realized I didn't love her. Could have been one of your dad's plays."

It could have been. I was about to tell him so when Jerome walked by with his Canon and snapped some pictures of us. Then he gave me a little wave and moved on.

"So you're okay with everything?" I said. "The way it turned out with Ana?"

"Yeah, I am." He straightened the knot in his tie. "I feel like I got a lucky break. And now I have a clean slate."

A clean slate. Funny how he said what I was thinking. "I kind of feel the same way, with my sister. And Carter." I thought I saw something flicker in David's eyes. Something that made the cinnamon brown even warmer. "Maybe we should get a couple of drinks and toast to clean slates," I said. I hoped he'd stay a little longer.

Aunt Bootsie wobbled toward me in her pink suit, a silk flower on her lapel, her silver hair brushed back from her face. She grabbed my arm and, with drunken breath, whispered, "Who's the hunk?" before heading inside.

"I'd like to make that toast," David said. "But there's something I want to do first. How about a dance?" He nodded toward the floor, packed with gyrating bodies, Mariel and Carter among them.

He wanted to dance. With me. I felt fizzy and light, as if I'd been transfused with champagne. Everything inside me began to whirl. Or maybe it was the patio that was moving. The band started to play "I've Got You Under My Skin," and I thought about Dad and how he loved that song, especially when Sinatra sang it. It was another one of his favorites. And now it was one of mine.

"Sure," I said. "I'd love to."

David smiled, took my hand, and led me into the crowd.

THE ROLLING PIN'S FAMOUS ORANGE CHOCOLATE CHUNK COOKIES

2¾ cups all-purpose flour
1 teaspoon baking powder
¾ teaspoon baking soda
¼ teaspoon salt
1 cup (16 tablespoons) unsalted butter, softened
1 cup packed light brown sugar
¾ cup granulated sugar
1 tablespoon orange zest
2 large eggs
1 teaspoon vanilla extract
¾ teaspoon orange extract
4 ounces bittersweet chocolate, chopped into chunks
4 ounces milk chocolate, chopped into chunks
4 ounces semisweet chocolate, chopped into chunks

1. Whisk flour, baking powder, baking soda, and salt in a bowl and set aside.
2. In another bowl, using an electric mixer, whip butter, brown sugar, granulated sugar, and orange zest until creamy, about 2

minutes. Add one egg and mix until combined. Add second egg, vanilla extract, and orange extract and mix until combined.

3. With mixer at low speed, slowly add flour mixture and mix just until combined. Stir in chocolate chunks.

4. Shape dough into large balls (about 3 tablespoons each), put them on plates, and cover with plastic wrap. Chill for 1 hour in the refrigerator.

5. Line cookie sheets with parchment paper and preheat oven to 350 degrees F. Transfer dough balls to cookie sheets and bake for about 14 to 16 minutes. Let cool on cookie sheets for several minutes, then transfer to a wire rack to finish cooling.

TIP: If you don't want to bake the cookies all at once, put some of the dough balls in an airtight container, with waxed paper between each layer, and freeze them. Then thaw and bake when you're ready.

ACKNOWLEDGMENTS

My team at Little, Brown is the best and they deserve a huge thank-you: Judy Clain and Miya Kumangai, my editors; Kirin Diemont, jacket design; Jayne Yaffe Kemp and Tracy Roe, copy-editing; Katharine Myers, publicity; Ira Boudah and Lauren Hess, marketing; Laura Mamelok, subsidiary rights; and the folks in sales and audio who I didn't have the pleasure to work with directly, but who were integral to the publishing process.

Several people let me pick their brains about various topics: G. Alexander Carden, M.D., Elizabeth MacKinnon Haak, Dianna Kebeck, Captain Mick Keehan, Frank Sargenti, Captain Gino Silvestri, and Kathleen Timmons, DVM. Thank you all.

My early readers provided much helpful feedback. My appreciation goes to Suzanne Ainslie, Peter Helie, Rebecca Holliman, Christine Lacerenza, Kate Simses, and Mike Simses. I'm also indebted to Jamie Callan for her invaluable observations and suggestions along the way.

Finally, the biggest thanks of all go to the two most important people in my life: my husband, Bob, and my daughter, Morgan. I couldn't do this without them.

ABOUT THE AUTHOR

Mary Simses grew up in Darien, Connecticut, and began writing short stories as a child. She spent most of her life in New England, where she worked in magazine publishing and later as a corporate attorney, writing short stories "on the side." Mary is the author of *The Irresistible Blueberry Bakeshop & Café,* adapted as *The Irresistible Blueberry Farm* for the Hallmark Movies and Mysteries channel, and *The Rules of Love & Grammar.* Mary enjoys photography, old jazz standards, and escaping to Connecticut in the summer. She lives in South Florida.

marysimses.com
Facebook.com/MSimses
Instagram.com/marysimses
Twitter.com/marysimses